Blasting Trumpets

Also by Carole Bailey

The Morgan Chronicles
Ancient Boundary Stone
Chariots of the Clouds
Destiny Rising

The Locket Chronicles
BOK

The Locket Chronicles

Blasting Trumpets

CAROLE BAILEY

authorHOUSE®

AuthorHouse™
1663 Liberty Drive
Bloomington, IN 47403
www.authorhouse.com
Phone: 1-800-839-8640

Scripture taken from the NEW AMERICAN STANDARD BIBLE®, Copyright © 1960,1962,1 963,1968,1971,1972,1973,1975,1977,1995 by The Lockman Foundation. Used by permission.

THE HOLY BIBLE, NEW INTERNATIONAL VERSION®, NIV® Copyright © 1973, 1978, 1984, 2011 by Biblica, Inc.™ Used by permission. All rights reserved worldwide

Cover design and photographs by Caleb Hale

Published by AuthorHouse   03/25/2014

Edited by Nan Holloway

ISBN: 978-1-4918-7127-0 (sc)
ISBN: 978-1-4918-7126-3 (hc)
ISBN: 978-1-4918-7125-6 (e)

Library of Congress Control Number: 2014904588

This book is printed on acid-free paper.

Contents

TO AMERICA

ONE NATION UNDER GOD

When you go into battle in your own land against an enemy who is oppressing you, sound a blast on the trumpets.

Then you will be remembered by the LORD your God and rescued from your enemies.

Numbers 10:9

BLASTING TRUMPETS

Kate Phillips—Pilot/wing walker. Cousin to Jen Fillmore
Jen Fillmore—Wing walker/pilot. Cousin to Kate Phillips
Raguel—Mentor to Kate and Jen in Bigna World

CHARACTERS IN APHABETICAL ORDER

Abi—Rubidus' Senior Centurion
Atasa—Ruler of Obex
Count Begi—Domare knight. Commander of one Division of Bigna warriors
Duke Nerkon—Domare knight. Commander of all Pilger warriors on The Mission
Elak—Rapio's sentry of the Senvolte River
Eldré—Wise elder of Bigna
Friar Tuck—Cephas Monastery monk. Mysta's number one aide
Lieg—Bigna Air Power knight. Taught Jen to fly the Maup bird
Lord Obile—Domare's greatest knight. Commander of two Divisions of Bigna warriors
Maltzurra—Rapio's personal knight
Mejor—Nerkon's Senior Centurion—First Cohort
Mysta—High Priest of Cephas Monastery
Onde—Rapio's high priest and self appointed King of Helig
'Ov—Friend of Raguel
Petri Meudy—Key monk for The Mission
Rapio—Dark Prince of Bigna
Raven—Rapio in bird-like form
Rocas—Rapio's servant. Twin of Raguel
Sir Rubidus—Domare knight who betrays his duty to The Mission
Taka—Bigna Air Power knight. Taught Kate to fly the Maup bird

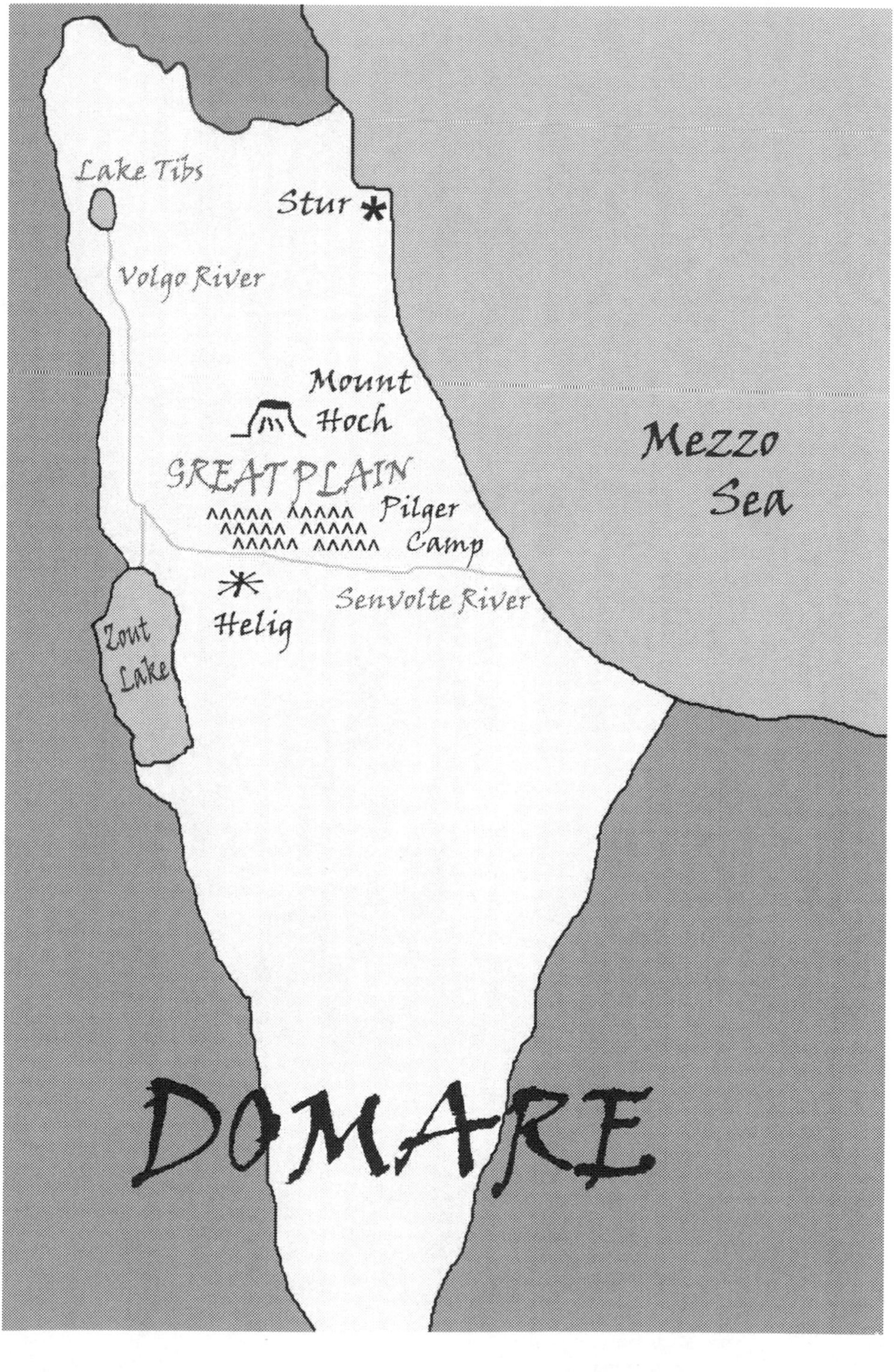
Lake Tibs
Stur
Volgo River
Mount
Hoch
Mezzo
Sea
GREAT PLAIN
Pilger
Camp
Senvolte River
Helig
Zout
Lake
DOMARE

Chapter One

S creeeech!

Squinting from the bright sunlight, Jen stopped mid-step and shaded her eyes with her hand so she could see the eagle circling above them. With his powerful brown and white wings stretched out to their fullest, his feathers caught the wind and took him heavenward. Knowing the peaceful solitude of flying free of earth's limitations, Jen felt the eagle was her kinsman.

"Fly high, my kindred spirit, fly high and free," Jen whispered into the air.

"Looking for a little jockey with copper red hair on the back of that eagle?" Kate asked, coming up alongside of Jen. She kicked a dirt clog off the black asphalt tarmac.

"Always," Jen smiled, but did not break her lock on the eagle's flight. "But, if Raguel has come to visit us, I haven't seen him."

"Remember, Raguel said he had visited us many times before he and the Eagle made their presence known to us." Kate scanned the sky to watch the eagle catch a thermal and soar upward.

"I know, but I can always hope to see them again." Jen continued to enjoy the fluid flight of the great bird circling aloft in the serenity of the rising warm air.

"Maybe the land of Gudsrika and the World of Bigna was a once in a lifetime event—a flash juncture of our lives and the Eagle," Kate said. Seeing a shiny object, she walked two feet onto the runway and stooped

1

down. "FOD," she commented. She picked up an aluminum washer and screw and dropped the foreign object debris into her jacket pocket.

"Thanks," Jen said, referring to Kate picking up the FOD. "Don't want anything to cause an accident."

"You know something?" Kate asked, continuing to walk beside the runway. "To this day Bigna doesn't seem real."

Jen shrugged again. "I suppose so, but you and I know it was." She looked at the graceful flight of the eagle. "Well, as real as a parallel world can be."

"Not a parallel world," Kate corrected. "Remember what Raguel told us about the two worlds—'*Bigna is its own world...connected to the Earth World we live in by the Obex.*'"

"I know. But, it is hard to not think of it as a surreal dream—and a parallel world," Jen shrugged. "And the Obex—I remember it as a surreal nightmare." She shivered at the thought of the eerie barrier between the two worlds—Earth World and Bigna World.

"Maybe it was a once in a lifetime experience going through the Obex from one world to another." Kate shared her thought aloud. "And maybe once is enough and all we will get."

"Maybe," Jen agreed. She unconsciously toyed with the golden heart-shaped locket that hung around her neck. She clicked the locket open to see if her grandparents' picture was still there. Slightly faded but still visible was the black and white picture of their Grandmother Annie and Grandfather Stewart in their World War II army uniforms.

"I just looked at mine, too," Kate smiled. "We're still in Earth World time."

Jen snapped her locket shut. "You are right, maybe just once..."

"Look!" Kate exclaimed, cutting Jen's thought off. "I can see both the sun and moon." She pointed at the sun, but the faded moon was reveling itself at the horizon. "It reminds me of the two moons of Bigna."

"Me too," Jen agreed. She put her hand on Kate's shoulder. "Me too."

For a moment they stood taking in a mental picture of Bigna.

"Bigna—Raguel—the Eagle—they all are like the vision of the two moons, almost illusions in our minds." Kate shook her head and gazed at the airfield around them. "We probably have reminisced enough about Bigna for the time being. This is our real word."

"You are right," Jen smiled. "And it is a great world."

They walked silently for a few minutes along side of the runway they would use in a few hours to take their Stearman into the air so Jen could perform her graceful gymnastics on the Stearman's wings. Swarms of people were posing for pictures beside the static display airplanes. Other individuals staked out places along the side of the runway so they would have a front row seat for the air demonstrations. For most of the people who were fascinated by man's ability to take airplanes to their envelope, watching the aerobatics of Jen wing-walking, while Kate held the Stearman steady, would be a first and the highlight of the afternoon.

"Look!" Jen pointed toward the crowd. "It looks like it's going to be a great audience for the air demonstration."

"And the day is beautiful." Kate sucked in a deep breath. "We are the two luckiest women in the world to be able to do this." She put her arms out and spun around, taking in every aspect of the airport.

"Agreed," Jen said. She glanced upward but could not find the eagle. It had flown to another place—another point in time.

"We'll soon be flying with that eagle," Kate said. Try as she might, she could not see the eagle either. "We might not see the eagle, but we know he is up there with us."

"Licet volare si in tergo aquilae volat," Jen said.

"A man can fly if he wishes, if he rides on the back of an eagle."

"Flying high and free," Jen smiled. "Yea, cousin, we are the luckiest."

Jen had not put on her wing-walking jumpsuit, but still wore the same type leather flight jacket as Kate. Both sported silk scarves around their necks—Kate's was white with a small blue triangle on it while Jen's was light orange with a small blue triangle on it.

The small blue triangles confirmed that their time in Bigna was real. After all, Raguel had presented them with the scarves when they learned to fly the Maup birds. Raguel had made it official—they were part of Bigna's Air Power. Once back to their Earth World, when the triangles didn't disappear, they changed the colors on their Stearman to reflect their experience and their love of flying the Maups.

Their Stearman's fuselage was an off-white that from a distance looked like the peach fuzz that covered the Maups' bodies. The airplane's wings and tail were orange. But, for them, the best part was the navy blue triangle painted on the belly of the Stearman. Inside the triangle was the profile of an eagle's head with a thunderbolt under it. The words *on the back of an Eagle* were printed underneath the triangle. They had changed their logo to match their hearts.

Jen scanned the sky around the desert runway and broke the silence. "Sunny and clear," she commented. "One small cloud," she pointed toward a cotton ball size cloud. "Good for flying and wing-walking unless the heat picks up."

Kate shaded her eyes and looked into the almost cloudless blue canopy above them. She picked up a handful of dirt and let the breeze blow it out of her hand. "It looks like the wind is kicking up."

"Well," Jen said, "the wind and the hot air coming off the ground could cause a few...a few interesting bumpy moments in the air." She smiled at Kate. "But, unless it gets worse, the show must go on."

The dust curled around them as it fell toward the ground, but it did not dissipate. Instead it swirled into an updraft, picking up more bits of sand as it gathered momentum.

Kate and Jen side-stepped to get out of the twisting dust, yet it moved with them, building into a full blown dust devil coiling around their bodies. The mini-tornado's strong vertical motion lifted their feet off the solid ground of the tarmac and pulled them into a forceful whirlwind.

"Kate!" Jen yelled. "What's happening?"

"I don't know," Kate shouted and reached toward Jen. "Grab my hand!"

Jen didn't need Kate to tell her twice. She stretched out and grasped onto Kate. "Hold on!"

The rotating column of thick dusty air pulled them into the vortex of the blinding storm. Sand blotted out their vision as they tumbled inside the twister. Hot air pushed them spinning upward in the chimney-like funnel formation. Forced to the outside of the spinning tornado, their backs hit a wall of an unseen force that grabbed them as metal against a strong magnet. Unable to move Kate and Jen grasped each other's hand tighter.

Their aviator sunglasses ripped from their eyes. Their faces unprotected, rice-size grains of rock pelted their skin like car windshields in a desert sandstorm.

"Close your eyes!" Kate yelled.

"Already done," Jen yelled back.

Even through closed eyes they could see the yellowish flashes of lightning. The sporadic flickering glow created ghostly imagines against their inner eyelids. Loud rumblings, sounding like a freight train barreling down the track at them, closed off any other sounds inside the sand tunnel in which they were trapped.

A blast of icy cold air rushed upward in the center of the rotating dust walls, causing the force holding them against the wall to release them, but they still rotated, though slower, inside the storm. The freight train rumblings gave way to a snake-hissing wind coiling around their senses.

Then silence.

They opened their eyes to get an orientation of what was happening. The lighting had stopped. The violent tornado was at a merry-go-round speed, with everything outside the funnel a blur. Kate looked upward and with her free hand she pointed toward a circular hole at the top of the funnel—blue sky shown through.

However, instead of continuing to go upward, suction pulled them downward and pushed them forward. Solid ground rose to meet their feet.

As sudden as it began, the storm dissolved around them. Ever so briefly, cool air brushed against their faces clearing away the dust particles that clung to their skin.

"Wow!" Jen said. "What was that?"

"Not sure," Kate answered. She bent down and retrieved two pair of aviator sunglasses. Studying them she handed one pair to Jen.

"Bent a little," Jen twisted one temple to straighten it out, "but still usable."

Kate put her glasses in her inside jacket pocket.

"Where are we?" Jen asked.

"Don't know that either," Kate answered, "but look around us. We're not on the tarmac of the air show anymore."

"Understatement," Jen said. She studied the early medieval building they were inside and the tunics, togas and laced sandals worn by the people surrounding them. "A very big understatement."

Chapter Two

*B*arely able to stand because of the mass of pushing people around them, Kate and Jen continued to hold each other's hand. The blue sky of the air show they were admiring just moments before had morphed into a domed, vaulted ceiling, decorated with figurative paintings. The soft murmuring of the crowd created a muffled humming reverberating off the walls.

"Where are we?" Jen whispered.

"I'm not sure," Kate answered. "But looking around the artistic architecture of the room, I'm going to surmise we are in a medieval cathedral."

Pressed into a stone pillar by men jockeying to gain a better spectator spot, Kate and Jen stood still momentarily to take in the interior of the stone building. The ceiling was arched five stories above them. Stone pillars, carved with intricate symbols and spaced evenly apart, framed the hall-like central section, which was thirty-five feet wide and extended the full four hundred feet of the building. Angelic figures, at the second-story level, were tucked into alcoves in the pillars. Behind the pillars on each side were hall-like areas about twenty-five feet wide that ran the length of the building. In the center section, three quarters of the way down, a huge oak pulpit rose.

In the pulpit, bigger than life, a priest held his hand up to quiet the crowd. His head had been shaved to show the thin band of hair of a clerical tonsure. A bushy boxed beard hid the expression on his aged face. The finely woven wool papal robe, draped around his body, revealed his leadership in a high ecclesiastical position. Nothing about his face or stature was out of the ordinary, yet when he spoke his words were elegant and powerful.

"Most beloved brethren…"

The shuffling for a better listening position stopped. All faces turned toward the priest in the pulpit. Each word he spoke drew the people deeper into his speech.

"…enter the road to the Holy Sepulchre…"

Only the movement of a small child broke the attention of the individuals listening to the priest. The people packed in the church seemed to cover the broad spectrum of social class. Sprinkled among the priests, monks, knights, bishops and abbots were laymen and peasants. Every inch of the cathedral was occupied by an eager multitude of men, women and children who gave their full focus to the man in the pulpit.

"…I call upon you, but not I but…" the priest's voice grew louder.

"If I didn't know better, "Kate whispered to Jen, "I'd say we're at the Council of Clermont in 1095AD."

"Either that or we're in a very realistic recreation," Jen whispered.

"Then the priest speaking must be Pope Urban the Second."

A young man, maybe in his late teens, standing close to them turned and gave them a *be quiet* look.

Kate, a little embarrassed, gave him a half-hearted grin. He went back to listening to the Pope.

Kate and Jen studied the people around them. The social positions could be guessed by the dress of those who filled the hall. Some sported linen caps, simple robes and sandals, suggesting they were of the working class, but most of the crowd wore clothing of an influential class. Velvet caps, silk purses, long cloaks and closed leather shoes reflected the elegance and high rank of the wearer. The young man who had given them *the look* wore extravagant shoes that curved up at the toe.

Jen pointed to the feet of the young man. "A member of a king's court?" she whispered so he could not hear her.

"It would appear so," Kate softly answered. She gave the man a once over and gave Jen a wink. "Looking at the grandeur of his clothing I'd say not the court jester."

Carefully edging through the crowd, they left the security of the pillar and moved closer to the pulpit.

"…All should go, rich and poor alike…" The priest in the pulpit paused and let the statement resonate among the gathering.

A roar of approval echoed off the walls.

Kate nudged Jen. Keeping her hand close to her body, she pointed to a man standing next to her. A small statured monk, wearing a long face and a grungy woolen robe tied at the waist with a coarse rope, clung enthusiastically to each of the Pope Urban's words. His face bore a mask of sadness, as one with years of internal torment would plaster on each day.

"Do you think it could be," Kate mouthed, "Peter the Hermit?"

Jen shrugged and mouthed back, "Ask him."

"What's to lose," Kate shrugged and turned to the man next to her. "Are you Peter…uh…Peter the Hermit of Amiens?" she dared to ask the monk.

The monk momentarily diverted his attention from the words coming from the pulpit to Kate. From under the hood thrown over his head his eyes quickly glanced at this oddly dressed stranger. "That is what they call me," he answered and then turned his attention back to the priest in the pulpit. The call for action was becoming louder and the crowd was becoming exhilarated with agreement.

"…Undertake this journey for the remission of your sins, with the assurance of the imperishable glory of the Kingdom of Heaven!"

His words were commanding. Even Kate and Jen were drawn in to the passionate plea from the priest.

"…Let none hesitate—they must march next summer. God wills it!"

The crowd again shouted their approval. The walls of the cathedral echoed with their agreement.

"The Crusades," Kate yelled over the crowd noise to Jen.

Peter the Hermit overheard Kate's comment. "Crusades? What crusades?" He shifted his weight from one filthy sandaled foot to the other.

"The Crusades," Kate answered. "And you will gather the laborers and country folk to follow you on your journey to Jerusalem."

"Crusades?" Peter the Hermit repeated. "I don't know anything called the crusades."

"The Crusades," Kate repeated. "You know—Pope Urban the Second urging the people to liberate the holy city of Jerusalem. And you will lead the first Crusade—the People's Crusade."

Peter the Hermit shook his head. "I don't know what you are talking about, but I do know that I am being called by God. I know it is God's will for me to lead a pilgrimage to Jerusalem and to fight a war on the Turks who have taken the city from us."

"But your followers," Jen stepped in. "Your followers will not be equipped to fight."

"My followers?" Peter the Hermit questioned. Without waiting for an answer he stated, "The people who join me will be on a pilgrimage to rescue the holy city. Deus vult—God wills it!"

"But you…" Jen began, and then she felt Kate's hand on her arm.

"No Jen," Kate said. "You cannot stop history. I don't know why we're here," she looked around the building, "but it cannot be to stop Peter the Hermit from leading the common people on the first Crusade."

"Crusade," Peter the Hermit shook his head and again gave them the once over. "I do not know where you come from. Your clothes are not like any I have seen in my travels, but I do know you have been brought here for a purpose."

For the first time, Kate and Jen realized they must look odd to Peter the Hermit and the rest of the medieval dressed people around them. However, most of the crowd was so engrossed with what Pope Urban the Second was saying they did not notice the strangers.

"I agree with you," Kate concurred with Peter. "We must have a purpose for being here." She looked at Jen, hoping she might have figured it out.

"Don't have a clue," Jen shrugged.

"Then you are on a journey like the rest of us," Peter the Hermit said. "Come with me to search for why you are here." Leaving Kate and Jen's side, he pushed his way through the crowd toward the pulpit. "Join us!" he yelled at them before he disappeared in a sea of people surrounding him.

From inside the crowd where he disappeared they could hear his commanding voice, "Deus vult! Deus vult!" His words, like a wave coming ashore, spread outward and grew louder as the crowd picked up his chant.

Deus vult!

Deus vult!

Deus vult!

Jen looked at Kate. "This doesn't make sense. We are actually in… actually in Earth World time…in Earth World history. It's like we've traveled backward through time. I don't get it."

"Me either." Kate watched the crowd being whipped up to a frenzied fervor to the call of war. "What I do get is that Pope Urban's speech changed the course of history, but we cannot."

Deus vult!

Deus vult!

Deus vult!

"What should we do?" Jen asked over the shouting crowd. "Should we join the monk on his first crusade?"

"I don't know," Kate raised her voice.

Deus vult!

Deus vult!

Deus vult!

For a moment they listened to the cadence of the crowd's echoing mantra until it became so loud they could not even yell over it. Jen pointed toward the door. Kate nodded in agreement.

Deus vult!

Deus vult!

Deus vult!

The chant tumbled out of the arched doorway ahead of them and was caught by enthusiastic peasants packed into the square in front of the church.

Deus vult!

Deus vult!

Deus vult!

Pushing through the crowd they made their way down one of the town's narrow cobblestone streets. Two story stone houses and places of businesses were smashed together, leaving little room, if any, between them. Stray pigs wandered around without their owners—some rolled around snorting in the drain channels that ran along side of the street.

Kate glanced around at their strange surroundings. A woman, stepping onto her second story balcony, lifted a wooden bucket over her head. Kate reasoned quickly at what was about to happen and yelled at Jen, "Watch out!"

She pushed Jen against the side of a building just as the woman threw the foul, chunky liquid downward toward the open drains. Missing the drain, the thick, filthy water splashed against the cobblestones and splattered over Kate and Jen's feet.

"Thanks," Jen frowned looking at her shoes. "That," she pointed at the unrecognizable muck on her feet, "could have been on our heads."

"You're welcome," Kate also looked at her grunge-covered shoes. "I guess it's better on our shoes than our heads." She grinned.

Jen knew in that moment they would be all right. Their feet might be covered in medieval filth, but they were together. She grinned back.

"Look!" Kate exclaimed. She nodded toward a man dressed in a bright purple peasant-like tunic over tight red pants. A red beret sat askew on his head. "A wandering minstrel."

As if on cue the medieval singer strummed his lute and warbled out a sing-song ballet.

> *Pope Urban is calling knights and peasants to take up their sword.*
> *Deus vult! Deus vult! Their battle cry before them.*
> *Every man undertakes this journey with one accord.*
> *Ride fast, ride fast for Jerusalem to gain your final reward.*
> *Ride fast, ride fast young man, for the devil is close, ready to condemn.*

"It seems Pope Urban's words have inspired everyone to join into the fight," Jen said. "The Crusades have begun."

"Yes, the Crusades have begun and we are standing in the middle of history," Kate said. "But we still don't know why we're here."

"And we can't change history, even though we know how the Crusades end, because we know the Eagle doesn't put us into the Earth World to change history."

"We don't know the Eagle brought us here," Kate observed.

"If not the Eagle, who…or what?" Jen rubbed her chin in contemplation. "This doesn't make any sense."

"Peter the Hermit was right," Kate offered. "We are here for a purpose."

"We just don't know what it is or where to look for answers," Jen said.

"The answers are somewhere."

"Someone or something brought us here, but who…why." Jen reached for her locket. Opening the golden heart, she commented, "The picture of Grandmother Annie and Grandfather Stewart are still in it."

"In mine too," Kate said. "So our lockets are not giving us any clues."

"At least not at this time," Jen said, hopeful that soon their lockets would give them guidance.

"Let's keep walking. Maybe we can find a clue or some sort of sign that will help us understand." Kate dropped her locket back into her shirt.

"Agreed," Jen nodded.

Chapter Three

Color was void on the cobblestone street where Kate and Jen walked. "Whatever our purpose is, it is extremely interesting seeing medieval history up close and personal," Kate observed.

"It sure is," Jen concurred. "And seeing all the businesses." She pointed toward a rough edged stone opening of a blacksmith shop at the corner of the street five feet in front of them.

Clink!

Clink!

Clink!

A blacksmith carefully struck a piece of iron and forged it into a steel knife blade. His leather apron protected him from the hot flying sparks of each stroke of the hammer. Behind him, a young boy pumped the bellows of the furnace to keep air blowing onto the fire so it would burn intensely.

"Keep the fire hot!" the blacksmith yelled at his apprentice. "More charcoal!"

The lad gave the bellows one hard pump before he picked up a battered bucket and carefully tossed charcoal into the stone fireplace. Scattering the dark grey lumps to gain an even heat, he went back to pumping the bellows.

Clink!

Clink!

The blacksmith gripped his tongs tighter and held the newly formed blade into the air so he could get a better look at it. Not satisfied with what he saw, he put it back onto his anvil and brought his hammer back into position.

Clink!

Clink!

Clink!

Kate and Jen watched a moment more before they ventured further down the street. Various venders, hawking everything from raw meat to silken cloth, vied for their attention. A few of the venders whispered to each other as Kate and Jen passed. They observed the strangers, dressed in odd clothes, with watchful eyes.

"What do you suppose we could use as money?" Jen asked. "I'm sure this won't work." She pulled a five-dollar bill from her pants' pocket.

Kate withdrew the aluminum washer and screw from her jacket pocket. "Maybe a bartering chip?" She held out the FOD she had picked up off the airport runway earlier that day.

"I'm sure they would not recognize anything we would offer," Kate smiled at the screw and washer.

"Just a thought," Kate laughed. "I'm sure you're right. But we're almost to the outskirts of town and we still haven't figured out why we're here." She tucked the screw and washer back into her jacket pocket.

A wooden cart stopped in front of them, blocking them from going any further on their walk. Woven baskets, half filled with fruits and vegetables, gave the rolling street side market a produce stand look.

Kate smiled at the vendor and looked over the sparse pickings. "Look!" She pointed to a group of golden yellow, pear-shaped fruits. "Quince."

"How do you know that kind of thing?" Jen laughed. "I would have called them puny pears."

Picking up a yellow quince from a cart, Kate jumped back.

"Oh!" she exclaimed.

A small copper red field mouse was underneath the piece of fruit—his black eyes stared at her.

"Squeak—Squeak—Squeak."

"What the..." the merchant muttered. Aghast that a rodent would invade his business, he grabbed a stick and whacked at the small furry object. His first swat hit the edge of the quince basket, spilling the five remaining fruit and the field mouse onto the ground. His next swing missed the mouse's head by a quarter of an inch.

The furry field mouse scurried away from the cart toward a narrow alley. Yelling at the rodent intruder, the merchant waved his hands in disgust. Unable to stop the retreating red mouse, he mumbled a few more indistinguishable words before he gathered up the spilled fruit and went back to selling his wares.

Gawking at the scene before them, Kate and Jen froze momentarily. Kate eased the quince back onto the cart and looked toward the alley where the mouse disappeared.

"Quince?" the merchant interrupted their thoughts. He wiped the fruit off on the front of his stained tunic and held it out as if the mouse never existed.

Kate shook her head no.

"What do you think?" Jen tugged on Kate's jacket sleeve to get her away from the merchant.

Kate scrunched up her face in uncertainty. She squinted down the seven-foot wide, shadowy alley. Stone buildings on either side of the passageway formed thirty-foot high walls—no visible way out once someone started down that path.

"That alley is pretty dark," she hesitated. "And we don't even know…"

Popping his head out from behind an overturned wooden bucket fifteen feet down the passageway, the mouse gave a quick glance at the angry merchant and then fixed his small marble-like eyes on Kate and Jen.

"I think the…the mouse…wants us to follow him." Kate said

"Do you think…could it be Raguel?" Jen asked

"I don't know," Kate shrugged, "but that red mouse is the closest thing to something familiar we've seen."

Jen laughed.

"What's so funny?" Kate asked.

"That you…we would think a red mouse running from a medieval fruit cart and hiding behind a wooden bucket is familiar…and maybe normal."

"You're right," Kate laughed. "It is a little crazy, but then so is this whole situation. I think we should follow the mouse and find out what is and what isn't real."

"I'm right beside you," Jen nodded.

Scurrying from behind the bucket, the mouse ran further into the darkening alley, up a flight of stone stairs and disappeared through a small crack in a wooden door in the side of a stone building.

Kate and Jen darted after the mouse, ignoring the gloominess of the alley. Slowly they climbed the twelve narrow steps until they reached the closed entrance. The wooden door, aged with mildew, gave a slimy green glow in the dim light filtering into the narrow alley. A dip was in the small stone porch, created from years of people coming and going from this building. They hesitated at the wooden door and glanced at the heavy beam above the door. A tracery of a small eagle was scratched into the masonry.

"What do you think, cousin?" Kate asked.

Jen exhaled a deep breath. "We're in a narrow, creepy alley...in a strange land...I think this is all weird, but I don't think we have a choice." Her locket began to radiate beneath her shirt.

"Jen!" Kate exclaimed. "Your locket!" At the same time she pulled her locket out and opened it.

"The pictures are fading," Jen said.

"Fading into where?" Kate pondered out loud. "There is no mist...no image...just our grandparents picture disappearing."

"I really think we don't have a choice now," Jen said. "We have to follow that red mouse through this door."

"Then let's do it," Kate concurred.

Creak!

The rusty door hinges suggested this entrance was not used much anymore. Whoever had created the worn spot in the stone porch had long since quit coming through this entry.

Creak!

Kate pushed the green glowing door open a little further. The dim light from the alley cast a yellowish streak across the wood-planked floor inside the doorway and highlighted a small figure.

The copper red mouse was gone. Instead, Raguel, with his beguiling smile and small round black eyes, welcomed them on the other side. He wore his hunter green knickers, long socks that cuffed knee-high, laced brown boots and a khaki Eisenhower jacket. On the jacket's left sleeve, just above the banded cuff, was an embroidered eagle flying toward two golden embroidered stars. His shoulder length, silky copper red hair curled around his small furry mouse ears and framed his chubby, freckled cheeked face.

"Raguel!" Jen gave a relieved yell. "We are so glad to see you." She felt like picking his stocky, four foot body up and squeezing him tight, but she froze because of the circumstances.

"And I am glad to see you, too," Raguel responded.

"Where are we?" Kate asked.

"No time to explain right now," Raguel said. "Just follow me." He hurried down a darkened hallway and through an arched doorway.

Kate and Jen raced after Raguel, but stopped short when they reached the doorway—nothing but an eddy of indigo blackness greeted them on the other side.

Badaroom!

Badaroom!

Chapter Four

*B*adaroom!
    Badaroom!

The rumbling bass-drum sound of thunder vibrated the air around them.

"Whoa!" Kate exclaimed. She stepped back from the pulsating threshold, pulling Jen with her. "That has the distinct feeling of the Obex."

"My feelings exactly." Jen craned her neck to see through the doorway, but didn't move her body forward.

Memories of their last encounter inside the Obex were all too real. Atasa, the monstrous dragon-like creature that was the sentry of the barrier between Earth World and Bigna World, flashed through Jen's mind. Vivid was the picture of the two large, bulging soulless black eyes, set in a scaly snake-like face. Its flaming three pronged, forked lizard tongue had lashed from a beastly mouth, when he chased them through the murky blue tunnel between Earth World and Bigna World once before. Teeth, ready to devour everything close to him, gleamed with acid-like saliva in his pursuit. Jen knew his mammoth 747 jumbo-jet size body still slithered across the Obex—its head moving to and fro in search of prey, ready to catch souls for eternity. And she knew that wherever Atasa was, Rapio the Raven, the mystical, magical dark leader of Bigna, would be close by—ready to control their spirits forever.

"Did Raguel disappear into that void?" Kate asked.

"It would appear so," Jen answered.

Instinctively Kate knew what Jen was thinking. She put her hand on Jen's shoulder for comfort. "We cannot think of Atasa and Rapio right now."

"You are right," Jen nodded. She put the picture of Atasa and Rapio out of her mind. "I think Raguel wants us to follow him."

"Then 1095AD in our Earth World might not be where we are going to end up."

"I guess not," Jen said. Her locket radiated with a pleasant heat.

"Jen," Kate said. "Look in your locket." At the same time she talked, she opened her locket.

Inside their lockets a mini tornado of misty blue vapor swirled around. But there was neither an answer nor direction for them.

"What do you think?" Jen asked.

"Well, we can't stay in this spot of history and we don't know how to get back to our time so…"

"So we have to follow Raguel," Jen finished Kate's sentence.

"Whew," Kate exhaled. She grabbed Jen's hand. "Hold on to your locket, cousin. This might be a rough ride."

"Holding it—as well as your hand—tight." Jen took a deep breath.

"Then let's do it."

"Ready?" Jen exhaled.

Kate nodded.

"Three—two—one—"

And they stepped into the swirling dark, indigo-black space after Raguel.

Flashes of flame swept out from the inky void, briefly giving their surroundings an orange-red color. Weightlessly, they disappeared into a shockwave of blue gel—thickish, yet at the same time transparent. They were again tumbling through the translucent blueberry jelly of the Obex.

Holding tight to Jen's hand, Kate twisted her head to get some sort of reassurance from her cousin that they made the right decision. An indigo colored, wave-like mist rippled between them.

Jen nodded the comfort Kate was looking for, but they both knew they were in enemy territory. Atasa could appear at anytime.

Aaargh!

The torturing sounds began.

It was faint for a moment—but only a miniscule moment—then the loud soulful cries of ghostly beings encased them.

Aaargh!

Wispy, humanlike forms soared by and reached out for them.

Invisible fingers from shadowy beings grasped them and pulled them toward the wailing cries. Though they struggled, they were in complete control of the unknown force.

Aaargh!

Kate felt a bone-crushing grip encircle her hand that held tightly to her locket. Without letting go of Jen she wrestled against the unseen vice. The more she fought the invisible force, the tighter the pressured grasp became. Kate felt her fingers loosening their hold on her locket.

"I'm losing the battle for my locket!" Kate yelled.

"Fight it!" Jen yelled back. "Fight it!"

Kate battled the unseen foe, but couldn't get the grip to loosen.

"Fight it!" Jen shouted again. She tightened the grip on her own locket. They could not lose both lockets to the wicked forces of Rapio.

The sensation was faint at first, but from within Kate's grip a white heat began to radiate. Though her locket grew hotter, she could not let it go. The more intense the new force became the tighter her fingers wrapped around her locket—her hand and the locket became one.

The locket is fighting back, Kate thought. Through her fingers she could see the golden glow of the powerful battle between the strength of her locket and the ruthlessness of the shadowy force.

Yowllll!

The loud howling, painful cry reverberated around Kate and Jen. As quickly as the energy had gripped Kate's hand, the golden flowing force released her from it. Her locket had won the battle.

But they were not out of danger. They were still encased in the Obex.

Aaargh!

The ear-piercing shrieks of agony continued from inside the pulsating dark walls. Pushed by a violent wind and pelted by icy golf ball size hail, they tumbled out of control.

A sudden flash of bright green lightning blinded them. Its roaring thunder shattered their hearing.

Kraa—Kraa—Kraa!

"The Raven," Kate yelled.

Jen's grip tightened around Kate's hand and pulled her close in. She encircled both arms around her cousin.

"Pray!" Jen yelled through the chaos. "Pray!"

Unseen, but felt by Kate and Jen, stereo waves of the tormented sounds coming from the wispy figures grew louder, mixing with the death-rattling call of the raven.

Kraa—Kraa—Kraa!

Aaargh!

The distant cry of the raven engulfed the other sounds.

Kraa—Kraa—Kraa!

Dry ice heat sucked the air from around them.

Kraa—Kraa—Kraa!

The raven was in the Obex with them—close enough that Kate and Jen felt their lungs crying out for the life-giving oxygen being squeezed from them.

Screeeech!

"The Eagle!" Kate managed to choke out.

"I hear him," Jen's words of relief echoed through the Obex. "Our prayers…he heard our prayers." She craned her neck to get a view of him, but it was no use—she could not find him through the dark mist whirling around them.

Screeeech!

The Eagle's protective cry surrounded their bodies, blocking the asphyxiating breath of the raven, and filled their lungs full of air.

Screeeech!

The dark blueberry gel Obex crashed around them, but they could feel the presence of the Eagle protecting them in the eye of the cyclone.

Kaboom!

Prbttt!

The undulating indigo darkness crashed behind them. Flashes of lightening exploded in one last turbulent defiance before the chaos stopped. The Obex had spit them out from its sinister mayhem into a blue sky calm world.

Screeeech!

With the Eagle screaming above them, Kate and Jen tumbled headlong onto a patchy green and brown carpet of moss and clay. Roots, from a large oak tree rising high beside them, protruded through the ground and spread out like octopus tentacles around them.

Cough…cough…cough!

"Are you okay?" Jen asked.

"I think so, but…" Kate coughed. "But I still need a little more oxygen." She inhaled deeply.

"Where are we?" Jen stood, a little wobbly, but kept herself upright. She offered her hand to Kate.

"Well, this tree looks familiar," Kate said taking Jen's outstretched hand, "but I don't see a butte with a cave or anything else familiar." Pulling herself up, she took another deep breath.

"I know," Jen said. "Except for the tree everything is different."

They stood at a mountain edge overlooking an enormous flat, grassy plain. In the distance, a three hundred foot-wide river separated the green prairie from a stone-walled city. Between them and the river was a tent city, dotting the grassland with temporary lean-to housing. Soldiers with medieval clothing milled around the campground.

"This looks like the oak tree that guided our landing in Bigna last time we were here," Kate said, moving toward the tree, away from the edge of the cliff.

"If this is Bigna." Jen followed Kate's lead toward the tree. "We don't know where we are, only that we pursued Raguel into the Obex. We don't even know if we landed in the same place as Raguel."

Screeeech!

The long wings of the Eagle controlled his circling above them.

"No, we don't know, but at least we know the Eagle is here with us," Kate pointed toward the sky.

Screeeech!

Jen nodded. "And we are together."

"Yes, we are," Kate smiled. "And we have our mighty oak beside us." She swung her arm up and pointed at the oak tree. She looked at the full foliage of the forty-foot tree. Each branch was filled with golf ball size acorns. Carefully, she jumped over the massive roots that spread out from the trunk of the oak tree until she was under its huge branches.

Jen followed Kate's steps and joined her under the thick green leaves. Hopefully, she looked upward, into the dense shrubbery.

"Welcome back to Bigna," Raguel said from a gnarled branch ten feet above them.

"Raguel!"

Raguel pushed himself off the branch and tumbled to a landing in front of them. He sprang to his feet.

"Raguel!" Kate did not hesitate this time. She rushed forward and hugged the four-foot being before them. "You are a welcome sight." She twirled him around once and then put him down.

"And so are the two of you," a smiling Raguel said. He pulled on the hem of his tunic to straighten it out from Kate's enthusiastic greeting.

Screeeech!

The cry of the Eagle beckoned them from beneath the shade of the tree and into the sun.

Screeeech!

Dipping one wing, the Eagle circled once above Kate, Jen and Raguel. The Eagle's gaze never broke from Kate's and Jen's eyes. Like a digital camera, his deep brown eyes clicked snapshots of their very souls. Neither

Kate nor Jen wanted to break their silent connection with the Eagle. He had brought them back to Bigna for a reason.

Screeeech!

With one long high pitched cry the Eagle momentarily became a freeze frame, and then quickly disappeared into the bright sun.

Chapter Five

Quickly, Kate and Jen turned their attention from the sky back to the elf-like being next to them.

"Raguel!" Jen exclaimed. "You haven't changed one bit."

Raguel's beguiling smile grew up his cheeks.

"Where are we?" Kate asked, looking at their surroundings.

"Bigna," Raguel said.

"Bigna?" Jen asked. "Except for this huge oak tree, nothing looks like the Bigna we left."

"Bigna World is like your Earth World—big, diverse and made up of many lands. When you were here last you landed in Gudsrika. This time when you came through the Obex…"

"Obex!" Jen spit out. "It is still unpleasant."

"I'm sorry," Raguel said. "The Obex is still Rapio's domain—and Atasa still guards its gates. You are still protected by your lockets but…"

"Raguel," Kate interrupted. "Something almost pulled my locket from me." She reached for her neck for assurance her locket was still hanging there.

Raguel paled. "Remember what I told you before. Your lockets give you protection and connect you to the Eagle. When Rapio, Atasa or any of their minions get close to you, they will try to yank your lockets off. If any of them succeed, you will belong to Rapio."

Phew! Air escaped from Kate's mouth.

"But you still have it." Raguel's color slowly came back to his face. "Your locket is still around your neck." He reached over and touched Kate's locket. "Always wear it close to your heart."

"We always have, ever since our Grandmother Annie gave them to us when we were five years old." Kate opened the locket to gain the comfort of the black and white picture of their Grandmother Annie and Grandfather Stewart inside. "Jen! The picture of our grandparents is gone."

Jen's fingers quickly unsnapped her heart-shaped locket. "Their picture is gone from mine, too."

Both stared at the smoky blue haze swirling around in their lockets.

"Your lockets will serve you while you are in Bigna," Raguel said. "They will guide you and protect you."

Kate and Jen nodded. "We know," they said in unison, and tucked their lockets inside their shirts.

"Raguel," Kate looked around at the big oak tree and then glanced at the open flatland in the valley. "You say this is Bigna?"

"Yes."

"How can that be?" Kate asked. "We saw Gudsrika…Bigna collapse into the sea."

"Bigna was not destroyed. What you saw was Bigna disappearing."

"Disappearing?" Kate's eyebrow raised in a question. "Bigna disappears? From what?"

"It disappears from the Earth World connection, but it does not go away. It continues to develop its own history."

"So—during that time there is no correlation to the Earth World's history and Bigna?"

"Yes…and no," Raguel grinned. "During this time it is not necessary to be in union with the Earth World."

"So there are times it is necessary for the two worlds to join together," Kate stated trying to understand. "And when it is necessary…does the Eagle pull them together?"

"Simplistically said, but yes," Raguel answered. "There are times the two worlds must collide in order for the Earth World to survive."

"And did the Eagle bring us here?"

"Yes."

27

"So it is now time for the two worlds to…to…you said collide?" Kate asked.

"Yes," Raguel answered without explanation.

"I'm still slightly confused," Jen joined the conversation.

"Confused?" Raguel asked. "About what?"

"I suppose if the Eagle brought us to Bigna he has a purpose for us… and I'm sure you, or someone, will tell us what it is."

"In time…" Raguel began.

"I know in time we'll find out why we're in Bigna," Jen interrupted him. She remembered that Raguel always answered *in time* when he wasn't ready to reveal the whole story.

Raguel smiled at Jen's remembrance of how he deflected questions.

"Our purpose for being here isn't why I'm confused," Jen said, "I'm perplexed by why we had the intermediate stop at the Council of Clermont…in medieval Earth World."

"Ah, yes," Raguel smiled. "Well, Eagle knows you two have inquisitive minds and would be curious about what was on the other side of the Obex—on the Earth World side. So, he pulled back the curtain to give you context of your purpose in Bigna…and so you wouldn't be tempted to find out on your own—again."

Kate and Jen grimaced at Raguel's not so subtle reminder of the time they put their trust in Raquel's twin brother Rocus and followed him through the Obex between the Isle of Gudsrika in Bigna World and Ireland in Earth World.

"We wouldn't do that again," Jen said meekly.

"We know," Raguel confirmed her statement, "but you also needed to see the Council of Clermont to know what is happening in Bigna."

"So why are we here?" Kate asked. Before Raguel could answer she added, "And where exactly is here?"

"Domare—this is the land of Domare in Bigna," Raguel answered her second question and ignored the first one. "We are standing on top of Mount Hoch. The Great Plain is before you. The river you see across the plain is the Senvolte River. Follow the Senvolte to its beginning and you will see it is a tributary off the Volgo River that flows from Lake Tibs to the Zout Lake. On the far side of the Senvolte is the city of Helig—the holy city to the Quae Pilgers."

"Quae Pilgers?" Kate asked.

"The Pilgers are part of The Missioners on The Mission to take back Helig from the Indringers who…"

"Indringers?" Kate interrupted. I thought the Indringers were all killed…" Kate began. "…killed…uh…destroyed…"

"Were all destroyed at the Battle of Agor," Jen finished Kate's thought.

"No, they were not all destroyed. Rapio still needs the Indringers to fight his battles in Bigna. The Indringers we fight in Domare are descendants of those you fought in Gudsrika."

"Oh," Kate and Jen said.

"The Mission began four years ago, many miles and many lands from Domare. They came from all directions to the city of Stur, but the objective of The Mission has always been to march to Helig. For the Quae, Helig is considered the holiest of holy cities. All Quae desire to make at least one pilgrimage to Helig in their lifetime so they can kneel in the Holy Chamber inside the Helig Monastery. And most did make their pilgrimage until four years ago when the Indringers, under the command of Rapio's High Priest Onde, invaded the city walls and took control of the city. They mercilessly massacred the Quae and monks who resisted them. Onde declared the kingship his and crowned himself king of Helig. He ordered the Indringers to turn the monastery into a stable, smash the altars and destroy much of the Quae's ancient culture. After showing the outside world of Bigna what he would do, Onde closed the city gates and would not allow the Quae Pilgers inside to complete their journey to visit the Holy Chamber."

"I'm beginning to see why you and the Eagle wanted us to be reminded about the Council of Clermont in medieval Earth World," Kate said.

"Earth World and Bigna World collided again at the Council," Raguel said.

"And now the Quae Pilgers are marching to Helig to release it from the stronghold of the Indringers," Kate stated.

"Yes," Raguel said.

"Much like the Crusaders after the Council," Jen said.

"Yes, very much like the Crusaders," Raguel answered her non question.

"Why did the Pilgers go to Stur first?" Jen asked.

"Stur is where the leaders of all the Quae armies decided they would meet to formulate a plan. When the Pilgers arrived outside the city of Stur they were halted by the strength of the Indringers who occupied the city. The battle for Stur lasted a year before Friar Fara was sent to encourage the Pilgers. One night, while all the Pilgers slept, Friar Fara left the camp and snuck inside the Stur city walls and found the Holy Sword."

"The Holy Sword?" Kate asked. "What is the Holy Sword?"

"The Holy Sword is said to have existed since the beginning of time. It has magical and miraculous powers. It was kept at the Cephas Monastery but was stolen by the Indringers hundreds of years ago."

"Kept at the Monastery—like the BOK?" Kate asked.

"Yes, like the BOK," Raguel smiled at Kate's remembrance of the holy writings of Bigna. "Both are ancient relics protected inside the Monastery."

"Are there other holy relics inside the Monastery?" Jen questioned.

"The Monastery protects many things," Raguel answered.

"Protects?" Jen picked up the present tense. "The Cephas Monastery is still around?"

"Yes, but before we talk about the Monastery, I must tell you about the Holy Sword," Raguel said.

"Of course," Kate eagerly nodded. "We won't interrupt again."

Raguel smiled. He knew they would have more questions and would interrupt him many times before he was able to get the whole story told. The grin still on his lips, he continued, "As I was saying, late one night, while everyone except the outer guards slept, Friar Fara managed to gain entrance inside the city walls. Once inside he found the sword and took it back to the Pilger camp. The next morning Friar Fara waved it over the Pilger army and told them they would be victorious in the battle to take the city of Stur. Filled with miraculous faith, the Pilgers charged Stur.

"It was a bloody battle but under the supernatural powers of the Holy Sword, they overtook the Indringers and were triumphant at the siege of Stur. Filled with confidence of being able to defeat the Indringers, the Pilger leaders met and planned the attack on the holy city of Helig. That was a year ago."

"A year ago?" Kate could not help interrupting Raguel with another question.

Raguel shook his head. He was dealing with two inquiring minds and they would not be happy if he rushed through the details. "Yes, it took the leaders of the Pilgers time to agree on what to do, and even now they don't all agree."

"So what did they do?" Jen piped in.

"Later for that part of the story," Raguel again deflected the question. "What you see in the valley below you are the camps of Duke Nerkon and Lord Obile, two of Domare's greatest knights. Most of the thousands of Quae you see are their armies."

Kate and Jen looked at the hundreds of tents crammed tightly together and the Quae wandering around camp fires at the edges of the camp.

"Look! There's Duke Nerkon." Raquel pointed at a Quae who was a head taller than the average four foot Quae.

Even from their distant observation spot Kate and Jen could pick out the knight Raguel pointed toward. Duke Nerkon's tall stature gave him the look of a nobleman and leader. Solidly-built, with a stalwart chest, his Popeye-like, bulging forearms reminded them of a wrestler. They could tell he was strong beyond compare. His curly blondish-red beard and copper-colored hair that curled around his small mouse-like ears gave him the mark of his fellow Quae.

"And Lord Obile." Raguel pointed to the Quae next to Nerkon.

Walking beside Duke Nerkon was a shorter version of Nerkon. His reddish hair stuck out from under his knights' red, woolen hood. Lord Obile's walk, like Nerkon's was that of confidence.

"When the Pilger leaders gathered together after they conquered Stur, they decided that there needed to be one person in charge to lead all of the Pilger warriors on The Mission," Raguel explained. "They selected Duke Nerkon as their commander. But each of the other leaders still commands his own army into battle."

Joining the two knights was another Pilger, dressed in a royal purple tunic, tan knickers and cloth boots that laced up to his knees. A black patch covered his left eye.

"Who is that?" Jen asked.

"Count Begi," Raguel answered. "He joined Nerkon and Obile in the quest to rescue the holy city of Helig. And like their armies, Begi's Pilgers also refuse to cross the Senvolte River."

"He has an eye patch…" Jen began, but decided that it might be too personal.

"It's okay to ask," Raguel grinned. "The count may even tell you about the battle when he lost his eye. Close hand to hand combat…he even has a scar under the patch where the Indringer's short sword caught Begi by surprise. He wears the patch as a badge of honor."

A torrential storm cloud hung over the Great Plain where Nerkon's army was camped on the near side of the Senvolte River. It seemed to Kate and Jen that it would be a simple trek across the river to get to Helig.

"Why don't they cross the river and attack Helig?" Kate asked. "Is the river too deep?"

"Deep is relative," Raguel answered. "But the depth of the river isn't why the Pilger armies refuse to go across. It is because of some events that happened to other Pilgers who went before them. It caused the Pilgers you see to hunker down and huddle in fear."

"Events?" Jen's eyebrows crinkled in question. "What events?"

"Quae Pilgers coming from the river reported of the Bás Plague…"

"Bás Plague?" Jen interjected.

"The Bás Plague overtakes a Quae Pilger and changes the physical, mental and moral identity of that Quae. It has been consuming all the warriors going toward Helig," Raguel said. "It has unleashed a rampage of death and confusion across the Pilgers marching toward Helig. With the rumor that Quae were infected with the Bás Plague, and able to pass it on, the Pilgers are avoiding anyone who has been into the river. Terror has struck the hearts and minds of the men and women in the encampment. Many have abandoned The Mission. Many who have stayed do not trust anyone. Quarrels are breaking out between soldiers every day."

"How are the leaders handling it?" Jen asked.

"Duke Nerkon and Lord Obile have gathered the knights in charge of their army's divisions to discuss the problems, but they have not come up with a solution. The Quae are still in disarray and are discouraged."

Kate looked intently at the Senvolte River. A large gray, stone tower rose midstream, casting its dark shadow on the white caps of the choppy river water. One glassless window faced the bank where the Pilgers camped.

"That tower," Kate said, "has an ominous look to it."

"That tower has not always been there," Raguel said.

"When was it built?" Kate asked.

"Built?" Raguel shook his head. "I'm not sure it was built. It rose from the depths of the river the morning after the Indringers invaded Helig, but more on that later.

"And the tower just adds to the fear among the Quae Pilgers. It is said that the creature that lives in the tower lures any passersby into the Senvolte. Those who are not killed immediately by the creature are sucked under the water and thrown into the ominous chasms of the darkness below. When, and if, they walk out of the river, they have been transformed and fallen into the power of Rapio's darkness."

"Is it like the Mørket Forest in Gudsrika?" Jen asked.

"Very much like the Mørket Forest in the evil intent, but unlike the forest, there is no safe time to cross the river," Raguel frowned. "Everything caught up in the river adds to the fear of the Pilgers and has delayed the journey to Helig for months."

Kate continued to survey the Senvolte. "Look!" she pointed toward the campsite. "Three Pilgers are going toward the Senvolte."

The three Pilgers made their way to the edge of the river. One of the Pilgers was armored clad, sword at his side. The other two wore red linen tunics and tan breeches that disappeared into their mud-splattered cloth boots. Slowly the armored knight slipped his Great Helm helmet over the mail coif that covered his head. His eyes were hidden behind the narrow slits in the head protector, but Kate was sure there was anxiety behind the courageous demeanor shown by the Pilger. Taking a few steps away from his fellow knights, he stood ankle deep in the river. He glanced quickly over his shoulder at his fellow Pilgers.

To Helig! Victory!

The strains of his victory cry seeped through the small openings in his helmet.

His companions raised their right fist into the air and echoed his cry.

To Helig! Victory!

The armored knight drew his sword from its scabbard and thrust it into the air. "To Helig!" he yelled. "Victory!" and he rushed into the water.

He reached twenty feet out from the shore before the water turned deep plum purple and formed waves thirty feet high. Flashes of blinding lighting exploded from the window of the tower. The knight froze in terror. His companions ran from the edge of the river.

Kraa—Kraa—Kraa!

From beneath the angry surface of the water a creature rose. Bear-like claws engulfed the knight, pulled him from the churning water and held him high in the air. The knight flailed helplessly.

"It can't be!" Kate grabbed Jen's arm. "It can't be!"

"It is," Jen said as she stared at the beast.

The monstrous dragon-like fiend's two large black eyes, set in a scaly snake-like face, moved to and fro in search for another prey. A flaming three pronged, forked lizard tongue lashed from the beast's mouth. Teeth, ready to devour everything in its path, gleamed with acid-like saliva. Finding what it was looking for, it focused its bulging soulless eyes on Kate and Jen.

"Oh no," Kate gasped. "The creature is a smaller version of Atasa."

Agggggggggggg!

The Pilger screamed in agony from the tight grasp of the creature's claws digging through his armor. Dragging the knight with him, the junior Atasa slithered beneath the water, never losing sight of Kate and Jen. Its dark core radiated its desire to also consume them.

"Elak!" Raguel shuddered. "He is Atasa's guard of Senvolte River. And he is just as nasty and with the same evil intent as Atasa—to catch the souls of the Quae so Rapio can put them under his rule and power—the power to forever control their minds, their souls."

"Will we have to meet...fight...destroy that?" Jen asked.

Raguel shook his head to clear it from the scene that just happened. "Evil must be fought, but for now I must take you to see Mysta."

Chapter Six

Jen broke her hypnotic stare at the river to focus on what Raguel just said. "Mysta? Mysta is in Domare to help us understand?" She was excited that they were going to see their friend, the High Priest of the Cephas Monastery. "But how is he in Domare?"

"He is…" Raguel began.

"Will we get to see Eldré and …" Kate enthusiastically interrupted. Maybe all their friends from Gudsrika were here.

"So many questions," Raguel cut her short. "You two have not changed." He smiled, but he did not offer answers.

Cluk—cluk—cluk!

Cluk—cluk—cluk!

"And here comes the transportation you will need to get to Mysta." Raguel pointed to the sky.

Cluk—cluk—cluk!

Cluk—cluk—cluk!

Kate and Jen swung their gaze skyward. The welcoming tongue-clicking sounds of a hen clucking foretold of Maup birds flying somewhere above them.

Kate shaded her eyes from the sun so she could better see the birds they had learned to love when they were brought to fight for Gudsrika in the Battle of Agor. Flying above them were two birds, featherless except for their beautiful eight-foot orange feathered wings, tail feathers and a navy-blue feathered triangle on their chests. The Maup birds dipped their wings and made a rapid approach speed toward them. When the Maups got fifty feet from them their heads came up; they hovered to a stop, their legs unfolded from their hiding place under their bodies and the birds settled to the ground.

Cluk—cluk—cluk!

Cluk—cluk—cluk!

Jen rushed over and hugged the neck of one of the big birds. With one majestic motion of one of its mighty wings, the bird pulled Jen into its body.

"You remember me," Jen said. She snuggled closer to the Maup.

"I suppose you both remember how to fly," Raguel laughed.

"Yes, yes, yes," Kate said. She ran to the other Maup and snuggled into its outstretched wing. "Yes, I have missed you too," she whispered into the Maup's ear. Understanding Kate's words, the Maup pulled her closer into its fuzzy body.

"Wouldn't it be wonderful if Taka and Lieg were here?" Jen rhetorically asked, looking toward the sky for their *flight instructors.*

"You do not need them...for now," Raguel stated.

"For now? You mean we might see them?" Jen asked. She felt a small flicker of disappointment in not seeing Taka and Lieg who had taught them to fly the Maups. But she still hoped they might be in Bigna—in this time period.

"Maybe...I don't know," Raguel shrugged. "But I do know I must get you to Mysta. He is waiting for you. Are you ready?"

"Let's go," Kate said.

"Don't have to say it twice," Jen said. She boosted herself onto the back of her Maup. "No, they don't have to tell us twice, do they?" she said patting the neck of her jumbo flying, two-legged aircraft. Her Maup unfolded his long legs and rose off the ground, reading himself for flight.

"Kate, do you mind if I catch a ride?" Raguel asked. "I never have gotten the hang of steering one of these magnificent birds."

Jen could sense her Maup smiling, though his mouth did not move, at Raguel's words. She knew Raguel could fly anything—after all he flew on the back of the Eagle.

"Not at all," Kate said. She threw her body up on her Maup and squirmed around until she was in an upright position. Reaching just below the Maup's ears she felt the hard knots she would use to hang on to and guide the Maup. Feeling a comfort of familiarity, she reached down with her right hand. "Grab on," she instructed to Raguel.

"Thanks," Raguel said. He grabbed Kate's hand and lifted himself onto the Maup behind her. He put his arms around Kate and held on tight.

"Not able to steer a Maup?" Kate whispered to Raguel. "You fly on the back of the Eagle."

"Fly? That's funny," Raguel whispered back. "I hang on to the Eagle. It's simple survival. The Eagle flies and goes where he wants to take me."

"Oh," Kate smiled.

"Are you ready?" Jen yelled. She hugged the neck of her Maup one more time and then grabbed the hard knots on his neck.

"More than ready." Kate sucked in a deep breath and kicked her Maup. "Hold on, Raguel!"

Kate's Maup ran a few feet to gain speed and then became airborne. His legs dangled for a moment like a Cessna Cardinal gear retracting, and then the bird folded its legs and tucked them into its sleek body.

Cluk—cluk—cluk!

The Maup sounded his tongue-clicking cry as he took flight.

"See you at…at wherever Raguel takes us." She yelled back at Jen who was still on the ground. "Licet volare si in tergo aquilae volat."

Jen threw her head back and laughed. "A man can fly if he wishes, if he rides on the back of an eagle." She stroked the neck of her Maup. "You may not be an eagle, but you are close enough. You are my regal flying partner."

She gave her Maup a gentle kick and held on tight. The Maup responded to her prodding and began their take-off run. "Okay boy, time to catch up with them." She flattened herself into the peach-fuzz back of her Maup and nudged him with her feet.

Cluk—cluk—cluk!

Within minutes she caught up with Kate and Raguel and pulled back on the neck knobs to slow her Maup. "You've got the navigator so I guess I'll follow you."

Kate gave Jen a wave, tightened her grip and gave her Maup a slight tug. He responded immediately and went straight up.

"Whoa!" Raguel yelled, sliding backwards. Grabbing Kate's waist tighter he yelled again, "Give a guy some warning next time you are going to be a stunt pilot."

Kate leveled off and grinned. "Okay, Raguel. Just couldn't resist. You're in control now so point the way."

Chapter Seven

*T*he scattered green patches of Mount Hoch, with the mighty oak tree, became a distant view behind them. They flew over a land that was stunning—different than the lush green of Gudsrika—but beautiful in its own way. Farms and small villages that dotted the landscape soon gave way to rocky and desert sand valleys cupped beneath the mountains. The deep green scrub brush and small Acacia trees that were sprinkled around the barren land gave a sparse amount of color to the tan earth. Flowers on the hedge rows were closing for the night.

Dusk crept up the blue sky as they flew over the last mountain. Twinkling stars trailed the darkling horizon and scattered themselves onto the midnight blue sky. Cresting the last mountain they saw a lush forest before them. The two moons of Bigna, one a full moon and one a half-moon guided the Maups over a grove of Yew trees that stretched across the valley and crawled up the far hillside.

"Fid-neimid—the holy grove?" Kate asked Raquel, pointing to the familiar forest in the valley below them.

"Yes," Raquel answered. "Still the place where you can come to nourish your soul—the place where inspiration and healing take place."

"And still beautiful," Kate whispered.

In the mist of the grove Kate saw a magnificent stone monastery. From atop her Maup she could see over the forty-foot limestone walls. The courtyard inside was just like the one at the Cephas Monastery—a green oasis in the middle of the grounds where the monks could take a peaceful walk. Alone in their thoughts, they communicated silently in prayer.

A single oak tree beside the monastery towered over the Yew trees and dramatically leaned into the side of one of the towering outside stone walls. Majestically, its branches nobly rose skyward above the rooftop. Chills ran through Kate. *The eternal Evig Tree*, she thought. *And it still protects the monastery with its strength and wisdom.*

Before she could take in anything else within the walls, her Maup began a nose dive toward the monastery. She tightened her grip on the knobs on the side of his neck. He obviously knew where he was going, and she was along for the ride. Her Maup circled once over a clearing fifty feet from the outside wall and then hovered a moment before settling to the ground. Jen's Maup followed the same pattern and landed beside Kate.

Jen kick-tapped her Maup on the left side and it folded into a squatting position. She looked at the magnificent cathedral rising from the lush green undergrowth of the Yew trees.

"Wow!" was all she could muster out.

"Agreed," Kate said, still enjoying the view from the back of her Maup.

"Cephas Monastery?" Jen asked. She vaulted to the ground and looked at Raguel to get answers.

"Yes, Cephas Monastery," Raguel answered.

"But how…how can it be Cephas…how can the Fid-neimid and the Evig Tree be here?" Jen asked. "We are not on the Isle of Gudsrika…and this seems to be many years after we saw Gudsrika disappear into the sea."

"The Cephas Monastery—the Fid-neimid—the Evig Tree—they belong to Bigna," Raguel answered. "They don't belong to a place…a time. They have always been—they will always be. They will always keep alive the holy flame of ancient Bigna." He slid from the crouching Maup.

Kate gave her Maup another hug before jumping off to study the massive building. It looked just like the Cephas Monastery she remembered. With its forty-foot limestone walls, it looked less like a church and more like a castle with a picturesque medieval cathedral built atop it. At each corner of the building, a tall tower rose above the landscape. The towers neither had windows nor doors on the first three floors. No entrance could be seen into the Monastery.

"The leaded-glass window," Jen whispered. She pointed toward a window thirty-five feet up on one of the four towers.

"Race you," Kate smiled. She tagged Jen's arm and ran toward the monastery. Reaching the base of the tower she gave a hardy tug on the lanyard cord that hung from a bronze bell, aged green with time. The valley below echoed with the deep tone of the clapper striking the hand-cast bell.

"You're getting faster," Jen smiled as she came up beside Kate.

Kate smiled, but knew Jen probably let her win the race. Jen was much more athletic and could easily outrun her.

They both looked up toward the leaded-glass window. From three stories above the ground, the window swung outward and a man, draped in a navy blue monk's robe, appeared.

"Greetings, friends," the monk yelled down to them.

"Friar Tuck?" Kate yelled toward the monk. She took in the monk. With his head shaved to bear the thin band of gray hair of a clerical tonsure and a gray chinstrap beard, his cubby face had a picture frame look. His navy blue robe showed a broad scarlet strip on his left sleeve. Embroidered on the strip were four green stripes and two golden stars.

"Yes Kate," the monk responded. "Friar Tuck."

This time Kate and Jen did not smile because of his name, they smiled because he was the welcome sight of a friend.

"Greetings, Friar," Raguel yelled up to the monk.

A rope ladder appeared at the edge of the open window and tumbled down the side of the stone wall.

"Go on," Raguel urged Jen and Kate.

Jen tugged on the hemp rope before she put her foot on the flexible bottom rung. She scurried up the ladder and accepted Friar Tuck's hand helping her through the open window into the monastery. Unlike when he catapulted her into the room on the Isle of Gudsrika, Jen expected his sudden yank and landed on her feet instead of tumbling to a sitting position. Kate and Raguel hurried up the rope ladder after her.

"Kate," Jen whispered. "It's the same room."

For a moment they stood still taking in the rock-walled room. No furnishings, just Friar Tuck and Raguel. From beyond the walls they heard a familiar Gregorian chant.

"Yes, it is," Kate whispered back.

"And listen…the choir…it is still beautiful." Jen remembered what Mysta told them when they were in Bigna on their previous journey. *The monastery is built so that their music can be heard anywhere you walk, sit or meditate. They not only bring peace and calm all the time, their chants tell us when it is time for communion, to gather for a meal, for prayer—they call us to our daily tasks within Cephas' walls.*

"Yes, the choir is still wonderful," Kate agreed. The treble and alto notes drifted in the air with the lightness of a boys' choir singing Handel's Messiah.

"Are you ready to see Mysta?" Friar Tuck asked

"Oh, yes," Kate and Jen said in unison.

"What about our Maups?" Concern crossed Kate's face.

"Look," Friar Tuck said, pointing out of the window.

The two Maups were in flight, disappearing over the monastery's wall.

"They have their own living space at Cephas. They will be taken care of by a group of monks who have devoted their lives to the Maups and the other creatures at the Monastery."

"Friar Tuck," Kate began.

"You have a question?" the friar asked.

"I…I…" she stuttered as she studied Friar Tuck. "You look the same as when we left you…and that must have been…"

"Your Earth World would say hundreds of years," the friar smiled. "It is a question you must ask Mysta. Come. He will be waiting for you." Friar Tuck did not offer any more information, but scurried out the open door.

Up a flight of stairs and down a stone-walled hallway, they passed winged-angelic stone statues spaced about fifteen feet apart. Behind the musical notes of the Gregorian choir, Kate and Jen heard the whispering singsong sounds the statues blew over them as they passed each one.

Comforting warmth flowed over Kate and Jen. Instinctively they knew they were safe with the statues praying over them.

Minutes passed before they came to the heavy wood plank door they were anticipating. Behind it, they hoped, would be where they would be united with their friend Mysta. Friar Tuck swung open the door and pointed for them to go into the oval shaped room. He moved to one side of the door, as this was as far as he would take them.

"Mysta's chambers," Kate said.

Jen nodded excitedly.

"Go on in," Friar Tuck said. He would wait in the hallway.

They stepped into the room. Friar Tuck gently closed the door behind them. The sparsely furnished room was just as Kate and Jen remembered. A heavy, round oak table in the center of the room was still the only furnishings. A single vellum scroll adorned the table. No pictures. No chairs, only the table and scroll. Dark wooden walls, carved with faces of animals, plants and creatures which they recognized from their previous trip to Bigna, curved inward like the inner surface of a bowl turned upside-down. The door they had come through was no long visible, but blended into the rest of the concaved panels. The carved wood ceiling was high and as they stared upward it shifted, changing dimensions.

"Yes, this is Mysta's chambers," Kate said grabbing Jen's arm for stability. With the moving ceiling she felt a twinge of vertigo.

"It sure is," Jen agreed. She took one step toward the center of the room and stopped. "The carvings on the wall are watching us."

"I get that feeling also," Kate said.

Jen stared at one lion face. Its eyes did not move from her.

"The carvings?" Raguel smiled. "Like you learned before, not everything in Bigna is what you might expect. And yes, the carvings are watching you."

"Will we learn the secrets of Mysta's chambers this time?" Jen asked Raguel.

"That is not up to me," Raguel smiled. "That is up to…"

"To me," a familiar voice said.

Kate and Jen spun around at the sound of the deep, resounding voice.

The lean monk, four-foot in stature, seemed to materialize from thin-air. He wore a solemn navy blue monk's robe, tied with a single scarlet cord around his waist. The scarlet stripe on his left sleeve contained an embroidered eagle, wings outstretched, flying toward two golden embroidered stars. With candlelight behind him, his full head of copper blond hair and chest length Van Winkle beard created an aura surrounding his upper body.

"Mysta!" Kate stepped forward to hug him but stopped, not knowing if it was appropriate.

Mysta made the first move and hugged Kate.

"It is good to see you again," he leaned over and pulled Jen into his hug. "It is so good to see the two of you again." His bass voice was contradictory to his small stature.

"And it is good to see you, too," Kate sighed.

"And you want to learn what secrets my chambers hold," he smiled.

"Well…uh…" Jen was embarrassed she had been so brash.

"And you shall," Mysta laughed. "At least some of its secrets."

"Mysta," Kate started. "Friar Tuck said you would help me…us with one thing that is confusing."

"What is it?" Mysta's smile flattened into a fatherly look.

"I'm a little confused. Since Jen and I left Bigna it seems like many hundreds of years have passed. You and Friar Tuck have not aged. How is that possible?"

"Oh we have," Mysta laughed. "But we live within the walls of the Cephas Monastery. Years—age—are relative here. You live in the Earth World where each day is twenty-four hours. When you are in Bigna the Eagle divides your time into something you feel comfortable with—a twenty-four hour-like day. For us who live at Cephas—well—the Eagle gives us a thousand days—a thousand years, it is all the same for us."

"Raguel explained to us that the Monastery was timeless, but he didn't mention that the monks who live here are also timeless." Kate glanced at Raguel and raised an eyebrow.

"You didn't ask," Raguel offered.

"Is it the same for all Quae in Bigna?" Kate asked.

"No," Mysta smiled at Kate and Raguel's interchange. "Most Quae live in a measurable time. We who live at Cephas fulfill a different purpose than most Quae who are on Bigna. We are here to serve the Eagle—we've served him from the beginning and will be with him until the end."

"The end?" Kate picked up on Mysta's statement.

"Look!" Mysta ignored her question. Instead he waved his hand in a circular motion and pointed toward the carved lion on the wall.

The lion's eyes looked closely at Kate and Jen. Seeing what it wanted to see, the lion's gaze softened and the panel he was on slowly slid upward, exposing an entrance to a stone-walled corridor. The lion was giving them permission to go past him into the unknown passageway he guarded.

"Wow!" Jen exclaimed.

"Jen," Kate whispered. "Look! The rest of the figures are watching our every move. We may have the lion's permission to go into that passageway, but the others are also standing guard."

"You are so right," Mysta said. "The lion is wise and strong, but so much wiser and stronger when he combines his strength with the others."

"I see your point," Kate agreed.

"Come," Mysta said. "I want to show you something."

Chapter Eight

T he lion's eyes continued to focus on the strangers Mysta took past his sentry post and into the passageway he had guarded since the beginning of time.

"Thank you," Kate whispered to the lion when she stepped across the threshold he watched over.

"Keep an eye on where you step," Mysta offered. "The path is uneven and filled with obstacles."

"Oh," Kate said, stumbling over a raised cobblestone. "Yes, it is." She stopped to let her eyes adjust to the dim light.

"Are you okay?" Jen asked.

"A little embarrassed but okay," Kate answered.

Whoosh!

The fiery torch Mysta lit in an iron sconce on the wall provided an eerie light in the darkened corridor, but at least they saw where they needed to step on the uneven stone walkway.

"Oh!" Kate said, moving closer to Jen. "My eyes are playing tricks on me in this flickering light. I thought I saw the stone move."

"Then my eyes are playing the same tricks." Jen let her eyes adjust to the wavering glow given off by the torch. "All of the stones are moving. The whole pathway floor is shifting."

"Yes, it is," Raguel said. "But, if you step solidly you'll be all right. The stones do not want you to stumble, so the larger stones will get out of your way." He stepped solid, yet fast, to show Kate and Jen how to navigate the walkway. With each step a stone scooted toward the walls.

Whoosh!

Whoosh!

Mysta, five yards ahead of them, lit two more scones. The stones no longer moved but were now along the side of the path, giving Kate and Jen a clear way down the corridor where Mysta and Raguel had stopped. Before them was a massive oak door, but it had no handle or hinges.

Jen looked at Kate and shrugged.

Kate shook her head in an *I don't know either* gesture and then whispered, "You asked to learn the secrets of Mysta's chambers."

"Then let's go learn," Jen smiled. They traveled the distance between them and Mysta.

Mysta put his finger to his mouth, indicating he wanted complete silence.

Kate, Jen and Raguel stood motionless.

Mysta laid the palm of his hand in the middle of the oak barrier and whispered words Kate and Jen did not understand.

Viip!

The door whirled inward and disappeared into a void. A cool, but pleasant, breeze puffed through the opening.

"This is the Fís Chamber," Mysta stated. He stepped to one side so Kate and Jen could scrutinize the place where the door had vanished.

Slowly they edged their way to the door and stared into the dimness. The room was a perfectly circular bubble. The Acacia wood walls had no seams and no edges on their highly polished, smooth surface. Unlike Mysta's chamber, there were no carvings or any markings on the walls. The room glistened from emptiness, except for one item. In the middle of the room was a table made of Acacia wood—eighteen inches wide, thirty-six inches long and twenty-seven inches high. A light from an unseen source radiated off the glossy glass-like top. To them it looked like a glowing square tree stump.

"Go ahead," Mysta urged Kate. He pointed at the open door. "Go inside and explore for yourself."

Kate did not see anything on the tree stump-like table, but she knew magic happened inside the walls of the Cephas Monastery. She took one step forward and realized there was no visible floor.

"Whoa!" she pulled her foot back onto the solid stone path in the hallway.

Mysta and Raguel laughed.

"It is all right," Mysta said. He stepped through the door and walked across the floorless chamber to the table. He walked on air.

It was then that Kate and Jen realized that the table was floating freely inside the room.

"Come on," Mysta said. "All you need is a little faith."

Kate looked at Jen and took a deep breath. "Here goes." She put her right foot out and stepped into the air, but did not put any weight on it.

"Come," Mysta held out his hand. "Come to me."

Kate dragged her left foot from the security of the solid footing of the stone hallway and set it astride her right foot, as a soldier would on the parade field standing at ease. She sank a couple of inches into the nothingness.

"Faith," Mysta encouraged her. "Believe you can walk to me."

Kate closed her eyes and slowly put one foot in front of the other. Three steps inside the room she opened her eyes. She was no longer sinking but walking as if she were on solid ground. She continued to put one foot in front of the other until she reached Mysta.

"Wow!" she exclaimed. "What a kick."

"Go ahead," Raguel told Jen. "Just remember—have faith."

"You can do it," Kate encouraged Jen. "Just like wing-walking—without the wing," she grinned.

Jen followed Kate's path toward the floating table where Mysta and Kate stood.

"It is just like wing-walking," Jen smiled and spun around. "But no safety harness." She looked down. Far, far below her was the Acacia wood flooring of the bubbled room.

"We don't seem to need one," Kate said. She stood next to Mysta, shifting from one foot to the other enjoying the new sensation. "Secure, yet like walking on…on marshmallows."

"Marshmallows, indeed," Jen said coming up beside Kate. "And you are so right—it's a huge wow and a real kick!" Like Kate she shifted from one foot to the other to enjoy the new phenomenon.

Raguel joined them at the Fís table but did not partake in their merrymaking. Instead he just smiled at their new-found activity.

Mysta did take pleasure in Kate and Jen's joyful movement, but he knew they were in the Fís Chamber to learn about their purpose in Bigna, not the secrets of the Cephas Monastery. Looking upward he whispered the same words he spoke to open the massive oak door of the Fís Chamber.

Viip!

As quickly as the door had whirled inward and disappeared into a void, it reappeared and spun across the bubble room and sealed the entrance of the Fís Chamber.

Kate and Jen quit shifting their feet. It was clear Mysta was giving them the signal they were brought to the Fís Chamber for a reason beyond having fun.

Kate turned her attention to Mysta. "What is this?" she pointed to the floating Acacia stump beside her. "You called it a table?"

"This is the Fís," Mysta said. "The Fís Table."

"What does it do?" Jen asked.

"It is a table of vision." Mysta leaned over and put his hand on the top. A thin blue mist formed from under his fingers and covered the table top, but the blue vapor did not flow over the sides.

Kate and Jen took a step closer to the table.

Mysta lifted his hand. The mist instantly disappeared and the shiny wood top reflected Mysta's face.

"Wow!" Jen exclaimed again.

"Rub the top," Mysta urged.

Jen reached out to the polished wood top but nothing happened.

"Both of you," Mysta said. "You must rub it together to see what it has to show you."

Kate and Jen leaned forward and rubbed the glistening top. Mist swirled around their fingers, making their hands disappeared. Reflexively they pulled their hands from the table top. The mist instantly disappeared and the glossy wood top reflected their faces.

"What was that?" Kate asked.

"That was the Fís learning about you," Mysta said.

"Learning about us?" Kate questioned.

"Once it understands and knows whether you are friend or foe it will decide if it will let you come into its realm," Mysta answered. "Put your hands back on it and give into the Fís so it can learn who you are. Once it knows you are a friend, it will then reveal its visions to you."

Obediently Kate and Jen put their hands back on the top of the table. Instantly the blue vapor formed around their hands.

Ziiip!

A force beneath the mist electrically shot through their bodies with chalk-screeching-on-a-blackboard chills.

Kate shivered slightly, but the Fís did not give them time to think about their reaction. It pulled them inside the blue mist and transported them to an observation point high on a hill.

The ground beneath their feet moved slightly. Above them the clouds traveled fast west to east. They stood on a hill that overlooked the last scene from their previous trip to Bigna. Quae were disappearing into the blue Gudsrika Sea. Other Quae were going through the rumbling tumult Obex into the Earth World. But unlike when Kate and Jen left Bigna they now stood alone—no Raguel—no Mysta—no Eldré—just the two of them watching the familiar scene.

Then they heard it—the maniacal squealing of Rocus, who at birth was Raguel's mirror image twin brother. But after giving his soul to Rapio, his diminutive, mouse-like features gave way to harsher rat-like traits.

Skreek—Skreek—Skreek!

The tiny elf-like Quae rode atop the giant ink-black raven Rapio.

Skreek—Skreek—Skreek!

Rocus twisted and turned his small statured body until his form was no longer a two-legged creature but a four-legged rat. His rodent body sported copper red hair, but it was dulled by the darkness within his soul. He let his body-length tail drape over one ink-black wing of Rapio.

Kraa—Kraa—Kraa!

The raspy echo of Rapio's cry drowned out Rocus shriek.

In the distance, Kate and Jen saw Indringers, who stood on the balcony of the Gäer Fortress, swallowed up by the Obex. The Indringers of Bigna, whom they had defeated in battle, vanished before their eyes.

Rapio turned his focus on Kate and Jen. His eyes, void of life, blazed from somewhere inside his dark spirit.

Swoosh!

Rapio's fifteen foot wingspan cast a dark shadow across the picture before Kate and Jen as he flew over them.

Kraa—Kraa—Kraa!

The low, guttural sound of the raven disappeared into the eerie rumbling of the pulsating dark indigo blue-swirling Obex.

Instantly Kate and Jen were pulled away from the misty vision and were again in the Fís Chamber with Mysta and Raguel.

"Gudsrika—the Fís took us back to Gudsrika," Kate stated, refocusing her eyes to the dim light of the Fís Chamber. "Is that where we are going?"

"That was what you left," Mysta said.

"But…Gudsrika…is that why…" Kate stammered looking for the right question. "Were we brought back to Bigna to continue the battle we fought…didn't we win…did something go wrong?"

"No, that battle is finished," Mysta offered.

"But we saw the Indringers of Gudsrika vanish," Kate said. "But Raguel said the Indringers who hold Helig are descendants of the ones we fought at the Battle of Agor."

"Yes, they are. After The Battle of Agor, the Indringers appeared in a province in the Northern Bigna waters. After a few years they advanced overland, fighting anyone who got in their way, until they arrived in Domare. After they conquered the city of Stur, they continued their war across the country and advanced to the gates of the holy city of Helig. The inhabitants of Helig were peace-loving so they did not have the means or heart to go to war with the Indringers. They were crushed without much of a fight."

"So we are here to help the Quae Pilgers take back Helig?" Jen asked.

"Although that may happen on your journey, that is not what brings you back," Mysta answered. "To find out why you are here you must continue crossing into the Fís."

Kate grabbed Jen's hand. "This time I want you a little closer."

Jen nodded.

Together they placed their hands on the Fís Table. A drifting fog rose from the glistening wood and curled around them.

The fog from the Fís Table that twisted around them dissipated to a small cloud around their feet and settled them atop a mountain overlooking the city of Stur. Outside the city gates the Quae Pilgers were in disarray. The battle for Stur was going against the Pilgers in favor of the Indringers who were entrenched inside the walls of the city.

From the outer edges of the camp a friar, clothed in a navy blue robe with a broad scarlet strip on his left sleeve, stepped upon a remnant of an overturned cart. His head was shaved to bear the thin band of dark brown hair of a clerical tonsure and a brown chinstrap beard. With two hands, he carried a sword above his head.

"Do you think that is Friar Fara and the Holy Sword?" Jen asked.

"It could be," Kate answered. "He is younger than I imagined he would be."

"Let's listen. Maybe we can figure out what is going on."

"Fellow Pilgers," the monk spoke. "We are saved!" He made a complete circle, with the sword high in the air, to show it to everyone. "While I was inside the city walls the Holy Sword appeared before me. I was able to move quickly and quietly past the Indringer guards and bring it back to you."

Friar Fara paused to let his words sink in, all the while pointing the shining blade of the sword toward the sky. His hand now had a golden glow.

The Holy Sword!

The Holy Sword!

The roll of the words waved over the crowd as the Pilgers mumbled to each other. In awe, they pressed closer to the friar to hear his words.

"Yes, the Holy Sword," Friar Fara stated. "This is the very sword that has existed since the beginning of time! The Holy Sword that was stolen from our sacred monastery hundreds of years ago! The Holy Sword that has miraculous powers—the power to lead us to victory this very day."

The Pilgers stood in silence, waiting for Friar Fara to explain how this could be true.

"It is not by your own strength, but by your faith," Friar Fara offered. Two-handed he brandished the silver blade of the Holy Sword above the crowd. He pointed it at each of the four cardinal directions of the compass and stated, "From the north—the south—the east—and the west, a mighty force will fall upon you. Fall upon you to strengthen your body— strengthen your mind—strengthen your mission—strengthen your faith. The enemy will not defeat you, but you will crush them."

Friar Fara again allowed the sound of silence to ripple across the land.

"And your great knights Nerkon and Obile will lead you," he continued. "They will lead you this day to victory."

The silence of the crowd was broken by a single voice.

Sir Nerkon!

Sir Obile!

The hush of the crowd burst and quickly rose to a roar.

Nerkon!

Obile!

Nerkon!

Obile!

The throng of Pilgers pushed the two knights from their ranks until Nerkon and Obile were standing before Friar Fara.

"Kneel, our great leaders," Fara said.

Nerkon and Obile took a knee before the friar.

"Your destiny is clear," Fara said. "Great knights, you will lead our army to victory." He tapped Nerkon and Obile on their heads with the Holy Sword and raised the tip of the sword toward the heavens above.

An aura of light began at the grip of the sword, spread upward to the tip and blasted over the Pilgers toward the four cardinal points of a compass.

Badaboom!

Badaboom!

Badaboom!

Badaboom!

Silence fell upon the scene.

Slowly at first, and then an eruption was heard.

Onward to Stur!

Onward!

Victory!

Victory!

The Pilgers were energized. They knew the victory was theirs.

Nerkon and Obile rose and took their places before their armies.

"Onward Pilgers to Stur!" Nerkon yelled.

"Onward Pilgers to Stur!" Obile confirmed.

Without hesitation, the Pilgers followed their leaders and charged the gates of Stur.

Onward to Stur!

Victory!

Victory!

The Pilgers battle cry echoed across the plain.

From their mountain-top position Kate and Jen watched the Pilgers pound the gates of Stur with a tree-trunk battering ram. Within the Stur city walls shouts of confusion from the Indringers rose. The sudden charge from the Pilgers took them completely by surprise.

The Pilgers swung the huge oak log back and forth, crashing it into the wooden gates, until the metal gate locks holding back the invasion snapped. Once the gate was breached, the Pilgers spilled into the city.

The battle was swift and bloody, but that day the Pilgers crushed the Indringers and captured Stur.

Once again, Kate and Jen were pulled away from the misty vision and appeared in the Fís Chamber with Mysta and Raguel.

"I'm still confused as to why we're here," Kate said.

"Likewise," Jen echoed. "It would seem the Pilgers would now have a clear path to Helig."

"You would think that was true," Mysta offered. "And after the victory at Stur the Pilgers did plan the attack on the holy city of Helig. That was a year ago."

"What happened?" Kate asked.

"After the victory, the Pilgers forgot what brought them victory—strength in their faith," Mysta explained. "They abandoned their moral compass. The Holy Sword had bestowed on them a great victory, but they threw themselves onto the altar of depraved celebration. Rapio seized the opportunity. He sent Onde, his high priest, into Stur with his legions to infiltrate the city and take advantage of the moral decay spreading among the Pilgers. Rapio's army created havoc by rapidly spreading the Bás Plague among the Pilgers. Each day thirty or forty Quae died. Those who didn't physically die, but were infected by the plague, were changed. Those who still resisted, and the legions couldn't change, Onde and his soldiers brutally killed."

"This high priest Onde," Kate frowned, "doesn't sound very holy to me."

"He is Rapio's high priest—a priest of darkness," Mysta said. "He once was a Quae and a priest at Cephas Monastery, but he turned and went to the dark side. He took on the looks of Rapio, except for his feet—they still are that of a Quae."

"Feet of a Quae?" Kate asked. "Why?"

"Rapio wants Onde to be reminded every moment of where he came from and that Rapio has the power to send him back—broken."

"Couldn't the leaders of the Pilgers stop Onde and Rapio's legions?" Jen asked.

"The cause of the plague was not immediately known. Slowly the Pilger leaders realized the plague was not only lethal by physical death, but those who survived had gone to the dark side of Rapio's domain. Across the board, in all groups, Quae Pilgers died or were infected, including Friar Fara, who was now trying to guide the Pilgers away from the depraved style they had chosen."

"Wasn't Friar Fara from Cephas Monastery?" Kate asked. She remembered seeing the scarlet strip on the sleeve of his navy blue monk's robe, indicating he served at Cephas.

"Yes," Mysta answered.

"Then how could he die? You said for the monks who live within the wall of Cephas time was limitless."

"Friar Fara asked to be sent to the Pilgers at Stur," Mysta said. "He was young and still did not have all the powers of Cephas. He knew once outside the walls he could be vulnerable to the measurable time of all Quae."

"How brave of him," Jen said.

"Yes, he was brave, but his faith drew him to this. He believed it was his purpose to go." Mysta paused a moment, shook his head and then continued, "Exhaustion and an unusually hot summer finally got to the friar and he succumbed to a physical death caused by the plague. He died treating and trying to cure others infected."

"Then no one could be guaranteed protection from the plague," Kate said.

"That's true," Raguel said.

"And knowing this, the Pilger leaders became wary of staying in Stur but, were afraid to go on to Helig," Mysta said.

"So what made them finally leave Stur?" Jen asked.

"They left mainly because of the emperor's personal knight, Sir Rubidus," Mysta explained.

"Then Sir Rubidus encouraged them to leave?" Jen inquired.

"Not exactly," Mysta answered. "The emperor mistakenly put his faith in Rubidus' loyalty to him and the emperor's kingdom. He gave Rubidus the freedom to carve out some land for himself, thinking his personal knight would take a little land and create a huge territory for the emperor.

But Rubidus, whom they call the Red Knight because of his ruddy complexion and cherry red cheeks, is a selfish and self-indulgent knight. He thought The Mission was a waste of time and secretly laughed at the Quae Pilgers' faith in their quest. But he saw The Mission as a way to gain more land and power for his own. The longer he stayed in Stur, the more his soldiers became restless and implored him to leave the city and march on to Helig. Over half of his division of five-thousand warriors had succumbed to the plague. He knew, if he didn't do something to rally those who still stood loyally around him, all his plans to increase his personal power would be lost.

"When Friar Fara died, Rubidus was with him. Thinking he could gain the miraculous power of the Holy Sword, Rubidus took the Holy Sword he found next to Friar Fara's body. He assembled his soldiers outside Stur's city walls. Raising the Holy Sword above his head he told his army the sword would protect them and assure them victory, just as it had at Stur. With his convincing speech, his army suited up and marched toward Helig. Arrogance rode with Rubidus that day. He was convinced he would be seen as a heroic conqueror by capturing the city of Helig, and that the Pilgers would name him the king of Helig. As king, he would use the Pilgers' burning devotion to The Mission as a ploy to set out to conquer other lands for himself."

"What happened to Rubidus and his army?" Kate asked.

"The Fís will answer that question," Mysta answered. "You must go with it again while it shows you what happened."

Kate gripped Jen's hand tight and nodded. They placed their free hands onto the glowing top of the Fís Table. Instantly they were standing atop

Mount Hoch overlooking the Great Plain. The mighty oak sheltered them and a misty cloud covered their feet.

"Isn't this where we tumbled out of the Obex and saw Raguel?" Kate asked. There was comfort in seeing the mighty oak.

"Yes," Jen answered. She leapt over the roots of the tree and made her way to the edge of the mountain, the cloud continuing to mask her steps. "And below us is the Great Plain."

"There are the Senvolte River and the city of Helig on the far side of the river." Kate joined Jen at the mountains edge.

Below them, dust swirled around two thousand warriors hurrying across the plain toward the river. The army rode hard toward their goal—Helig.

"But that is not the army we saw before," Jen said. "This one is much smaller and doesn't have an encampment."

The knight in the lead raised a sword and yelled, "To Helig!"

To Helig!

To Helig!

The army behind him echoed his words.

"Is that the Holy Sword?" Kate whispered.

"It must be," Jen whispered back. "So that must be Rubidus."

Knight Rubidus hesitated but a moment before he charged into the Senvolte River. "To Helig!" he yelled again.

To Helig!

To Helig!

His army yelled again and then rushed into the Senvolte River behind their leader.

Without warning the water of the Senvolte rose into forty-foot towering waves, that quickly crashed down on the unsuspecting army. Rubidus and his men were knocked from their steeds into the violent undertow created by the sudden, turbulent squall.

Heavily armored Pilgers thrashed about in the river trying to stay atop the white-capped water. Screams of fear rolled across the valley as the warriors, one by one, lost their battle with the malevolent force and were sucked under the hammering river storm. With one last victory echo, the river bellowed a rock-pounding crash against the shoreline and then sucked its liquid weapon into an ever dwindling whirlpool.

As suddenly as it had started, the storm calmed and the water was again still.

Silence.

"What just happened?" Jen asked.

"I don't know," Kate answered.

Moments passed before anything moved.

"Look!" Kate said, pointing toward the river.

Walking upright and horseless, Rubidus emerged from beneath the water. He still wore his suit of plate armor, but no longer carried the Holy Sword.

"Where is the Holy Sword?" Jen whispered.

"It must rest somewhere at the bottom of the Senvolte River," Kate guessed.

Rubidus wandered away from the shoreline and took off his can-shaped, flattop helmet. A few hundred of his warriors surfaced behind him. Dazed, they fell upon the muddy river bank and stared at the indigo water with ghostly eyes.

Kate and Jen's attention was diverted to a cloud of dust that rolled across the Great Plain. Two knights rode their horses hard in front of the rolling dust cloud.

"It's Duke Nerkon and Count Obile," Kate said. "They must have gathered their armies together and ridden after Rubidus."

"And their armies make up the thousands of Pilgers we first saw when we stood on this mountain with Raguel," Jen commented.

Duke Nerkon and Count Obile reined their horses to a stop and held up their arms.

"Halt!" They shouted.

"Look," Nerkon shouted at Obile. "Rubidus." He pointed to a disorientated Rubidus who wandered aimlessly away from the river—away from Helig. Instinctively, Nerkon knew something was wrong.

"Halt!" He shouted again to his warriors.

The mass of Pilger warriors behind Nerkon and Obile obediently pulled to a stop. The plume of dust created by the pounding hooves of their horses slowly dissolved into the plain and the sights of the valley came into the warriors' view. In the clarity of day they no longer looked to their leaders for their next move. Instead they were entranced by their unobstructed view across the Senvolte River—the Holy City of Helig was within their reach.

Enthusiastically the warriors raised their voices in a battle cry.

Helig—Helig—Helig!

Onward to Helig!

Onward!

"But they cannot go into the river," Jen yelled. "We must stop them!"

"No," Kate put her hand on Jen's arm. "I don't believe that the Fís brought us here to stop them. Remember, this is but a vision."

Nerkon turned quickly to see what was pressing his army into a frenzy. Realizing they were hypnotized by the sight of Helig, he knew he must do something to put order in their enthusiastic run toward Helig.

"Wait!" He yelled at the armies rushing toward the river. "Halt!" Nerkon rode hard to stop his warriors. "Halt!"

But it was too late to stop the delirium of joy that burst out amongst the first soldiers at the river's edge. Throwing their heavier weapons to the side, they shouted louder and louder as they rode their horses into the river so they could get to the holy city.

Helig!

Helig!

Helig!

They did not see or hear their leader yelling at them to halt.

Helig!

Helig!

Helig!

The first Pilgers rushing into the water were sucked under and disappeared. When they did not surface, the Pilgers behind them stopped, terrified of the dark blue-green water. Somewhere, far beneath the depths of the river, a guttural roar bubbled up toward them. Fear-struck, they backed away from the water's edge.

"It is cursed!" Nerkon yelled at Obile. "The river is cursed!"

The cloud at Kate and Jen's feet rose and swirled them back to the Acacia wood-bubble room of the Fís Chamber.

Mysta's face showed wrinkles of concern.

"Now you are almost up to date on what is happening in the land of Domare," Mysta said.

"Is that what we saw when we tumbled out of the Obex onto Mount Hoch today?" Kate asked Raguel.

"Yes," Raguel confirmed. "Although what you saw today is actually a few months beyond the vision you saw in the Fís table."

"When Rubidus walked out of the river, he was confused and delirious. Nerkon found him and nursed him back to a physical health," Mysta said. "For the next few hours after Rubidus came out of the river, a handful of his soldiers continued to trickle out."

"What happened to the Holy Sword?" Kate asked. "When we saw Rubidus come out of the river, he no longer had the sword with him."

"We know Rubidus lost the Holy Sword when he was taken to the bottom of the Senvolte River. Beneath the river's surface lies a porthole to Rapio's domain. So, whatever miracles the Holy Sword can produce, it is now is in Rapio's hands."

"Is the sword still in...beneath the river...in Rapio's domain?" Jen asked.

"We don't for sure," Raguel said, "but we don't believe it is."

"Where is it?" Jen asked.

"When Rubidus rode out of Stur, Rapio's high priest Onde and his legions followed him," Raguel said.

"We didn't see anyone but Nerkon and Obile's armies following Rubidus," Kate said.

"Onde and his mercenaries followed him out of the city of Stur, but they flew to the Senvolte River."

"Flew?" Jen questioned.

"On Acchims," Mysta answered.

"Acchims!" Kate shivered at the thought of the deep chestnut-brown, bird-like creatures, with the twelve-foot red feathered wings. "There are still Acchims?"

"Yes, and still used by Rapio's warriors. And by flying out of Stur they went into the Senvolte River before Rubidus came to the water's edge. Onde and his mercenaries were already beneath the water's surface by the time you arrived on the mountain."

"You said you don't believe the Holy Sword is still beneath the river… in Rapio's domain."

"Word has spread that Rapio sent the Holy Sword with Onde and his mercenary soldiers to the city of Helig."

"Then the Holy Sword is behind Helig's fortified walls," Kate stated.

"Yes," Mysta confirmed his belief. "And once inside Helig, Onde slaughtered the Indringer king and declared himself emperor of Helig."

"But if the Holy Sword is magical and can produce miracles, why didn't it protect Rubidus?" Jen asked.

"Because Rubidus did not understand how to invoke the power of the Sword," Mysta answered.

"And Onde knows how to call up that power?" Jen's curiosity was heightened.

"Mostly," Mysta hedged. "Onde only knows how to invoke some of the magic of the sword. But Rapio knows the supreme strength within the sword and he knows how to bestow the power to his legions at his will. Of course, Rapio does not want any being to be as powerful as he so he will only grant that magical ability for short periods of time. Because of this, Onde only has limited power."

"But can Onde pull enough energy and magic from the sword to defeat the Quae Pilgers?" Jen asked.

"Yes."

"Why did Duke Nerkon and Obile follow Rubidus out of Stur?" Kate asked.

"The reason they gave their army was because they did not know how to stop the Bás Plague in Stur. Nerkon and Obile took their faithful out of Stur and followed Rubidus in hopes of leaving the Bás Plague behind them. They wanted to join Rubidus in the assault on Helig. When Nerkon caught up with him, he realized somehow, somewhere Rubidus had been exposed to the plague. But as each day went by Nerkon hoped Rubidus had escaped the lasting effects."

"And Rubidus has not escaped it?" Kate asked

"Nerkon believes he has," Mysta answered.

"And you?" Kate raised one eyebrow.

"We know he did not," Mysta frowned.

Chapter Nine

*K*ate shook her head. She had so many questions. "What happened to the Quae? When we left Bigna they were happy and peace seeking. They never quarreled among themselves."

"There is a cancer spreading through the Quae—the Bás Plague," Mysta explained. "Though you saw Rapio fly away just before you left Bigna, Rapio left evil behind to fester. Unfortunately, we did not discover it in time to stop it before it leached its horror into all walks of life." Mysta shook his head. "Nevertheless, Rapio's main targets are the knights—the leaders of the Quae. That is why infecting Rubidus was so important. If Rapio gains the leaders' allegiance, the leaders will bring their troops to his dark side."

"And that is why the Eagle brought you back through the Obex to Bigna," a steady voice said.

Kate and Jen whirled around to face the wise elder of the Quae.

"Eldré," Kate and Jen said in unison.

Eldré's ocean blue eyes were fixed on them. Her composure was the same as they remembered—dignified and straight face. Kate took a step toward Eldré and stopped, unsure of Eldré's reaction. When they last saw her she was disappearing into the Gudsrika Sea with the elfin 'Ov clinging to her hand.

Eldré nodded to Kate. Her magnificent ground-length, red silk robe glistened in the reflecting light of the Fís chamber.

"Amicis," Eldré said. She took the five steps between them and grasped Kate and Jen's hands. "My friends, you have come back. It is good to see you. It has been too long since I walked away from you and into the Gudsrika Sea."

"We agree," Kate said. "Much too long."

"And it looks as if the Eagle found you again nearby your flying machine." Eldré gave Kate and Jen's leather jackets and silk flying scarves a once-over look and then smiled. She softly touched Kate's white silk scarf. "You have kept the blue triangle of the Mymybids. Taka and Lieg will be proud."

"Taka and Lieg?" Jen said enthusiastically. "Raguel said we might see them."

"Perhaps later," Eldré shrugged. "For now you have other things you must learn."

"We're ready," Jen offered. She was disappointed that they would not see Taka and Lieg soon, but knew they were not in Bigna for a social event.

"The Eagle called you back to Bigna because of Rapio's success in infecting the Quae Pilgers with the Bás Plague at Stur and the events afterwards."

"Events afterwards?" Jen asked. "You mean Rubidus stealing the Holy Sword and losing it in the Senvolte River?"

"Yes, that, but much more," Eldré said. "We have a problem with the Bás."

"Raguel told us a little about the Bás Plague infecting the Quae Pilgers on The Mission," Kate said.

"The Bás Plague has swept across the Quae of Domare, not just the Pilgers on The Mission," Eldré frowned. "What else did Raguel say?" she glanced at Raguel.

"He said that the Bás Plague overtakes a Quae and changes the physical, mental and moral identity of that Quae," Jen said. "But you make it sound even worse."

"What Raguel said is true," Eldré nodded at Raguel. "And it is much worse. It is Rapio's curse upon the Quae. Rapio has found a way to use the Quaes' weaknesses to submit to him and to turn on each other."

"Weaknesses?" Kate asked.

"Each Quae—like each of your Earth beings—has a weakness. Pride—desire for power—greed—so many things. And Rapio uses those weaknesses to deceive the Quae."

"What can we do?" Kate asked.

"You have been brought to Bigna to stop the spread of Rapio's Bás Plague from being spread any further—to end it at this time," Eldré stated without directly answering Kate's question. "If Rapio can conquer the Quae with the Bás Plague, he will not have to fight the final war—Război."

"Război…" Kate began.

"Look into the Fís," Eldré directed. She waved her hand above the glistening stump top, but she did not touch it. A mist rolled from the center, off the edges and encircled their feet.

"Do you want us to…are we to…" Kate began.

"Do you want us to put our hands on the Fís?" Jen finished Kate's sentence. "Are we going back into the Fís?"

"Not this time," Eldré answered. "This time you only need to see the wickedness of Rapio's curse."

Kate and Jen followed Eldré's instruction and looked into the top of the Fís. The mist continued to fall from the edges until a clear picture formed deep within the stump. Before them was a burnt out medieval street in the city of Helig. Brick buildings crumbled onto the blood red mud that oozed from beneath the cobblestone street. Shutters hinged loosely to windows from long ago vacated houses, banged erratically in the wind.

Bweee—Bweee—Bweee!

Bweee—Bweee—Bweee!

Two, five-foot tall, green, luminous scorpions walked upright on their hind legs, crushing the stones beneath their heavy, clawed feet. Blazing from their chests were blood-red silhouettes of a raven head inside a triangle.

"The scorpions," Kate whispered. "They have a red triangle on their chests much like the Acchim birds."

"But with the addition of the raven head. It is the mark Rapio puts on his Elite Troopers," Eldré's soft voice explained through their mist-filled journey.

Bweee—Bweee—Bweee!

Bweee—Bweee—Bweee!

Rapio's heartless hit squad continued down the cobblestone road, their crusty heads wagging to and fro looking for victims. The sky crept over the building tops in a pulsating dark indigo blue swirling mass. The Obex was coming to envelop the city. Adult Quae scurried about, gathering up their youngsters, trying to flee the horror overtaking them.

Squeek!

A door slowly opened, and an adult Quae stared out. Darkness in the room behind him cloaked any movement from inside the building. Seeing that the Elite Trooper scorpions had passed, he carried the body of a Quae out and laid it among the debris scattered on the street. Hurrying back inside, his two hollow eyes could be seen, vague as they were, peering out of a grimy window. A wooden cart, pulled by a gaunt centaur, stopped and put the body into the cart. The centaur glanced at the two dazed eyes behind the window and nodded. The eyes disappeared. There was nothing more either the centaur or the Quae behind the eyes could do.

Kraa! Kraa! Kraa!

Above the scene, in a disfigured skeleton of what was once a mighty oak, a raven sat observing the chaos.

Over the top of the Fís table the mist quickly enveloped the scene in a fog.

Poof!

The glistening top of the Fís once again reflected the faces of Kate and Jen.

"What was that?" Kate asked.

"It is the future of Bigna—the final time of the Quae—if you cannot stop the Bás Plague," Eldré said.

"It was horrid," Jen stated.

"Yes, it could be, but you have the power to stop it," Eldré stated. "And now you have one more thing to do while you are in Bigna."

"More?" Kate questioned. "I...we don't know how we can even match Rapio in stopping the Bás."

"Once Friar Fara found the Holy Sword after it was lost for so many years," Eldré stated, "he was going to bring it back to the Cephas Monastery. The Bás Plague in Stur delayed his trip back. When he died, and Rubidus took the sword, it was lost to Cephas again. You must find and retrieve the Holy Sword from Onde, Rapio's High Priest. You must find it and give its power of miracles back to the monks at Cephas."

"Where do we even begin?" Jen questioned.

"How do we find out what we should do?" Kate asked.

"Your lockets," Eldré whispered. "Listen and follow your lockets. They will show you the way."

Instinctively, Kate and Jen put their fingers around their lockets.

"But first," Mysta interjected, "we must get you a change of clothes, something to eat and a good night's sleep. Come."

Division	5,600		# Warriors	Others	Total # in army	
Tent party		8				
Century	10 tent parties of warriors		80		80	Leader—centurion
Cohort	7 Centuries of warriors		560		560	Leader—First Centurion
Division	10 Cohorts of warriors		5,600		5,600	Number one Cohort is made up of elite warriors. Its commander is the **Senior Centurion**, the highest ranking knight and most respected of all the Centurions because he has proven himself in many battles.
	Each Cohort has a trumpeter					Number one Cohort has **Senior Trumpeter**
In Nerkon's Army	2 Centuries of horsemen—Centaurs		**160**		**160**	Leader is **First Centaur**—has proven himself in many battles
Total			5,760		5,760	
Bigna Air Power	Maups/ Mymybids		**80**		**80**	Senior Centurions— Leaders of Mymybids— —Taka and Lieg
	2 units-40 each					
Nerkon	2 Divisions	11,200		& Mymybids	& 160 Centaurs	
Obile	2 Divisions	11,200				
Begi	> 1 Division	> 5,600				
Rubidus	> 200 warriors	> 200				
	Total--about	28,000				

QUAE PILGER WARRIORS ON THE MISSION

Chapter Ten

Kate banked her Maup bird right so she could see below. "Look!"
Raguel, ridding behind Kate, tightened his grip around her
waist. This was no time to fall. He had so much to teach Kate and Jen.

"I see," Jen yelled back. "It's the mighty oak atop Mount Hoch." Her
Maup made a lazy eight, descending toward the brilliant green hill top
and the full foliage forty-foot oak tree.

The sunrise flight across Domare, atop their Maups, was beautiful.
A hue of orange-reds burst forth over the jagged mountain tops, pushing
the blue-gray of night in front of it. Strips of dark green hedge plants
sped by underneath them as they flew over the countryside. The valleys
they had flown over at dusk the night before had taken on the color of a
barren desert. Now, they opened their plant lives' colorful bloom to the
coming day.

Kate's loose-fitting, cream colored tunic fluttered in the wind. She
smiled at how the clothier at Cephas knew their exact sizes. When they
laced their leather boots up over their green knickers, it was as if they
had not left Bigna. From a secrete place inside her leather flight jacket she
pulled out a pure white, one-inch stone and slipped it into a small pocket
inside the top of her boot. She glanced over at her cousin.

A big smile filled Jen's face. She too had slipped a pure white stone into
her boot and commented, "The stones King Malki gave us in Gudsrika to
protect us and give us entrance to anywhere in his castle."

Raguel had laughed at the two of them. He had pulled up his knickers far enough to show that his white stone was still tucked into a small pocket in his boot. King Malki and his castle were far behind them, but no one knew when the magic of the stones might be needed.

And now they flew over the land they loved—Bigna. Kate kicked up one leg to see her boot. The stone was not visible, but the small budge in the top of her boot assured her it was still there.

Jen waved at Kate. "Fits like we never left," she yelled, raising her left arm and letting her tunic's long sleeve ripple.

"My thoughts exactly," Kate yelled back.

Within a half-hour of leaving the monastery, the mighty oak appeared on the horizon, glowing from the morning light. Fiery reflections bounced from the smooth shells of the golf ball size acorns that filled its branches.

When Jen was fifty feet from the tree, she pulled back on her Maup's neck knobs. His head came up, he hovered a moment and then settled to the ground. She stroked the orange peach fuzz on his neck. "We're still one, boy." She smiled before she jumped off. Her Maup nuzzled her shoulder with his soft head. "I know. It is good to be back with you, too."

"There is something I want to show and explain to you before we go down to the plain," Raguel said, sliding off Kate's Maup. He walked toward the edge of Mount Hoch. "Look at the Great Plain."

Kate and Jen joined him. The first light of day cast an orange tinge on the Great Plain spread out before them. The encampment of the Quae Pilger armies was a fury of activity, readying for the daily routine.

"It looks just like it did yesterday," Kate said. "The valley is filled with the camps of Duke Nerkon and Lord Obile."

"True," Raguel said, "but what I want you to understand is how each army is made up. It will make a difference in the part you play."

"Part we play?" Jen queried. "Are we going to be part of their army?"

"Yes and no," Raguel smiled.

"Yes—no—," Jen said. "Why did I expect a definite answer? We always seem to be caught between the yeses and nos."

"It is indeed the camps of Nerkon and Obile," Raguel ignored Jen's comment. "However, it is also the camp of the armies of Count Begi and Rubidus…"

"Rubidus still has an army?" Jen interrupted.

"Small, but yes he has an army that follows him," Raguel frowned. "And don't turn your back on his followers."

"Why?"

"Because Mysta believes they all have been infected by the Bás and are loyal to Rapio, but that is still to be proven."

"So what part and whose army will we join—or sort of join?" Kate asked.

"Nerkon's, but he will tell you more about that. What you need to know before we go down to the plain is how each army works—how it is organized."

"Sounds good to me," Kate said. Her tightly analytical mind kicked into gear. Organizing the armies would be right up her thinking.

"The army of Nerkon consists of two divisions. Each division has five-thousand, seven-hundred and sixty fighting warriors plus their officers."

"Wow! That's a lot of warriors for Nerkon to herd into battle," Jen commented.

"It is, but each division is broken down into parts. Start with eight warriors as a tent party. Then put ten tent parties together for a Century— seven Centuries make a Cohort and ten Cohorts make the Division."

"That sounds very much like the way the Earth World's Roman army was structured," Jen mulled over.

"I suppose it is," Raguel said. "Yet, it is a logical way of managing a large army. It gives the commanders—in this case Nerkon—complete power over their troops."

"That is only five-thousand, six hundred," Kate was still thinking about the numbers Raguel had thrown out and quickly added them in her head.

"Very good," Raguel smiled. "Each of Nerkon's Divisions also has a unit of one-hundred sixty Centaurs. Obile has two divisions, but he does not have any Centaurs."

"So much for the Roman army," Jen smiled and looked at the thousands of Pilgers encamped by the river. "That is a lot of warriors to lead into battle."

"The officers who lead also have a ranking order—one Centurion over the Century, a First Centurion over the Cohort and a Senior Centurion over the whole Division. The Centaurs have a Senior Centaur as leader, but he works directly under the Senior Centurion. And each of these leaders has officers under them to help lead."

"And Count Begi's army?" Kate asked.

"After the Battle of Stur, and losing so many to the plague at Stur, he has been left with less than one division. Nevertheless, he and his army are strong in their belief of The Mission. They follow Nerkon in his quest to gain back Helig."

"And Rubidus?" Jen asked. "Nerkon lets him and his followers stay in the camp?"

"Nerkon believes Rubidus was not infected to the point he cannot be healed. Since there are only about two hundred Pilgers who still follow Rubidus, Nerkon doesn't feel threatened. And Rubidus keeps his *army* on the outskirts of the main campground. If you ask me, they are more like a band of ruffians than an army."

Kate gazed at the mass of activity picking up among the Pilgers on the plain. She could see how each army was laid out—organized by groups of ten tents and dirt walkways around those tents. "I see now," she said to Raguel. "The campground in laid out by Centuries."

"That's right, and each Century is kept together under their flag." He pointed to the different pennants waving in the morning breeze. "All the purple flags signify Nerkon's Divisions. When you get close, you will see they may all be purple, but each Century has a different emblem on them. The yellow flags are Obile's."

"What are the green and red flags?" Kate asked.

"The green flags are Count Begi's. His army is much smaller than Nerkon's. He has less than a division left after everything that happened at Stur."

"Then the dark red flags closest to the river must be Rubidus' followers."

"Yes—Rubidus and his followers," Raguel spit out. His lips tightened. "Do not trust any of them."

Jen watched a minute at the activity on the stage below them, but became impatient to find out what roll she and Kate would play. "So what are we suppose to do in Nerkon's army?" She could not imagine Kate and her being foot soldiers and they certainly weren't Centaurs.

"Oh, I forgot to tell you," Raguel allowed a sly grin to form on his face. "Nerkon's army has a special unit attached to it."

"A special unit?" Jen's eye brow rose.

"Bigna Air Power…"

"Flying?" Jen could not contain her enthusiasm. "We get to fly our Maups again? We get to fly with the Bigna Air Power again?"

"Yes…"

"Raguel," Jen hugged his small body, "you are wonderful."

"Not me. I just follow what I'm told."

"Where is the rest of the…the…Air Power Unit?" Kate asked.

"Not to worry. They will be here soon. And now it is time for you to go down and officially meet the Pilgers who are on The Mission."

"Great!" Jen said. She started toward her Maup.

"Not so fast," Raguel said. "We will be flying into the camp, and though we are on friendly Maup's and not Acchims, we will still be met by Nerkon's personal guards."

"What do you want us to do?"

"Before you land, circle above the campground so they can see we are not armed and mean no harm to them."

Kate felt like a helicopter caught in a holding pattern. Their circling above the encampment had not gone unnoticed by the warriors below. Instead of aimlessly wandering about, the warriors now scurried with purpose, picking up their weapons and readying for any assault their air-bound intruders might bring down on them. Swords drawn, they stood their ground.

"Duke Nerkon!" Raguel yelled down. He tightened his grip on Kate with his left arm so he could free his right one to wave at Nerkon who was jogging toward their landing spot.

"Raguel," Nerkon yelled back. With his muscular Popeye-like arm, he motioned for them to land and waved off the Pilgers who encircled him, on guard to protect their leader.

Nerkon's warriors obediently backed away and sheathed their swords. But they kept one hand on their swords' hilt ready for battle if the foreigners made any advancement against the Duke.

Their Maups made one last circle before they began their hovering-settling landing.

"Raguel!" Nerkon rushed to meet the three foreigners. "Welcome to our camp. Mysta sent word that you were on your way."

Raguel did not wait for Kate. He slid off the back of her Maup and landed, feet first, with a thud in front of Nerkon.

"Duke Nerkon," Raguel said. "It is good to see you. I'm glad his message got to you."

"We have so much to talk about," Nerkon said.

"So I understand," Raguel responded. "You have brought many Quae Pilgers to the Senvolte River to release Helig from the Indringers...from Rapio's High Priest Onde."

"That is why The Mission began. Look around at how many Quae have gathered. Yet we cannot go on."

Kate and Jen sat atop their Maups taking in the scene before them. They were unsure as to what they should do. The conversation of Raguel and Nerkon did not include their existence in the camp. The Pilger warriors who were the first to draw their swords had given away to another group of Quae. Those warriors, a tight grip on the hilts of their swords, now surrounded Kate and Jen. Suspicious glances at them were interspersed with apprehensive murmuring.

Sensitive to Kate and Jen's awkward situation, Raguel stepped back from his discussion with Nerkon and pointed at them.

"Kate—Jen!" Raguel said, motioning for them to join him. "Come down and meet Duke Nerkon and the Pilger Knights."

Without hesitation Kate and Jen leapt from their birds and made their way past the wary warriors until they stood safely beside Raguel. Still unsure of the proper etiquette for meeting a Duke and his knights, they did not speak.

"Welcome," Nerkon nodded slightly. His curly blondish-red beard and copper-colored hair glistened in the morning light.

"Thank you," Kate and Jen nodded back.

"And this is Lord Obile and Count Begi," Nerkon said, stepping aside so the other two Pilger leaders could join their growing group.

Obile and Begi stepped inside the inner circle and nodded. Though polite, they gave Kate and Jen a thorough once-over with their eyes.

Kate and Jen nodded back at them. From this close up they could see that Count Begi's black leather eye patch bore scratch marks of many battles. Raguel was right—a visible scar stretched out from the top of the patch and disappeared into his hairline. Hopefully, someday he would tell them of that battle.

"And you will get to know each of our knights soon enough." Nerkon pointed toward the Pilgers who had surrounded their Maups, but now gave them a wider breathing space.

Kate and Jen were surprised at the height of the Quae knights. At five and a half feet tall, they were about six inches taller than the average Quae, but still shorter than Kate and Jen. Though small in stature they were muscular. Unlike Raguel, their ears were less mouse-like and more elf-like. Their red, silky hair hung shoulder-length instead of curling around their ears. Their clothing was a little more elegant and colorful than the average Quae Kate and Jen remembered, but they still wore loose-fitting, long sleeved shirts and baggy pants that were tied down by the leg laces of their leather moccasins. Cinching their shirts at the waist was a leather belt with a long knife tucked into it on one side and their sword in its sheaf attached on the other side.

"Raguel," Nerkon said. "Bring Kate and Jen to my tent and we'll talk about everything that has happened. I'll meet you there. I have to take care of something first." His lips formed a crooked smile as he turned his attention to Kate and Jen. "From everything Mysta has told us, you two have come back to Bigna to help us defeat Rapio."

Before Kate or Jen could speak, Nerkon turned away and disappeared through a drawn opening of a long tent. His knights quickly followed him. Lord Obile and Count Begi nodded one more time to Kate and Jen before disappearing into the tent.

"Come," Raguel said. "Soon enough we will find out their strategy. I'm sure Nerkon is doing a…what do you call it…oh, yes, a pep talk."

"Pep talk?" Jen asked.

"Yes," Raguel smiled. "Though you were sent by Mysta, I'm sure Nerkon just got the message and now must inform his knights as to who you are and why the Eagle brought you to Domare."

"And then the knights will pass it on to the Quae Pilgers under them?" Jen was a little concerned that they might not be accepted.

"Yes, but trust must be earned so you both will have to prove yourselves to these Quae. They are descendants of the Quae you met when you were in Bigna many years ago, but they have only heard of you. They do not know you personally. Most of these Quae are battle-hardened Pilger warriors and do not take to strangers—even those from their forefathers' passed-down stories.

"How…" Kate began.

"You will learn to fight alongside of them. All of that will unfold to you soon. Let me show you the camp from ground level."

The straight dirt road they walked on formed a separation between small stretched, heavy-wool wall tents on their left and larger tents on their right. Kate and Jen were silent and tried to put an organizational form to the layout of the camp they had observed from Mount Hoch.

"The tents to your left are where the tent parties are quartered," Raguel explained. "You know, eight Pilgers to a tent. Each block of sixty tents makes a cohort."

Kate counted the double rows of five until they came to a smaller road, where another tent party's quarters began.

"See the three larger tents in front of the rows of tents?"

"Yes," Kate said.

"That is where the Centurions are quartered. Each Centurion commands eighty men. The outer two tents have three Centurions in them. The center tent is the First Centurion's quarters. He is the commander of the whole cohort—four-hundred and eighty Pilgers."

"Who lives there?" Jen asked. She nodded toward a dark purple and white stripped tent that sat behind the First Centurions quarters. Though it was smaller, it was much more colorful and drew attention to it right away.

"Ah," Raguel smiled. "That is the Trumpeter's quarters. Each Cohort has a Trumpeter who calls the Pilgers in their Cohort together."

"Much like the choir at the Cephas Monastery and their Gregorian chants," Kate observed staring at the circus-like tent.

"Yes, the Trumpeters serve much the same purpose, but they also will blast their trumpets in battle," Raguel explained, "to begin the battle—to show strength—to give courage."

"They sound important," Jen said.

"They are very important," Raguel concurred.

"And the colors," Kate observed aloud, "are very fitting for musicians."

"The larger tents on your right are the Centaurs' quarters. Their tents are larger because…"

"Because the Centaurs are larger," Jen interrupted and smiled. She knew the Centaurs' half horse-like and half Quae-like bodies would demand more space for billeting than the much smaller Quae Pilgers.

Raguel smiled at Jen's interruption.

They walked minutes without talking. After passing two more cohorts, Jen's curiosity got the better of her.

"Where is the Bigna Air Power unit? Where are the Mymybids and Maup birds?" Jen searched the camp. Excitement was bubbling up from deep within her with thoughts of seeing their friends Taka and Lieg again.

"They are behind the Centaurs," Raguel said. "Needless to say, they take up even more room than the Centaurs."

"Will Taka and Lieg be…?" Jen began.

"Ah," Raguel interrupted. "The First." He pointed at the next group of tents ahead of them.

"The First?" Kate questioned.

"Yes, the First," Raguel emphasized. "The First is what the number one cohort is called. It is made up of four-hundred eighty elite warriors— Nerkon's best. Its commander is the Senior Centurion, the highest ranking knight and most respected of all the Centurions because he has proven himself in many battles. Notice he also has the number one Trumpeter." He pointed to a small tent behind the Senior Centurions tent. Like the other Trumpeters' tents it was deep purple and white-striped but, from the center pole, it flew a purple banner with a silver trumpet—golden stars tumbled upward from its bell.

"I am sure this will be this cohort that Nerkon chooses to train you."

"Train?" Kate asked.

"You have to learn to use *today's* weapons and the Pilgers' way of battle," Raguel smiled. "Ah ha. We have arrived at Nerkon's tent."

Before them was a multi-sided, heavy wool pavilion, secured to the ground by ropes pulled taunt from the pole rising from the center of the conical roof top and eight wooden spokes that poked through holes at the roof line. Purple and white striped; it looked like a much larger version of the Trumpeters' tents to Kate and Jen. But the flag that flew from the center pole gave no doubt as to the difference of importance to its occupant. An eagle—wings outstretched, flying toward two golden stars—blazed from the deep purple background of the pennant.

"Kate," Jen said. "The Eagle and two stars."

"Like Raguel's and Mysta's," Kate said. "His tent sits beneath the eagle and stars."

"Yes," Raguel answered their unasked question. "Nerkon does fly toward those stars, but only for a short time. Unlike Cephas, neither he nor his tent will be forever."

The Quae Pilger who stood at the entrance did not budge as they approached. His bulky, five and a half foot body, dressed in a loose fitting tunic, baggy kickers, a leather helmet and breast plate, blocked their access. His drawn sword placed across the cloth draped doorway made them stop short of the entrance.

Kate stepped closer to the guard. His eyes narrowed at her bold intrusion, but his sword did not move from across the entrance. Kate glanced over her shoulder at Raguel. He stood firm, but did not approach the guard. Kate took one step back. The guard was not going to be her first battle in Domare. She would have to wait to go inside the tent.

"Let them in," Nerkon spoke from inside his tent.

With that, the guard raised his sword, pulled back the heavy wool cloth that acted as a door and stepped to one side. But his sword remained outside his sheath.

Kate's feet sunk into the thick brown fur rug that acted as a floor covering inside Nerkon's tent. She was unsure what she expected for the inside of Nerkon's tent, but she was sure she expected much more than what surrounded her—after all he was a duke and leader of The Mission. The octagon tent's side walls rose twelve feet to meet the slopped ceiling. Both the walls and ceiling were colorful hues of purple. In the center of the tent a vertical oak poll, about ten inches in diameter, held the conical roof upright eighteen feet in the air. On one side of the room, a six-inch high pallet, covered with blankets, served as Nerkon's bed. On the opposite side of the room a small writing table with a saddle chair, covered with a padded purple pillow, waited for Nerkon to sit and write his commands. Six unadorned wooden saddle chairs lined the edges of the tent.

"Wow!" Kate said. She took another step into the tent.

Clank! Clank! Clank!

Crash!

Kate barely made it inside the entrance before she stumbled, knocking over the line of weapons that leaned against a saw horse made from yew tree branches. Before she could stand upright the guard pushed Jen and

Raguel out of the way and was inside the tent. He grabbed Kate by her arm and, even though he was shorter than her, pulled her straight up, feet off the floor.

Legs dangling she forced out, "I'm sorry."

The guard didn't loosen his grip.

"Put her down," Nerkon calmly said. "I am all right. Go back to your post."

The guard dropped Kate and retreated from the tent.

"Let me help you up." A small Quae hand reached out to her.

"Thank you." Kate took the hand that appeared out of nowhere and pulled herself up. She studied the Quae whose hand she briefly held before he let go.

A small-statured monk stood beside her. He wore a long face and a grungy woolen robe, tied at the waist with a coarse rope. His face bore the same mask of sadness as Peter the Hermit she had met at the Council of Clermont.

Taken aback at the resemblance, Kate mumbled, "Peter?"

"Petri—Petri Meudy," the monk nodded. "Have I met you?" He pushed the hood of his robe off his head, exposing his elf-like ears and shoulder length red hair.

"No. No, I suppose not," Kate smiled. "But you remind me of someone I once met." With the exception of his Quae ears, he could be Peter the Hermit.

"Amazing likeness," Jen said joining Kate inside the tent. "Amazing."

"And you two are…" Petri began. He did not know what they were mumbling about.

"Excuse our impoliteness," Kate said. "I'm Kate and this is my cousin Jen." She grabbed Jen's arm and pulled her toward Petri.

"Yes, I know who you are," Petri peered at Jen. "What I was going to say is that I don't remember meeting you before now, but I do know you two are the ones the Eagle brought to Domare to help us." His sad expression did not change.

Redness crept up Kate's face because of her interruption of Petri.

"I suppose we are," Jen smiled at Kate's embarrassment. "We have a lot to learn."

"And I am here to pray for you," Petri's long face seem to lengthen with each word. His eyes darted between Kate and Jen analyzing the two strangers the Eagle had brought to Domare for him to pray for. "Yes, a lot to learn—a lot of prayers."

"Come sit," Nerkon said. "We have so much to discuss."

Chapter Eleven

*T*he tale Nerkon wove for the next hour about what happened at Stur was more colorful than what Kate and Jen had heard from Raguel and Mysta. Even experiencing the visions of the Fís Table was not as explosive as Nerkon's story. He and his army had endured much to get to the Great Plain and put the holy city of Helig in sight—three years battling their way across many lands to get to Domare, only to be stopped at the city gates of Stur by the Indringers. After Friar Fara gave them the faith and strength to forge on into Stur and defeat the Indringers, they relaxed and thought their battles were over, at least until they fought for Helig. But their worst battle was within the city walls—the Bás Plague.

"I watched my warriors die—both physically and mentally. So many succumbed to the plague..." Nerkon dropped his head in thought for a moment. "When Friar Fara died and Rubidus took the Holy Sword, I knew we had to gather everyone still healthy and loyal to The Mission and leave Stur. It was painful to leave our dying, but we have pledged ourselves to The Mission."

Silence hung in the tent.

"But now," Nerkon's face creased with concern, "even with Helig just over the river, we cannot succeed with The Mission."

"We will find a way," Obile interjected. He and Begi had joined the gathering in Nerkon's tent. After Nerkon had consulted with them, they went to their senior centurions and related who Kate and Jen were and

83

why the Eagle brought them to Domare. Those centurions would take the message back to the warriors they commanded.

"Yes," Begi nodded. "We will find a way."

Nerkon breathed a heavy sigh. Rising from his saddle chair, he slowly walked to the entrance of his tent and pulled back the heavy cloth covering.

"Our armies are waiting for a way." He sighed again. He starred momentarily at the many Pilgers milling around the camp. "Faithfully they wait." He let the covering drop back into place—again closing them off from the outside world. Without turning around he stated. "A way... the Eagle has sent these two Earth World beings to us to show us a way." He turned and waved at Kate and Jen.

Kate and Jen were silent.

"Since childhood I have heard of the two of you, but I always thought that your daring feats in Gudsrika were exaggerated. Well, I suppose we'll find out."

"Doesn't sound like he has a lot of confidence in us," Jen whispered to Kate.

Kate wrinkled her eyebrow in agreement.

"The Eagle knows what he is doing," Nerkon continued. "So I know you two will be able to fulfill his confidence in you."

Kate instinctively reached for her locket and grasped it tightly. All eyes in the room were on her and Jen.

"Yes, they will," Raguel interjected. "But the Eagle wants you to do your part, too."

"Our part?" Nerkon raised one eyebrow.

"They need to be trained...to learn the lay of the land...the customs of a Pilger," Raguel said.

"Of course," Nerkon nodded. "My First will train them in weapons and strategy."

Kate took a deep breath. Dare she ask about the Bigna Air Power? That was where her heart was and she knew the Maups were part of his army.

Your First," Raguel agreed with Nerkon. "Very good choice. When it comes to handling the shield and sword there are none better."

"And they are the best with a bow in battle," Begi added. Though he himself had an elite number one cohort, he knew Nerkon's First were superior to any other warriors in the camp. They always won in the Games.

"Once they've learned everything the First can teach them," Nerkon hesitated a moment, focusing his eyes on Kate and Jen. "Once the Senior Centurion gives them their sword and shield we'll turn them over to the Air Power."

Jen exhaled a sigh of joy.

Obile and Begi nodded in agreement.

"And after you get through all that," Nerkon stated, "you'll be ready for knighthood."

"Knighthood?" Jen couldn't silence her thoughts any longer. Her mind was spinning with everything the three leaders were laying out for her and Kate.

"Of course," Obile finally joined the conversation. "From what we've been told, you two will make excellent knights."

"Knighthood?" Kate repeated Jen's surprise.

"Yes," Nerkon agreed with Obile. "Live up to the stories pass down to us about you and you both will be knights in the highest order."

Phew!!! Kate exhaled. A lot was being expected of Jen and her. She prayed they could live up to the Quae expectations.

Chapter Twelve

*T*he bury blacksmith greeted Kate and Jen with much enthusiasm. "Ah," the blacksmith said. "I am honored to be the one to fit you with your knighthood armor."

"Thank you," Kate responded. "We're still trying to get used to the idea."

"The idea and the pressure," Jen stated. "Thinking we can become knights in such a short period of time."

"The Eagle would not have brought you to Domare if he didn't think you were up to the task," Raguel smiled.

"Still, such a short time," Jen responded. She raised one shoulder to shift the chainmail tunic she wore. It amazed her that the blacksmith was waiting for them as soon as they left Nerkon's tent.

Hanging from pegs stuck into the center pole of the blacksmith's tent were their waist-length chainmail tunics they wore in Gudsrika. He made minor adjustments, but the chainmail slipped over their linen cloth tunics perfectly. As nice as it was that they didn't have to be fitted for their chainmail, they did have to stand still while the blacksmith fit them with tailor-made bronze Bascine Helmets and plate armor suits.

"I hope they are to your liking," the blacksmith said.

"Oh yes," Kate said. "You've made them perfectly."

"These still remind me of the intricate knitted dollies our great aunts made," Jen said of the chainmail tunics they wore.

"Me too," Kate laughed. "Remember when they tried to teach us to knit?"

"Disastrous," Jen joined Kate in laughter. Turning to the blacksmith she added, "So glad you made these instead of us."

The blacksmith measured, hammered metal into flat sheets, measured more and after a couple of hours sent them on their way. The next morning, hanging outside their tent, were two full suits of armor.

For the next five days, dawn to dusk, they joined Nerkon's First to learn about Quae Pilger customs, weapons and how to use them in battle and why these Quae believed in The Mission. Each night they fell into their pallet beds exhausted.

"Will we ever get use to the weight of these helmets?" Kate asked Raguel.

Though they had practiced a few times in full armor, this day—day six of their training—they were down to their chainmail tunics and helmets. Despite the fact that the visor of the helmet was detachable, they practiced with it on and down—which partially blocked the targets.

"When you are in battle you will not think of the weight," Raguel said.

"Raguel," Jen began. "You never wear armor—aren't you afraid in battle?"

"I wear the armor of the Eagle at all times. I am always protected," Raguel smiled.

Jen gazed at her friend. *Of course he is*, she thought. *Of course he is.*

"The full armor and helmets are different than the protection we wore in Bigna before," Kate said, "but the Pilgers' swords and shields are not much different from those of the Quae of Gudsrika." Kate tilted her head to see better though the slits of her visor. "And neither is my bow and arrows." She held her bow over her head. The tight tension of the hemp string pulled the yew wood taut, ready for Kate to put in another feathered arrow, but the quiver on her back was empty. She had shown her skill of shooting nine arrows in one minute.

For the umpteenth hour, they stood on a football field-size, flat area on the outskirts of the camp practicing. Crude targets, made to look like Indringers on Acchims, were seventy-five yards from their position.

Nock! Mark! Draw!

Over and over Mejor, the Senior Centurion from the First Cohort, yelled at them. Being the best of the best longbow Pilgers, he did not let up on their training.

Nock! Mark! Draw!

And over and over again Kate and Jen would put the notch of the arrow onto the string, mark their target, draw the arrow back—and then wait for the final command.

Loose!

With Mejor's yell of *loose* their arrows flew toward the targets. Most arrows hit somewhere on the mock Indringer that, if they were in actual battle, would do harm to the enemy.

"Not bad," Mejor nodded at Kate. "Not bad at all. You emptied your quiver in one minute." His training had paid off. Although these two Earth World beings could not match his fifteen arrows in one minute, they were already better than most Pilgers.

"Excellent!" Jen exclaimed. "You beat my time." Emptying her quiver of nine arrows had taken just over a minute. "Maybe I'll win next round."

Kate smiled at Jen's challenge, "Maybe." Without waiting for Jen to respond she asked Raguel, "Swords, bow and arrows—are there any other weapons we need to learn?"

"Lances," Raguel responded.

"Lances?" Jen asked.

"That's right." Raguel pointed at two eight foot ash wood, steel tipped poles leaning against a yew tree at the edge of the clearing. He jogged over to the six pound poles, balanced one under each arm and jogged back to where Kate and Jen stood. "One for each of you."

"Not as heavy as I thought lances would be," Kate observed, steadying her lance on both hands.

"Wow!" Jen exclaimed, looking up at the glistening steel point of the long rod she held. "That could do a lot of harm."

"Yes, it can, but you will be trained to stay away from it and become skilled in deflecting it with your shields."

"Are you going to teach us?" Kate looked at Mejor.

"No," Mejor's intense face did not break a smile, but his eyes glimmered with a private joke. "No, it is time you move on to where you will be when we go to battle."

Kate cocked her head in puzzlement. "Where we will be in battle?"

"How about learning to use them while you fly your Maups?" a familiar voice proposed from behind them.

"Taka!" Kate yelled while turning to see her flight trainer and friend.

"It is good to see you again," Taka said.

"And you too, Jen," Lieg addressed his former flight student. "We have been waiting for you."

Jen dropped her lance and ran to Lieg. Overjoyed to see him, she gave him a hug. "You are here."

"Of course we are," Lieg said without trying to loosen Jen's embrace. "And it is time for us to train you for the upcoming battle on Helig."

"Oh," Jen said, letting go of Lieg. "I guess I'm a little more than happy to see you."

"It is all right," Lieg said. "I understand. And Taka and I would not want anyone else to supervise your training on Maups."

"Thank you," Jen said.

Kate took a step back and studied Taka and Lieg. "It really is you." Surprise and curiosity filled her words.

"Yes, it really is," Taka confirmed.

"You have not aged. Do you stay…live at the Cephas Monastery?"

"Yes," Taka laughed. "We need to live close to our Maups at the Monastery. I believe Mysta told you that we who that live within the walls of the monastery count a lifetime different than you on the Earth World. Time is even different for us at Cephas than those Quae who live outside the Monastery walls."

"He did explain much to us, but it is still hard to grasp," Kate said.

"Just think of it like this—we are on Bigna to serve the Eagle—we've served him from the beginning and will be with him until the end."

"Those are Mysta's exact words," Jen observed.

"Are you ready to learn how to fight using a lance?" Lieg asked. Kate and Jen would learn more about the secrets of the Monastery soon enough.

He and Taka did not have much time to teach them the art of using a lance from the back of a Maup.

"With you two," Jen said enthusiastically, "more than ready."

"Then it is time," Lieg said.

"Not yet," Raguel grinned. "You will need these."

"These look like the 1920's flight helmets we wear when we perform our wing-walking aerobatics at air shows," Jen exclaimed.

"Somehow it wouldn't be right seeing you fly your Maups with a bronze helmet of the ground forces, even those of knights. I recalled that when you were in Bigna before you missed your flight caps...helmets, so I watched you closely in the Earth World when you were doing your aerobatics and duplicated what you wore."

"Of course you watched us," Jen grinned. "We never doubted you were somewhere around us."

"They have a navy blue triangle on the front," Kate said taking off her bronze helmet and shaking out her long, sable hair. "They are beautiful." She quickly pulled the leather helmet on. "It fits."

"And," Raguel continued, proud of his handy work, "I smuggled a couple of pairs of goggles from the Earth World."

"How..." Jen's head cocked to one side. She now wore her new headgear. "How did you get them..." she tried to imagine a small copper field mouse carrying two pair of goggles—three times his size—from the Earth World to the Bigna World. "How..." but she couldn't even formulate the question.

"A little Bigna magic," Raguel smiled at her visualizing him smuggling the two giant size pair of goggles on his back. "A little Bigna magic."

Chapter Thirteen

*F*rom a distant tent, unfriendly eyes focused on Kate and Jen.

"Just look at those two, Abi." Disgust flowed from Rubidus' lips. He stood ridged, watching Kate and Jen on the practice field. "Look how they shoot their arrows at the fake enemy."

"Yes, Sir Rubidus," Abi responded. "But they cannot match our longbow warriors when we go to battle."

"No, they cannot," Rubidus tightened the grip on his sword. "They will soon feel the wrath of our reach."

Abi, Rubidus' Senior Centurion, did not respond.

"And now they have been joined by the Senior Centurions from the Bigna Air Power," Rubidus spat. Like the rest of the Quae on Bigna, as a child Rubidus had learned of the exploits of the two beings who had come from the Earth World many years before and saved Bigna. *Just fables handed down from one generation to another,* he had always assured himself. But here they stood, in *his* camp. But even with all the stories, his arrogance did not let him believe they were as good as the stories made them to be. Surly they were not as good of a warrior as he—and he was definitely sure they were not nearly as cunning. "They will soon learn just who has the power in this camp—in Domare."

"That would be you," Abi stated, playing into Rubidus' ego. "And you will soon defeat them."

"Yes, I will." Rubidus glared out his tent door a few more moments. "But we have to make sure that they never get the chance to show their skill." He turned to his Senior Centurion. "Abi, I want you to find the two most loyal warriors from our army and bring them to me."

"Every one of your fighters would gladly give up their life to obey your order," Abi nodded.

"Cutthroats, one and all," Rubidus offered.

"But eager to follow you and do whatever you ask." Abi still did not know what his leader was asking of him.

Rubidus meditated a moment on his newly-organized army. Most of his soldiers had followed him from Stur and into the Senvolte River. He shuddered mentally remembering his time below the water's swift current—the first heat of the blistering sting of a Bás Scorpion behind his left ear, the need to sleep and waking up vowing to kneel down in obedience at the altar of Rapio. He walked out of the river with a new master—a master who had left an overseer forever embedded in his neck and soul.

And before him was his militia. Those who had walked out of the river behind him had the same reminder, the same black mole and swelling of an implanted Bás Scorpion, on their neck. A few other rebellious Quae Pilgers had joined his army, but all of them were never-do-gooders. He did not care about their brutal debauchery. He let his ruthless soldiers do as they pleased because they followed him with complete submission to his will. *Let them fill their hearts with their dark pleasures now, for their eternity belongs to Rapio.*

"I know any one of them would do what I ask," he finally responded, "but I only want the best two. I have a special assignment and do not want anyone else to know my plans."

"Plans?" Abi asked, hoping to find out more. He too felt the heat of a controlling scorpion squirm underneath his skin.

"They will unfold to you soon," Rubidus glared at Abi. "You will know soon enough. I count on you to bring me the best."

"Yes, Sir Rubidus." Abi did not hesitate any longer to obey his leader's command. He scurried out the tent door before Rubidus' anger fell on him.

Rubidus's eyes followed Abi's path until he disappeared into his Senior Centurion's tent. His head twitched from a searing pain he felt behind his left ear. Gritting his teeth he swallowed hard the sound of pain he felt rising in his throat.

The Bás Scorpion, which lived inside the dark growth on his skin, intensified its stimulation.

Aaargh!

Rubidus could not force down the sound any longer. He grimaced once more as the scorpion shot more venom into his soul. His hand went to the spot of the throbbing and he felt the creature squirm—hot to his touch.

He shifted his gaze back to Kate and Jen. *They will not escape you, my lord.* The creature writhed with every stroke of Rubidus' touch.

Bwoorm!

An explosion of wind exploded into the room. From between his fingers a deep reddish-purple glow flashed out and filled the tent with a sulfur stench that sucked the oxygen from the air. He inhaled deeply, the scorpion glowed with delight.

Pushing back the sleeve of his tunic he saw the encroaching hard shell-like scales of the creature living inside him beginning to take over the physical part of his body. Soon his hands would turn to pincher-like claws. He knew his time as a Quae was limited. When he walked into the Senvolte River his life was changed forever. He no longer fought for The Mission and the Quae—his mission was that of Rapio. Soon he would live in Rapio's domain as one of his scaled, encrusted servants.

Rage rose from Rubidus' depths. He would not even be one of Rapio's Elite Imperial Knights—the most trusted in Rapio's army. At least he had been promised the status of Elite Trooper—at least he would be able to walk upright on his hind legs and crush everything that stood in his way.

Vroo-vroo!

A low-pitched whistling wind whirled around the tent and blew the stench from the air. The Bás scorpion within Rubidus went still. The creature's needs had been fed. Rubidus closed his eyes to gather his composure. A drop of sweat tricked across the mole on his neck, found its way under his collar and slid down his arm and over the waxy substance that coated his increasing scales. His overseer was content for the moment.

Clack!

Clack!

Clack!

The sound of dashing footsteps hitting the rocks twenty yards from his spot made him open his eyes to the reality before him. Abi was approaching his tent, two Centurions in tow.

"Sir Rubidus," Abi bowed down. "I have brought you two of your finest warriors. I handpicked them from my personal elite guard. This is …"

"I do not need to know their names," Rubidus stated. "All I need to know is that they are the ones whom I can trust for my purpose."

"You can…" Abi began.

Rubidus held up his hand and quieted Abi. He looked at the two burley warriors in front of him. Though slightly shorter than he, their barrel-like chests gave them a menacing look of strength. Unruly hair tumbled around their necks, meeting the beards from their unshaven faces. Their brown woolen, thigh-length tunics were belted at the waist. Tight kickers disappeared into their knee-high, laced boots. Each of them had a fourteen inch, two-edge bladed dagger tucked into their belts on one side and a long sword sheathed on the other. A quiver, full of arrows, hung on their backs.

But it was their eyes that convinced Rubidus that Abi had chosen the right two deviants for his quest—black craters that looked out from the abyss. He did not hesitate to commission them to carry out the task of eliminating Kate and Jen.

"You have heard of the two intruders in our camp," he stated.

The two curled their lips but did not move.

"Good," Rubidus took their expressions as confirmation of their distaste for Kate and Jen. "They are a threat to our lives—our mission. I have chosen you to do away with that threat." He stopped so his words would sink in.

Seconds passed, turned into a minute—then two minutes.

Outside, the clamor of Pilgers going about their daily tasks filtered in through the heavy wool door of the tent. Abi and his two selected warriors stood rigid and silent, waiting for Rubidus to make the next sound.

Writhing inside his body, Rubidus felt his overseer flare up. Anger filled his thoughts and quickened his pulse. The fury of a raging tornado filled his eyes when he finally bellowed out his command.

"They are to vanish from the camp—from Domare."

"Killed?" Abi asked.

"I do not care," Rubidus growled. "But they are never to set foot in Domare again. They are never to be a threat to me again."

"It will be done!" Abi stated. He glared at his two chosen warriors. "It will be done tonight."

"Tonight," the two warriors grunted in agreement.

"Tonight," Rubidus sneered. "Yes tonight, but away from the camp. No one can ever know it was me..." he hesitated. Searing pain in his neck crimped his thoughts. "You must not speak my name—ever!"

The eyes of the warriors sank deeper into the abyss.

"If you are caught, I will personally put you to death."

"They will not be caught," Abi offered. "They have much experience in this kind of...of disposal."

Rubidus glared at the murderers. *Yes, they are the right ones.*

"They will do it tonight," Abi restated. "The two intruders from the Earth World will be disposed of, and no one will know who did it or what became of them."

Rubidus thrust his face toward the two warriors and hissed, "If it is not as Abi says, do not let me see your faces again. You will not fail—their lives or yours!"

"Yes, Sir Rubidus!" the soldiers snapped to attention. The void craters that served as their eyes radiated a depraved fear.

"Go!" Rubidus thrust a silver coin in each of their quivers. "Two more for each of you when you send word and proof the deed is done."

Without hesitation, the two Quae soldiers scurried out of the tent and raced across the campground. They would make their plans for the night raid on Kate and Jen.

"You have chosen well, Abi," Rubidus' voice softened slightly, but continued to invoke a sneer.

"By tomorrow you will no longer have to look at the faces of the two aliens from the Earth World," Abi gloated. "And then you can proceed to defeat Nerkon."

"Nerkon!" Rubidus laughed. "His zeal to complete The Mission and take back Helig has blinded him to us. He thinks, because I have told him, I am still pledged to The Mission and that I will follow him into Helig."

"But instead he will follow you into the river," Abi snickered.

"The river!" Rubidus snorted. "Yes, he will follow me into the river and never return. He will become Rapio's for eternity—for eternity the same as you and me, Abi, the same as you and me."

His deep, snorting laughter seeped out of the tent and fell upon his guard's ear.

The guard squirmed and cast an uneasy glance at the cloth-draped door. The laughter he heard was not of joy but of depravity. He had followed Rubidus into the river—he knew his time in Bigna was short, but he hoped not too short.

Chapter Fourteen

A cool breeze blew across the knights and Pilgers who gathered for the evening meal. It was the time of the day everyone could relax and share stories of their day.

"Wow!" Jen exclaimed. "It has been quite a day."

"It sure has," Kate agreed. She pushed her empty wooden bowl, that minutes before held a vegetable stew, a few inches toward the center of the table.

"You two learned the art of using a lance in battle faster than many of my warriors," Nerkon stated.

"Maybe because when we first learned to wing walk..." Jen began.

"You walk on the feathered wings of your Maups?" Obile questioned.

"No, no, no," Jen laughed. "In the Earth World we fly...we fly..." How could she explain a metal airplane to someone who was unfamiliar with machines? She settled for the simple. "Our birds are different. We can walk on our Earth World's birds' wings."

"Strange," Obile said, but did not pursue an idea so foreign to him.

Jen waited for a moment for another question. However, Obile was silently trying to picture Jen walking on a bird.

"In our Earth World, before we climbed on the back of our *birds*," Jen hesitated knowing Obile was still struggling with the idea of them walking atop a bird, "we would practice our balancing techniques on a thin beam by using a pole about the size of these lances."

"Strange" Obile said again.

They sat at a table outside Nerkon's conference tent. Nerkon, Obile, Begi, Rubidus and their highest-ranking knights sat at the table. All their other knights sat at tables in front of them. Most who were in attendance enjoyed partaking in the evening meal with the two Earth World beings they had been told about for all their lives. Murmuring to each other about the daily activities, they waited for Nerkon to speak and inform them as to what they were to do now.

Clink! Clink! Clink!

The hard surface of Mejor's metal dagger striking the outside of his goblet was the signal that Nerkon was about to speak. A hush fell over the knights.

Clink! Clink! Clink!

Nerkon rose and held up his hands. His acceptance of the role as leader of all the knights, no matter whose army they represented, meant he needed to give them an informational and encouraging speech.

"As you all know, we have been on a long trek to accomplish The Mission—to take back Helig from the Indringers. Many of you have been with me…with us," he pointed to Obile, Begi and Rubidus, "from the beginning. You have fought many battles along the way, including the battle of Stur." He stopped for a moment to think of his next words.

"Now we are within sight of our destination, the final part of our journey. Helig is just across the river. As you know, the river is controlled by Atasa's guard—Elak." He paused.

The knights at the table gave Nerkon their full attention but didn't comment.

"Elak can be conquered!" Nerkon exclaimed. He looked into the eyes of the knights. Some eyes radiated fear—others belief.

From the outer outskirts of the camp nightly sounds were heard, but from the group of knights no one uttered a sound.

"Sir Rubidus and some of you, his mighty warriors, have entered the river and come out. We all can do the same." He looked at Rubidus with approval. "Sir Rubidus shows us that Elak may think he can prevent us from going across the river but we know we can cross over and take back Helig."

Helig!
Helig!
Helig!

The words of The Mission rose suddenly from the knights.

Nerkon raised his hands and quieted the knights. "And to lead us to victory, the Eagle has sent us the two from the Earth World that we all learned about when we were growing." This time he pointed to Kate and Jen. "They have trained with the best knights we have and are ready to take us over the river and to the gates of Helig."

Helig!

Helig!

Helig!

"Rise," he instructed Kate and Jen.

Slightly self-conscious they stood and smiled.

"Mejor has informed me that they are ready to join our ranks—they are ready to become knights."

Knights? Jen mouthed to Kate.

Kate shrugged. So Nerkon was serious when he said they would be knights.

"The battle for Helig is ahead of us, but tomorrow we will be jubilant. Tomorrow we will have a grand pageant and knight them into the Royal Knights of Bigna," Nerkon stated. "They will wear the colors of the Bigna Air Power."

Taka and Lieg lips turned upward into a grin. Their pride in Kate and Jen could not be contained.

But on the other end of the table Rubidus turned his smiling lips into a sneer. *I will be jubilant tomorrow, Sir Nerkon, but not for the reason you think.*

"Knighthood," Kate shook her head.

"I cannot even imagine being in the Royal Knights of Bigna," Jen agreed. "But then I could not imagine this." She pointed around the tent where they lay under the heavy covers of their beds, which were more like giant pillows than a bed. A multicolored rug floor pushed its way up the sides of the wool wall tent. Though much smaller than Nerkon's tent, it was ample for two people. Two saddle stools were pushed underneath a rough sawn wood table. A candle lantern, hanging from one of the cross poles, flickered its dim light across the room. Their swords, bows and arrows, lances and armor were propped against a sawhorse made from small branches of yew trees.

"Me either," Kate yawned. The day of flying, practicing with lances and a huge dinner were taking its toll. Her body was craving sleep.

"I wonder what kind of ceremony we will go through to become knights?" Jen mulled aloud.

"Mmmmmm," was all Kate could muster out.

"Do you think we'll be called 'Sir'—Sir Kate—Sir Jen?"

Heavy breathing answered Jen's question.

"Sleep well," Jen chuckled to herself. "Sleep well."

Not five minutes passed before Jen had joined Kate in a deep sleep.

Chapter Fifteen

Heavy breathing from inside Kate and Jen's tent assured the two malevolent Pilgers that it was time for them to carry out Rubidus' order. Black executioner masks covered their faces, making their heads disappeared into the darkness of their hooded cloaks. Emerging from the shadows they eased their daggers from their belts.

Vippp...vipppp...vipppp!

The razor-sharp blades of the short fighting weapons quickly cut through the side of the tent, until there were two slits large enough for the two to sneak through. Once inside they quietly crossed the tent, each with a destination in mind—one hovered over Kate, the other over Jen.

"What....who..." Kate's words were muffled quickly by the dark hood that was pulled over her head. Her flailing hands quickly were wrenched behind her back, a coarse rope looped around them and pulled tight.

Fighting back became a mute point as she was jerked from her bed and dragged out into the cold air.

"Jen..." Kate tried to cry out.

But Jen was suffering the same fate and could not hear Kate.

Once outside, Kate and Jen were easily thrown over the shoulders of the two burly kidnappers. Running swiftly past Nerkon's tent, the kidnappers held tightly to the squirming cousins and threw them onto the back of waiting dark chestnut-brown centaurs. Jumping behind their hostile bundles, they rode away from the camp.

Flumpp!
Flumpp!
Kate and Jen hit the ground hard.

Before either could move, strong hands grabbed their tunics and towed them across rock-strewn ground.

Flumpp!
Flumpp!
They were dropped a second time.

Crunch! Crunch! Crunch!
Crunch! Crunch! Crunch!

The footsteps grew fainter but the mumbling of the two assailants could still be heard.

"We're far enough from the camp. We can kill them now," one of them said.

"Hmmm," the second one responded.

"Slash their throats and send their heads back to prove we have accomplished our deed."

"I don't think so," the second kidnapper mulled over aloud.

"I want my two silver coins."

"Let me think," the second one grumbled.

"Don't take long. I want to get this over with and ride on."

"Make the fire and let me think."

Kate and Jen heard one of their assailants mumble something indistinguishable. Sounds of wood being thrown together filtered to their location.

Whoosh!

The fire lit.

"Kate," Jen whispered.

"I'm here."

"We've got to do something before they decide we are no longer any use to them."

"I know," Kate said. "Work on your ropes."

"Already on it," Jen said. Her captor, in his hurry, had tied the ropes around her wrists loosely and she was able to pull one hand partially through.

Whoosh!

Another log was thrown on the fire.

"I've got it," the second kidnapper stated. "We'll ask for more silver. If these two are the ones we've heard about for so many years, they must be worth more than three pieces of silver."

"I don't know…" the first kidnapper started

"If Ru…" the second captor cut him off.

"Do not say his name!" The first kidnapper's voice wavered in fear. "He said he would kill us if anyone found out who hired us."

"But of course," the second one laughed. "He will personally kill us." He mocked Rubidus' words.

The first captor didn't respond to the mockery.

"Well, if he won't pay us, there are many other rebels that will," the second captor continued on with his double-crossing plan. "I think we will be able to get much more."

"I don't know…"

"Are you afraid of …" the second captor laughed. "Oh yes, I cannot say his name. Are you afraid of the traitor in Nerkon's camp?"

"No." But fear was still heavy in the first assailant's voice. "But he is not someone to make fun of. His soul belongs to Rapio…and I do fear Rapio."

"Rapio did not tell us to dispose of the two intruders," the second kidnapper spat. "And we will not be touched as long as we hide these two. We will not cut off their heads just yet, but we will cut off a finger and take it back to the camp. He will pay us more and then we will kill them."

"It sounds right," the first kidnapper shrugged. "But why not a hand?"

"Ah, that is why I am the one who makes the plans. If we cut off a hand we would make these two less powerful and able to battle at their full strength. They would be less of a threat to…to the one who pays us. But a finger—now a finger just shows they are still alive and we are in control of their fate."

The first captor looked into the fire and nodded. His fear was still within him, but now he was afraid of his fellow captor as well.

"Let's eat and then we'll take off one of their fingers," the second kidnapper mumbled.

"Jen?" Kate said. "How are you coming? It doesn't sound like we have much time."

"Working on it cousin—working on it." Jen's small hand was almost out, but once she freed herself they needed a plan. "Kate," she whispered. "I'm almost free, think of what and where we will go once we've gotten the ropes and hoods off."

"Keep working on your ropes," Kate whispered back. "I've been listening to the sounds those two are making. I think they are about fifty yards from us. The centaurs are even further away. Once we get free we'll have the element of surprise, but we'll have to formulate a direction as soon as our hoods are off."

"We seem to be in a forest with mesquite brushes around us." Jen continued to work on freeing her hands.

"I think so too," Kate said. "I can smell the oily mesquites mixed with heavy oak."

"Two more fingers and one hand will be out of the ropes," Jen assured Kate. "Just a few more tugs and both hands will be…"

Snap!

The sound of a twig breaking froze Jen's movement.

Not yet, she prayed. *Not yet.*

"Kate," Jen whispered. She tugged harder to free her hand.

Snap!

Snap!

The unseen entity was getting closer.

She tugged hard once more.

Phtttt!

Jen's hand slipped from her bonds. Quickly she reached for the hood covering her face so she could see a reference as to what she needed to do next. But a hand grabbed hers and stopped her movement.

No! She yelled inside.

Shhhhs!

The hand quickly pulled back Jen's hood.

"Ov?"

Shhhs!

Her elfin friend held his finger to his mouth. His mouse-like ears pricked forward, listening and looking intently at their surroundings. He tipped one ear back in anticipation of an aggressive move from their captors.

Jen was stunned to see 'Ov. The last time they had seen him he was with Eldré, his small hand in hers, disappearing into the Gudsrika Sea. She did not let her surprise slow her thinking. She reached over and pulled the hood from Kate's head. 'Ov was already working on cutting the rope binding Kate. The sharp blade of the eight inch dagger easily cut through the hemp rope.

"Quick!" 'Ov whispered. "Follow me."

Kate glanced at their kidnappers. They were so involved in filling their stomachs they did not notice the activity fifty yards away from where they gorged on a recently killed small animal.

Kate and Jen crawled a few feet before they stood upright. Seeing 'Ov dash into the darkness of the twelve-foot high bushes that surrounded the clearing where they were held captive, they followed without hesitation. The dim light of the two new moons of Bigna barely forced a small sliver of light through the heavy wooded area. What light that did filter was focused on 'Ov.

'Ov dashed fifteen feet ahead of them—suddenly he vanished in an eight-foot high bush that was unlike the other mesquite. It had the same gangling branches and smell but it glimmered once 'Ov disappeared into it.

With no clear path ahead of them, Kate and Jen's footsteps followed their instinct and 'Ov.

Thud!

Kate tumbled head first to the ground as her foot hit a rock and tripped her. Instinct had failed her moving feet.

Jen, two steps ahead of Kate, stood with one foot into the glimmering bush where 'Ov disappeared. She stopped mid-step. Turning to help Kate she saw the noise of Kate's fall had aroused their captors.

"What the…" one yelled, throwing his food onto the ground.

"They've gotten loose."

"Get them!"

"Kate!" Jen yelled. "Take my hand." She yanked Kate up and pulled her into the unknown of the bush where 'Ov had vanished.

Jet ink blackness surrounded them.

"Where do we go?" Kate asked. They had stepped into a place void of all color—they could not see 'Ov—they could not even see each other.

"I don't know," Jen answered. She groped the darkness for Kate. Finding her, she grabbed Kate's hand. "But we are together. We'll make it."

Outside of the blackness they heard their captors getting closer.

Crunch! Crunch! Crunch!

Crunch! Crunch! Crunch!

"Where did they go?" One yelled.

"This way, but I don't see them." Fear radiated from the second captor's words.

"We have to find them! They couldn't have gotten far."

"I saw them. They went into these bushes."

Crunch! Crunch! Crunch!

Crunch! Crunch! Crunch!

The heavy footsteps grew closer to where Kate and Jen stood. They did not dare to move as they had no guidance as to which way was safe.

Crunch! Crunch! Crunch!

Crunch! Crunch! Crunch!

Then silence. Their two captors had stopped moving.

Kate squeezed Jen's hand. Though she could not see their kidnappers, their pungent, unbathed odor put them within ten feet of where she and Jen stood.

"Ohhh," Kate gasped.

"What was that?" a kidnapper yelled.

Kate felt the small hand of 'Ov over her mouth, sealing any other unwanted noise.

"It came from over here," one of the kidnappers yelled.

Swoosh!

Swoosh!

Swoosh!

Rushing air from the swinging long sword of the kidnapper brushed Kate's cheeks. 'Ov's hand tightened but Kate did not even breathe.

Swoosh! Swoosh! Swoosh!

"You are swinging at nothing but a scraggly bush and wasting time. Come on. We have to find them. Remember, it is their lives or ours."

Crunch! Crunch! Crunch!

Crunch! Crunch! Crunch!

The sounds of their fleeing footsteps grew weaker until they could no longer be heard.

Kate and Jen waited for 'Ov to explain, but he offered no explanation.

"Hold to each other," 'Ov said. "Must get you back to Raguel."

"Sounds good to us," Jen said, squeezing Kate's hand. "But how do we see…"

'Ov joined hands with Kate and Jen and held on tightly. "Your lockets.—Raguel said your lockets."

"Kate?"

"I feel it too."

Around their neck their lockets warmed and then glowed blue. From the blackness where they stood crystal snowflakes fell, giving off a sparking glow. The blue light from their lockets flashed a ray to each falling flake, seeming to search out its origin. With each pulsating burst of light, the snowflake the ray hit glistened with a blue glow from within.

"What is happening?" Jen asked.

"I think our lockets are finding out which one snowflake to follow," Kate surmised.

"Do you think each one has a different direction?"

Before Kate could answer, the blue lights from their lockets locked onto one small, tumbling blue flake far in the distance. Their light beams merged into one bright cobalt blue beam.

"I think we've found our way back to the camp," Kate said.

"I still can't see anything but the blue beam," Jen said. She looked in the direction that she heard Kate's voice but could not see her cousin.

"Me either." Kate squeezed Jen's hand. "Faith—I think we're being called to trust and have faith."

From between them, they felt 'Ov's feet leave the ground as he swung his tiny body between them.

"Yes 'Ov," Kate said. "You've done what you were sent to do. Now it is time we get you back to camp and Raguel."

'Ov took one last swing and let go at the height of the swing, landed on his haunches and ran into the blue beam.

"What are we waiting for?" Jen asked, watching the small, shadowed figured of 'Ov running before them.

"Let's go," Kate said. She did not let go of Jen's hand as they followed 'Ov toward the blue speck in the distance.

Nothingness surrounded them as the deep blue glassy surface of the beam from their lockets drew them along the lighted path. With each step they took, the glow of the flake grew bigger and brighter.

"Ov," Kate yelled. "Wait for us."

'Ov's tiny body was moving much faster over the shaft of light than Kate and Jen. What was once the void of color in the blackness they ran through, the small blue speck had grown until it now illuminated everything around them so bright that even their clothes glistened. Kate and Jen easily saw each other but did not slow down to enjoy the halo effects of the lighting.

From the center of the blue snowflake they ran toward the intensity blazed brighter with each step they took.

Boosh!

"Ov!" Jen yelled.

But he was gone—disappeared into the sudden flash of the blazing blue light.

Jen pulled on Kate's hand to stop their momentum but a force beyond the blazing blue light latched on to them and drew them inside. Their legs and feet no longer moved, but the force surrounding them continued their forward movement.

"Hold on to me," Jen yelled, and then realized her voice echoed in the quietness.

"I am," Kate almost whispered. "Where are we?"

"Don't know, but it is beautiful." Jen searched the cavern size passageway they were traveling through.

Kaleidoscopic effects of a noon sun dancing off millions of Marquise cut diamonds threw strobe lights radiating around them. Spring fresh, cool air brushed over their faces. Their lockets radiated streams of light and touched each surface. It was staggering to their senses, yet peaceful.

Boosh!

The force that had pulled them into the blue light, gently nudged them out onto the football field-size flat area on the outskirts of Nerkon's camp. It was where they had learned the art of becoming knights. Their lockets, once again, were quiet around their necks.

"There you are!" Raquel exclaimed. "So glad you are safe." 'Ov peeked out from behind him.

"Raguel," Kate said. "What happened?"

"You were kidnapped," Nerkon said. He and all Nerkon's knights were standing around Kate and Jen.

"Who…how?" Jen asked.

"We don't know," Nerkon answered, "but we are going to find out. We are glad you were not harmed."

"There were two of them," Kate blurted out. "Whoever they were, they were paid by someone in this camp to kill us."

"Are you sure it was someone from this camp?" Nerkon asked.

"That is what one of them said," Kate answered. "He said it was a traitor in Nerkon's camp. One of them seemed very afraid of the traitor, but the other one wanted to cut off …" she shuddered a moment. "…to cut off one of our fingers and send it back to the traitor."

"Why?" Rubidus was intensely interested in what happened to them and butted into the conversation.

"They said they were paid one silver coin and promised two more when they killed us. But one of them decided to hold out and get more silver. He felt we were worth more. The finger was to show they had us and could do whatever they wished. If the traitor in this camp didn't pay more they were going to sell us to a higher bidder somewhere outside the camp."

"Did you see them?" Rubidus inquired.

"No," Jen answered. "They put hoods over our heads. When 'Ov took off the hoods and set us free we were thinking of getting away, not slowing down to look at them."

"Unfortunate." Rubidus' show of concern came from anger inside him. He would find the two rogue warriors he hired and make them an example of what happens when he was crossed.

"Yes, Rubidus," Nerkon said, "it is very unfortunate, but we will find out who did this."

"And you are back in our camp." Rubidus forced a smile. "Now we can go on making you knights tomorrow."

"Yes," Nerkon agreed. "I will put guards around your tent tonight. Tomorrow we will go on with your knight ceremony and the Festival of

Games." He raised his hands toward his knights who stood around him. "Knights of Bigna! Tomorrow you will fight for the honor of the banner you serve under."

A roar of approval went up from the knights. Tomorrow, after Kate and Jen were dubbed knights, many of the existing knights would either challenge or be challenged by another army's knight in one of the many contests held. Each knight nodded his head thinking of the glory to be had in victory.

"I'll walk you back to your tent," Raguel said.

"Raguel?" Kate began.

"You have questions about tomorrow?"

"Yes, tomorrow and becoming knights holds many questions," Kate said. "But I have an even more curious question."

"That's why I'm here—to answer your questions."

"When 'Ov showed up and rescued us... Kate paused, her eyebrow raised in a question. "He said you sent him."

"Yes, I did."

"How did you know...?" Kate asked.

"How did I know where you were?" Raguel interrupted.

"Yes."

"The Eagle," was Raguel's explanation.

"Okay." Kate accepted the answer. "But why 'Ov and not you?"

"'Ov is very cleaver in getting in and out of places stealthily," Raguel smiled at his small friend who walked beside him.

"That he is," Kate agreed.

'Ov grinned with the compliments.

"About that," Jen said. "When we ran into the bush after 'Ov it was... was a black void."

"That was the Vanishing Bush," Raguel explained. "When you saw 'Ov disappear into the bush, what you saw was the surrounding bushes images—reflecting to give the appearance of one bush."

"But we went into the bush after him," Kate said.

"Sort of," Raguel smiled. "You followed him into the image."

"How could we follow him into an image?" Kate scoffed. Without waiting for an answer she said, "Of course we could—this is Bigna."

"Why couldn't the kidnappers see us or follow us?" Jen asked without giving Raguel time to answer the rapid questions coming from Jen and her. "Couldn't they have come into the bush after us?"

"'Ov closed the porthole behind you."

"Porthole?" Jen questioned.

"Let me explain from the beginning," Raguel said. "After you were kidnapped, the Eagle found you and set up the Vanishing Bush close to you so 'Ov could get to you quickly and safely. 'Ov left the porthole open when he went to you and untied you. Then, running ahead of you, he was ready to seal off the passageway as soon as you two came through it."

"And the kidnappers?" Jen pursued her question.

"They did indeed see the image of the Vanishing Bush, but the three of you were already hidden by the magic of the bush."

"So the bush is a cloaking...cloaking thingamajig." Jen had no idea what to call a bush that made them invisible.

"It does cloak whatever goes into it," Raguel said, "but it mostly acts as a portal for the passageway—the one that got you back to us."

"You mean the huge cavern filled with thousands, maybe millions, of falling crystal snowflakes?" Jen asked.

"Yes. Like your snowflakes in the Earth world, each of those flakes is different, in this case a different place—a different destination."

"When we first went into the bush...into the porthole, it was ink black. We couldn't see anything," Kate jumped into the conversation.

"The snowflakes are translucent and colorless. Until a light hits them they remain imperceptible."

"And that is why we could see them after our lockets lit up?" Jen asked.

"Yes," Raguel answered.

"Our lockets put out a blue light that seemed to search for one particular flake," Kate said. "And both lockets focused in on the same flake at the same time."

"Your lockets are very sensitive to direction and your journey while you are in Bigna," Raguel said. "They needed to get you to the other end of the...the cavern so you could come though the porthole at this end of the Diamond Passageway."

"Diamond Passageway?" Kate's head tilted and her face skewed up in a question.

"That is what the cavern…passageway you traveled through is called," Raguel explained.

"I will say this," Jen smiled. "Going through the Diamond Passageway from one place to another was much more pleasant than going through the Obex."

Raguel shrugged. "I'm afraid the Diamond Passageway only works on Bigna. To go from the Earth World and Bigna there is only one way."

"The Obex!" Kate gritted her teeth. "Not a pleasant thought."

"Then no more thinking of it tonight," Raguel said. "We are at your tent. I see Nerkon has already stationed guards around it for your safety."

"Completely around," Jen laughed. Standing hip-to-hip were guards surrounding their tent. If anyone tried to trespass and get inside their tent these guards would have to be torn apart by the virtual Velcro connecting them and killed first.

"And there is not much more time left for sleep," Kate said. "Dawn will be on us within a couple of hours. Good-night."

"Good-night, Raguel," Jen said. Her eyelids drooped in anticipation of much-needed sleep. "We'll see you in a short time."

"Good night," Raguel said. He waited until Kate and Jen went inside the tent. He thought for a moment to turn into his mouse persona and sit unnoticed inside the tent with them, but he decided to give them the privacy they wanted and needed.

"Come on, 'Ov," Raguel grasped 'Ov's small, elfin hand a little tighter. "They will not be harmed again tonight." He nodded toward the wall-to-wall guards around Kate and Jen's tent. "And we will not be far away."

They walked a couple of steps away from the tent's entrance, sat beneath an oak tree and closed their eyes. But sleep did not come to Raguel. His thoughts were of the traitor that tried to bring harm to his two charges—the two he was to safeguard. He knew, when he watched them walking along the side of the tarmac at the air show, they would be thrown into peril once they were back in Bigna. But he also knew he could not interfere too soon or they would not be able to carry out their mission in

Domare—the mission only they could finish. Opening his eyes he caught a glimpse of the Eagle's silhouette against the light of one of Bigna's moons.

"It is hard to stand by and watch them in the face of danger," he whispered upward.

The Eagle dipped one wing and disappeared into the night.

Chapter Sixteen

Crash!

Rubidus threw his lance across his tent, knocking over his other weapons that his aide had carefully lined up against the sawhorse made from yew tree branches. He was furious that the two Quae warriors he had sent out had not killed Kate and Jen. Abi had assured him they were the best covert soldiers in his army—and they failed. Now he had to watch the two Earth World beings become knights the next day.

"Abi!" Rubidus screamed.

The Bás Scorpion making its home in the mole behind his ear flared up. The feverous venom from the bug's anger scorched Rubidus' thinking.

"Abi!"

Furious, Rubidus' bellow could be heard throughout his camp. His controller burned deeper within him. He grabbed the spot on his neck and pushed hard. But the Bás spread its stinger and shot more toxic slime into Rubidus.

Aaargh!

Rubidus' pain turned into boiling rage. Why did the overseer think he would not take care of Kate and Jen? It was not his fault he was surrounded by incompetents.

It will be done!

Rubidus seethed that the creature inside him did not think he could handle the task at hand.

It will be done! I will do it myself!

He tugged at his gloved hand. The gloves he wore at all times covered his rapidly morphing body. Where his hands once had fingers, each hand now had five miniature pincers which soon would fuse together into a giant claw at the end of each arm. Underneath his knight's tunic he felt the scales of being half Quae and half scorpion—his life as an Elite Trooper was not far away.

"Abi!" Rubidus shrieked with burning anger.

"Yes, Sir Rubidus," Abi hurried inside the tent. His master was calling. With Kate and Jen still alive and back in camp, Abi knew Rubidus would take it out on him.

"Abi!" Rubidus gritted his teeth.

Abi stood still, waiting for Rubidus' wrath to fall upon him.

"They are still alive!"

Abi did not say anything.

"Your best was not the best!" Rubidus glared at his Senior Centurion. "Now I must take care of them myself."

Rubidus paced around Abi. Sulfur breath exhaled in invisible puffs from his nostrils, filling the tent with a stench of decaying eggs.

"How would you have me rid the camp of these foreigners?" He stopped behind Abi, put his clawed hands around Abi's throat and squeezed. "How, Abi, how?"

Aaargh!

Abi gasped for breath, but Rubidus' pinchers tightened their grip. The Bás within Abi's neck smoldered with furor but could not fight the power of the Bás that controlled Rubidus. Abi pulled at Rubidus' gloves but to no avail. He looked around the room for answers.

"I...I...know how..." Abi garbled out.

Rubidus pulled Abi close, until their faces were two inches apart. Rubidus' ruddy complexion and red cheeks flushed with an erupting volcanic crimson glow. He did not loosen his grip. Abi waited for the explosion sure to come from the small fiery dragon inside of his commander.

"You know how to what?" Rubidus' spit splattered over Abi's face.

"You...you can..." Abi tried to talk but Rubidus' pincher fingers around his throat cut off his words.

116

Rubidus' eyes glowed yellow and searched Abi's dark soul. Finding what he was looking for he threw Abi across the tent, releasing him from his death grip.

"You know how to what?" Rubidus repeated his question.

Cough! Cough! Cough!

Abi lay prone on the multicolored rug of Rubidus' tent. Gasping for air, he slowly worked his way to his knees and then stood.

"You can..." Abi sucked in a large gulp of air, "...you can defeat them tomorrow."

"And how would I do that with everyone focused on *them* tomorrow?" His Bás had temporarily quieted down. He knew with each violent outburst from the Bás there was a period of rest, but the next episode would be even fiercer—they always were.

Abi stumbled over to the lance Rubidus had furiously thrown against the rest of his weapons. "With this." He rubbed his fingers over the steel tip of the jousting lance.

"How will a jousting lance defeat them?"

"At the tournament tomorrow, you will challenge one of them to a match..."

"Only knights fight in a jousting match," Rubidus scoffed.

"True," Abi deliberately let his eyes drop to the ground. "So true, but tomorrow afternoon's games are because Nerkon is making the two intruders knights tomorrow morning."

"So," Rubidus sneered. "So, by the time the tournament begins, they will be knights."

Abi let his idea take roots.

"And once they are knights and serving under Nerkon, they can be challenged to a match." Rubidus rubbed his neck. The Bás was quiet. "Brilliant. I will challenge...which one shall I challenge, Abi?"

"I have been watching them. Both of them have learned quickly, but one of them seems more...more nimble than the other—the one they call Jen. I think the one they call Kate is a better match for you."

"Of course," Rubidus already liked the idea that he would be the one to kill the intruder. It would not be hard for him—after all wasn't he the best jousting knight in the camp? He had proven that many times over. And deathly accidents happened all the time in jousting matches.

"And to be sure," Abi offered, "after the first pass, I will exchange the lance tipped with the protective coronal with a lance tipped with the point of war steel-head."

"Why pretend?" Rubidus rhetorically asked aloud. "I will challenge, therefore I will also proclaim the rules."

Abi was silent. He wasn't sure where Rubidus was going with his thoughts.

"And I will write the challenge rules for the weapons to be those of arms and armor of battle—swords, lances and battle axes."

"With your skills you will be challenging her to death," Abi smiled.

"One thing," Rubidus pondered. "The match will only get rid of one of them. What about the other?"

"That is what is so great about this." Abi was gaining his confidence back. Rubidus was pleased at his plan and now he would focus on defeating Kate and Jen at the games tomorrow, not the failed attempt on their lives. "I've also observed that they work as a team. Once you take one of them out, the other should fall without any problems."

"I will crush them," Rubidus boasted. "And Nerkon will fall into my hands."

"You will be victorious," Abi said, his confidence now fully restored.

"One more thing, Abi," Rubidus mentally rubbed his hands together— at least the hands he remembered having before the Bás scorpion had changed his body.

"Anything," Abi bowed.

"You must be my attending Squire. We cannot let any minor mistake by an underling squire defeat us."

"Of course," Abi rapidly agreed. "I will be the one to prepare your weapons—your horse—your battle."

"Go, Abi," Rubidus laughed perversely. "Go prepare for tomorrow. Tomorrow is going to be a big day for me."

Abi bowed again. He grabbed the lance on his way out. There was much to do before the tournament. He had to have two lances that looked exactly alike—one harmless and one deadly. He had to make it look as if Rubidus did not intend to harm Kate.

Rubidus was pleased. This was better than the two Earth World beings just disappearing. After he won the match, everyone in the camp would know he was the leader—their leader. By tomorrow night he would lead Nerkon, and everyone who followed him, into the Senvolte River. He turned his gloved hands upward.

These will serve me one more day—One more day before I will become an Elite Trooper in Rapio's army.

He had accepted his fate, but he would defeat Nerkon before his body surrendered its service into Rapio's army.

Chapter Seventeen

*T*he brightness of the sun greeted Jen's eyes when she pulled back the cloth door of their tent. "Wow, Kate! Look at all the colors." Jen waved her hand around the campground. Overnight the campground had been turned into a festive faire ground.

"It is a time for everyone to honor their unit—their leaders," Raguel said. He quickly came up beside them as soon as he became aware they were awake and out of their tent.

"So many flags…so many colors," Jen said. She spun around taking in the brightly painted picture around her. Every tent displayed three pennants and a banner on a rod above the entrance.

"What do all the flags stand for?" Kate asked.

"The smallest pennant at the bottom of the pole on each tent is for that tent party. The next one up is for the Century and the third is their Cohort. Above all three is the banner for the Division to which they belong."

"This is really something." Kate's emerald eyes sparkled with excitement.

"Yes, it is," Raguel answered her non question. "Every one of the Pilgers who flies the pennants and banners is proud and wants to do honor for his unit."

"Honor his unit?" Jen asked.

"The Quae have not lost their love for big pageant and games. Nerkon has planned a pageant with mock war games so the Pilgers will not lose their battle skills while they are waiting to attack Helig. The jostling tournament is the highlight of the pageant that will pit the skills of knights from each unit against knights of other units."

"And today they put the pennants and banners out because of the tournament games?" Kate asked.

"Yes, but remember, the tournament games are being held today for you." Raguel rubbed his eyes to clear away the lack of sleep. Though 'Ov slept silently beside him all night, Raguel's mind had raced at what might have happened to Kate and Jen—and the future of Bigna.

"For us?" Jen searched for a clue that the campground was steaming with activity because of them.

"Today you will become knights," Raguel smiled. "Over there is where you will begin your journey into knighthood. It is the Knighting Castle." He pointed toward a circus-like tent that had sprung up overnight in the center of the camp. Its red and white striped paneled sides and conical roof made it stand out from everything else in the camp.

"Castle?" Kate questioned.

"It is a field castle—it has to do for a brick castle when knighthood is bestowed on the battlefield of a war."

"Whose banners are those?" Jen asked. Rising from the center of the field castle tent were poles with a variety of banners unlike the pennants and banners on the other tents.

"Those are for the knights who are in camp," Raguel explained. "See the ones with the Maups on them?"

"Yes," Jen cocked her head to take in all the banners. "I see one... two...three...four..."

"Those are the standards of knights in the Bigna Air Power," Raguel said. "Once we go inside the tent you will see the shields of all the knights hanging on the walls. Each has the heraldry of an individual knight."

"Heraldry?" Jen asked.

"It is the symbol that identifies the knight belonging in a certain family. In your world you probably call them a coat of arms."

"Will we have a coat of arms...a heraldry?" Jen asked.

"You will—you have," Raguel explained. "Your shields have already been designed and forged."

"Really?" Jen was excited. "Whose family…heraldry do our shields represent?"

"Soon enough you will find out," Raguel smiled. "During the presentation of your sword and shield, each knight will take his shield and join you, symbolizing they will be beside you in battle."

Kate took a deep breath. "This is really an honor."

"What you are about to go though is a big honor," Raguel said. "Most of the knights spend all of their youth in preparation to go through the knighthood ceremony."

"We have a lot to live up to if we are to do what is expected of a knight of Bigna," Jen stated.

"You will be everything a Bigna knight should be," Raguel declared.

"Will the knights resent us for jumping over some of the younger Quae who are still preparing for knighthood?" Kate was truly concerned.

"No, no, no," Raguel held up his hands to show the wrongness of Kate's question. "All of the warriors and knights have heard stories of you and your daring exploits when you came to Bigna before. They are honored the Eagle has brought you back to help them. You will find they respect you. Last night they were vying as to which one of them would be your sponsors."

"Our sponsors?" Jen asked.

"A sponsor is the knight who will hold your sword, spurs and shield—the one who will stand beside you during your knighthood ceremony. After you become knights, you will need guidance on the proper way to act and what is expected of a knight."

"You are our Consilliarius…our Counselor while we are in Bigna," Jen said. "You have always been our guide. It seems natural you would stand beside us."

"Thank you," Raguel smiled, "I will be close by, but I cannot be your sponsor for knighthood."

"Why?" Jen asked.

"Because I am not a knight. Your sponsor must be a Royal Knight of Bigna."

"And did anyone win…I mean…" Kate wasn't sure how to ask who their sponsors were, but winning didn't seem like the right word.

"We did," laughed Taka. He seemed to appear from nowhere. "And we were not going to let any other knights *win,*" he emphasized her word win in a dramatic nod, and then continued, "the honor of standing beside you."

"That's right," Lieg said, walking up beside Taka. "There never was any other choice as far as we were concerned."

"I will be next to you, Kate, and Lieg will be next to Jen," Taka said. "It is as it should be."

"That is wonderful," Jen blurted out, even though she did not really know what was expected of Taka and Lieg as their sponsors. But she did know she was glad they would be close by in this very important ceremony.

"What do we have to do?" Kate's pragmatic mind was twirling.

"Leave everything to us," Taka said. "We'll guide you through it all."

"Thank you." Kate was relieved that Taka would take care of the details.

"Let's find Nerkon," Raguel said. Churching inside him was concern about the traitor in the camp. Hopefully, he could find out who it was before Kate and Jen were put into any more unnecessary danger.

"Are you ready?" Taka asked.

"More than," Kate answered.

Jen gave a nod and thumbs up.

Kate, Taka, Jen and Lieg stood outside the entrance of the Knighting Castle. Kate and Jen, dressed in white vestures, black knee-high boots, black tight-fitting trousers, and draped with red robes, waited to be ushered into the ceremony.

Taka had explained the symbolism behind their ceremony dress. White was for purity, sacrifice and virtue. Red was for life and strength. Black was for the emptiness and evil that they would face. All Quae Knights before them had donned the same clothes for their knighting ceremony.

The noise level from the crowd encircling them was that of a low rumbling, oncoming thunderstorm. The Pilgers were excited that they were going to see the knighting of the two Earth World beings they had heard so much about all of their lives. They were also excited that the day would be filled with good food, joyous laughter, games among the Pilgers and a jostling tournament for the knights.

Chink! Chink! Chink!

Chink! Chink! Chink

The sounds of metal swords hitting against each other rang out from inside the tent.

"That's our signal," Lieg spoke in a loud voice. "The knights have put their swords together in agreement to be as one in knighting you." He nodded to the guard at the entrance.

The guard pulled back the wool door and bowed his head. Kate and Jen were about to become knights, a position that would mean he would follow them into battle when the time came.

Inside the tent Kate and Jen were taken aback at the scene. Knights knelt on one knee; they leaned on their swords drawn in front of them. One hand on the pommel and one grasping the hilt of the sword, they waited to give their blessing to the two new members of their elite group. The kneeling knights' surcoats, emblazoned with the knights' coat of arms, brightened the tent with a grand array of colors.

Shields hanging on the wool tent walls displayed unique heraldic designs that matched the coats of arms on the surcoats of the kneeling knights. Before the ceremony was over, each knight would gather up his shield and pledge their loyalty to the new knights, Kate and Jen.

From the corner of Kate's eye she noticed a shield hug upside-down. She nudged Jen and with her eyes asked the question 'why?'

Jen shrugged her shoulders.

Seeing the question on Kate and Jen's faces, Taka whispered, "Because the knight who owned that shield dishonored his knighthood."

"Dishonored?" Kate mouthed.

"He was caught conspiring with the enemy—an Indringer from Helig."

"A traitor?" Jen asked.

"Yes. The upside-down shield is the symbol of the knight fallen from honor—fallen from the grace given him."

Across the tent Raguel smiled at Kate and Jen. Their counselor would be close to them. They knew at that moment everything would be all right.

"Come forward Katherine and Jennifer," Nerkon's authoritative voice instructed.

Taka and Lieg stepped behind Kate and Jen and urged them forward.

Petri Meudy stood beside Nerkon, his head bowed and eyes shut. He muttered so low that Kate and Jen could not understand what he was saying.

"Kneel," Nerkon said, "to take your vows."

Following his command, Kate and Jen knelt on white wool pillows that were in front of Nerkon. Taka and Lieg stood behind them, one hand on their right shoulders. Kate finally understood enough of Petri's words to know he was blessing their knighthood ritual.

"Katherine…Jennifer," Nerkon began. "You are about to take the vows of the Royal Knights of Bigna. It is to be taken with upmost thought and consideration. Have you done this?"

Kate did not move her head but glance over at Jen. Their eyes met and they both nodded yes.

"Say it aloud," Taka leaned over and gave them instructions. "Everyone must hear your answers."

"Yes," they blurted out loudly.

Nerkon looked up to Taka. "Sir Taka, are you prepared to sponsor Katherine for knighthood?"

"I am, Sir Nerkon," Taka said.

"Sir Lieg, are you prepared to sponsor Jennifer for knighthood?"

"I am, Sir Nerkon," Lieg answered. He gave Jen's shoulder a slight squeeze.

Jen leaned her head slightly into Lieg's hand. She was comforted that he was close by.

"Katherine…Jennifer. The Code of Loyalty of Bigna is taken by all Bigna Knights—to protect the honor of Bigna—to serve humbly and justly—to refrain from giving aid to the enemy—to live with honor and for the glory of Bigna—to guard the honor of fellow knights—to turn your back on deceit and evil—to speak the truth at all times—to show resolution in all you do—to give hope to every other knight whose path you cross—to serve with valor. Will you follow the Code of Loyalty of Bigna?"

"I will," Kate responded.

"I will," Jen nodded.

"Royal Knights of Bigna," Nerkon addressed the kneeling knights. "Are you ready to accept Katherine and Jennifer into the Royal Knights of Bigna?"

"We are, Sir Nerkon!" the knights spoke loudly as one.

"Will you stand in one accord with Katherine and Jennifer?" Nerkon asked the knights.

"We will, Sir Nerkon!"

"Then gather your shields," Nerkon instructed the knights.

The knights quickly took their shields from the walls and assumed their kneeling positions, but this time one hand held their shield close to their chest and their other hand griped the hilt of their sword.

The guards, who had been waiting for the signal, rolled up the eight sides so the tent was now an open air pavilion. Now the crowd outside could see the ceremony taking place inside. They would be able to see the actual knighting of Kate and Jen.

Hurrah! Hurrah! Hurrah!

Hurrah! Hurrah! Hurrah!

The roar of the crowd as the sides went up filtered into Kate and Jen. The private part of knighthood was over. Everyone would now witness the two Earth World beings become part of them.

"Warriors of Bigna," Nerkon addressed the masses outside the tent. "Katherine and Jennifer have vowed to uphold the honor and loyalty with complete gallantry expected of a Bigna Knight. Their valor in times past has been told to each of us, and now they have been brought here by the Eagle to carry out his mission."

Hurrah! Hurrah! Hurrah!

Hurrah! Hurrah! Hurrah!

The shouts of approval and joy waved through the Pilgers. This was what the day was about—this is what they came to see.

Hurrah! Hurrah! Hurrah!

Hurrah! Hurrah! Hurrah!

Nerkon held up his right hand. The Pilgers quieted.

Kate sucked in a large breath. She stole a quick look at Jen. Jen stared straight ahead, biting her bottom lip in anticipation of the next unknown experience.

"Sir Taka," Nerkon said. "Sir Lieg."

Kate realized that Taka no longer had his hand on her shoulder. She wanted to look around to find him but froze in the moment.

"Bring forth the blessed shields and swords," Nerkon continued his instructions for Taka and Lieg.

Swuf! Swuf! Swuf!

Swuf! Swuf! Swuf!

The soft shuffle of Taka and Lieg's footsteps on the carpeted floor broke the silence.

Clink!

Clink!

Two silver swords glistened as they were laid upon an altar in front of Kate and Jen.

Clink!

Clink!

Taka and Lieg laid two silver shields atop the swords.

Swuf! Swuf! Swuf!

Swuf! Swuf! Swuf!

Taka and Lieg took their positions behind Kate and Jen.

"Katherine…Jennifer," Nerkon's voice wafted though the pavilion and out into the crowd. "Your shield, which you will hold over your heart, gives you protection from the evil and falsehoods you will face." He lifted both shields at the same time, giving Kate and Jen their first look at their coat of arms.

"The Eagle", Jen whispered to Kate. "Our heraldry is that of the Eagle." Jen smiled.

The silver shields caught the morning light and threw rays of brightness in every direction. The coat of arms in the middle of the gleaming shield was a navy blue triangle. Inside the triangle was the profile of an eagle's head with a thunderbolt under it. The words *on the back of an Eagle* were printed underneath the triangle. Both cousins' heaved a sigh of joy.

Taka and Lieg reached around Kate and Jen and raised their left arms. Nerkon brought the shields forward and slipped the grips over their arms and pushed the shield close to their chests.

"Always hold your shield close. It will quench the flaming arrows sent to destroy you."

Taka and Lieg again reached around Kate and Jen, this time raising their right hands. Nerkon brought the swords forward and placed one in each of their hands.

"Your sword shows your courage—your strength to stop the oppressor."

"Katherine…Jennifer," Nerkon said. "Do you accept your shield and sword of a Bigna knight?"

"I do," answered Kate.

"I do," answered Jen.

Swoosh!

Nerkon drew his own sword from its scabbard. He laid the sword blade on Kate's right shoulder and then her left shoulder. "I dub you Sir Katherine."

Kate exhaled the deep breath she held.

Nerkon took one step to his left. He laid his sword blade on Jen's right shoulder and then on her left one. "I dub you Sir Jennifer."

"Amen." Petri stopped his muttering. Their blessing was completed.

Jen glanced at Kate and grinned.

"Rise Sir Katherine! Rise Sir Jennifer!" He looked toward the Pilgers crowded around the pavilion. "Let the celebration begin in honor of our two newest knights."

Hurrah! Hurrah! Hurrah!

Hurrah! Hurrah! Hurrah!

The Pilgers were ready. Now the food, merriment and jostling tournament would begin.

Petri was the first to bow his head to Kate and Jen. "Serve with honor and faith." Simple instructions from the monk.

"We will," Jen said.

"Thank you for your blessing," Kate added.

Petri nodded and exited the pavilion.

"Come," Nerkon said. "It is time for you to enjoy your day."

Chapter Eighteen

*J*en gave Kate a big smile. "You really look very spiffy, Sir Katherine."
"As do you, Sir Jennifer," Kate grinned.

They walked among the cheerful Pilgers who stopped the two new knights to offer congratulations and blessings.

"Your…our coat of arms looks great on your surcoat." Kate spread Jen's silky surcoat out so she could see the total crest. "Yes, the same as we have on our Stearman."

"How did they know?" Jen twisted her head trying to see the triangle with the profile of an eagle's head with a thunderbolt under it.

"I hope you are pleased with your coat of arms." Raguel appeared from the middle of a group of well-wishing Pilgers. 'Ov's small head poked around from behind Raguel. He had a way of appearing and disappearing in a moment's notice.

"Raguel… 'Ov." Jen's smile spread across her face. "We couldn't be more pleased."

"Of course," Kate nodded with a new understanding. "You designed our crest—that is how it looks just like our logo on our Stearman."

Raguel gave them a crooked grin. "It seemed like the only one that you should wear. You are Royal Knights of Bigna and will serve with the Bigna Air Power, but you also will always have one foot in your Earth World—the world where you walk in the sky."

"You are wonderful," Jen exclaimed. She twirled in a circle, her surcoat flying out behind her. "Licet volare si in tergo aquilae volat."

"Indeed," Kate said. "We fly on the back of the Eagle."

'Ov slipped from behind Raguel and put his small hand into Kate's grip and squeezed tightly.

"And if it weren't for you 'Ov we would not be here to celebrate this day." Kate's praise brought a broad smile to 'Ov's elfin face.

"So true," Jen added. She gloved her hand around 'Ov's free hand. "You rescued us from those wicked kidnappers."

'Ov looked up into their faces and grinned. Picking his feet from the ground he swung freely between them, his elf-like body gaining a little more height each with each arcing movement.

"Yes 'Ov," Jen said. "This is going to be a wonderful day." She laughed at the childlike joy 'Ov displayed in a simple thing like swinging between her and Kate.

"Sir Katherine...Sir Jennifer!" Petri Meudy ran toward them. "I have unsettling news for you." His face flushed from running.

'Ov stop swinging, but held Kate and Jen's hands tightly. His mouse-like ears pricked forward, listening intently. One ear tipped back in anticipation of Petri's unwanted pronouncement.

"Slow down, Petri," Raguel said. "What has you so upset?"

"Sir Rubidus...the Red Knight," Petri spat out. "He...he..." Petri inhaled to catch his breath.

"He what?" Raguel didn't like the sound of Petri's tone.

"Sir Rubidus has challenged..." Petri again took a deep breath. "He has challenged Sir Katherine to a Joust. He struck his sword on Kate's shield at the Tree of Shields."

"No, no, no." Raguel shook his head in disagreement. He and Nerkon had hung Kate's and Jen's newly acquired shields on the Tree of Shields as a gesture, but they never believed either of the two new knights would be challenged in today's games. Raguel gritted his teeth. "No, he can't do that. He can't challenge her to a joust."

"I'm afraid he can," Nerkon sighed, joining the group. "It is in his right as a knight."

"Tree of Shields? A joust?" Kate asked. "What does that mean?"

"The Tree of Shields is where all knights hang their shield so that any other knight who wishes to challenge him in a jostling match in today's tournament may strike the shield with his sword. The knight whose shield is stuck must accept the challenge of the joust or be disgraced."

"And he has challenged me to a jostling match?" Kate queried.

"Yes," Nerkon stated.

"Why?" Kate was truly puzzled. She and Jen had just become knights. Surely no one believed either of them would deliver much of a match.

"Do you remember what I told you about the jostling tournament?" Raguel asked Kate.

"I think so," Kate cocked her head, searching for his words. "You said the jostling tournament is the highlight of today's celebration. That the jostling matches pit the skills of knights from one unit against knights of other units."

"That is correct," Raguel affirmed.

"But she just became a knight," Jen said. "She has never been in a jostling match before. We've barely practiced with a lance."

"I know," Raguel said. "We did not believe anyone would challenge either of you today...not the first day you became knights." He was sure that Rubidus had taken into account that they were new knights. He wanted to test Kate in the rigors of a jostling contest.

"But you are knights," Nerkon said. "And as a knight, any other knight can challenge you to a match."

"So I have to accept?" Kate asked.

"Pretty much so," Nerkon said. "Rubidus has already given the proclamation that he has sent the challenge to you. And because it is Rubidus that will be fighting you, it will be the main match."

"Main match?" Kate was puzzled.

"There will be other matches between other knights before you, but your match with Rubidus will bring out everyone."

"And he is good at jostling?" Kate's face skewed lopsided in anticipation of the answer.

"The best," Petri said.

"One of the best." Nerkon gave Petri a silencing glance.

"A lot is riding on it," Raguel said. He did not want to dwell on the fact that Rubidus' skill in the games was legendary. Only Nerkon had ever gotten the best of him.

"There is?" Kate's face still showed signs of a question mark. "Like what?"

"Usually the challenge is to defend the honor of one's division—the banner the knight flies in battle," Raguel said. "But I suspect there is more going on with Rubidus."

"What else could Rubidus challenge me for?" Kate asked. "I don't have any possessions worth fighting for."

"Rubidus could challenge you for the command of all the Pilger armies—for Nerkon's position as leader of The Mission to capture Helig."

"It is what Rubidus has wanted since The Mission began four years ago," Nerkon said. "It was always his terms when he and I fought in the games."

"Why didn't he challenge you then?" Kate asked.

"Rubidus cannot win in a match against Sir Nerkon," Raguel said. "And because Rubidus named the rules in the last match, which he lost, Sir Nerkon is commander over him."

"And I will no longer hang my shield on the Tree," Nerkon said. He did not elaborate.

"But it is your command, not mine," Kate said. "How can I joust to protect something that belongs to you?"

Before Nerkon could answer Petri spoke up. "Sir Nerkon," Petri said. "I was just handed this by one of Rubidus' warriors." He handed Nerkon a strip of parchment paper. "He has posted another one at the Tree of Shields."

"Hmmm," Nerkon said.

Everyone waited for Nerkon to divulge the contents of the note.

"It is from Rubidus," Nerkon said. "He is stating the rules for the challenge match between him and Kate." He handed the paper to Kate. "It is as I expected."

Quickly reading the rules, Kate shrugged her shoulders and handed the paper to Jen.

"What does it mean?" Jen asked.

"Let me see," Raguel said. He hastily read the note aloud.

Joust Rules
Knights
Sir Rubidus Sir Katherine

On the Field of Tournament
Weapons
Arms and armor of battle
Swords Lances Battle-axes
For the Command of The Mission Armies

"You are right, Sir Nerkon," Raguel said. "It is just as we suspected. His challenge is not for sport. His challenge is a very real simulation of the battlefield. He will use his sharpen sword and lance. If necessary, he will be allowed to use his battle axe."

"No," Jen said. "Kate can't agree to this."

"She is a Bigna Knight," Nerkon said. "Rubidus has challenged her bravery—her valor."

"But he is asking for your command," Kate inhaled deeply, putting the weapons to be used out of her mind. "How can my loss give him your command?" She still did not understand the rules of the joust.

"Because you are being sent in my place," Nerkon explained. "You are acting as my surrogate."

"Let me take her place," Jen quickly offered. "Let me be her surrogate."

Kate looked at Jen. Both knew Jen was the athletic one—much more competitive than Kate. Kate shook her head *no*.

"No," Raguel confirmed Kate's gesture. "Rubidus has challenged Kate." Raguel knew Rubidus had calculated which cousin was more vulnerable.

"I'll be all right." Kate forced a smile, and then added, "As long as you are close by me."

"Always!" Jen touched Kate's arm. "Always!"

"We only have a couple of hours to prepare," Nerkon said. "I will train you in everything I know about Rubidus' jostling skills." He knew he had underestimated the extent of Rubidus' desire for power and now Kate would have to go to battle for his error of judgment.

Jen tightened her grip on Kate's arm.

Kate saw the concern in Jen's eyes. "I'll be okay," Kate said to put Jen's mind at ease.

Jen gave Kate a half smile but she was not reassured. This was not a good situation.

Chapter Nineteen

Kate, Jen, Raguel and 'Ov walked toward Nerkon's tent. Inside Nerkon would lay out a plan for Kate on how she could defeat Rubidus.

"Why won't Nerkon hang his shield on the Tree of Shields?" Kate asked.

"Because in the last jousting match with Rubidus Nerkon won," Raguel answered Kate's question. "In fact, he has beat Rubidus every time he has been challenged by him."

"Then it would seem Nerkon would want to take part in the tournament," Jen forced a smiled.

"Nerkon has beaten everyone he has ever come up against," Raguel said. "But Nerkon's decision to not participate in the jostling tournaments against Rubidus any more began many years ago."

"How is that?" Jen asked.

"When they were both seven they were sent to become Pages at the Castle of Baron Slott. It is at the baron's castle they began their futures as knights. There they began their education in the use of horses, weapons and the discipline for battle. At that time they were also instructed in lessons of courtesy, honor and chivalry.

"As chance would have it, Nerkon and Rubidus were assigned to room together. Throughout those first seven years they became best friends. They were trained by the baron throughout their serving as Pages. Nerkon was a quick learner and he quickly became a favorite at the castle. Rubidus always fell short of the praise heaped upon Nerkon.

"At fourteen Nerkon and Rubidus were promoted to the next step to become knights—they became Squires in the baron's castle. Each was assigned a knight to serve under. As squires they served their knight's meals, cared for his horse and made sure the knight's armor and weapons were always spotless and prepared for battle. It was the knight's duty to teach the squire to handle a sword and lance while wearing the full weight of armor.

"Nerkon's skills and talent were much desired by all the knights so Sir Aristo, the best knight in Baron Slott's army, quickly snatched Nerkon up to be his squire. Rubidus went to a lesser knight."

"So they did not room together anymore?" Jen asked.

"They continued to be roommates for the next five years."

"That's a long time to learn together," Kate said. "Seven years as Pages and then five as Squires."

"It was a long time," Raguel said. "But normally, a knight-in-training is a Squire for seven years. During this time they put their skills to the test."

"Skills? Test?" Jen asked.

"Actually, there were many tests of their skills—not the least of which was the practice in the use of weapons and horsemanship by jousting."

"And Nerkon won?"

"Always—against everyone—whether it was in games to utilize their battle skills or at social events, Nerkon always came out on top," Raguel said. "All the other Squires accepted Nerkon's talent, but Rubidus sulked after each event—whether on the dance floor or at a jostling tournament. But those who were watching the closest saw in Rubidus' eyes an underlying malevolence building inside him. When Nerkon was rewarded knighthood two years early at nineteen for his bravely on the battlefield, we knew it was a matter of time before Rubidus' spitefulness boiled over."

"And Nerkon never saw Rubidus' bitterness?" Kate asked.

"Rubidus was his childhood friend. He didn't want to see anything except the good in Rubidus. Even at the beginning of The Mission it appeared they were still friends, comrades-in-arms. Rubidus was always ambitious and ruthless. When Friar Fara publically blessed Nerkon and Obile with the Holy Sword at the Battle of Stur as the leaders of The Mission, Rubidus changed outwardly. His dark side surfaced and his overwhelming desire for power took over. When the battle for Stur was won, and before the Bás Plague began, Rubidus challenged Nerkon in a jostling match for the command of The Mission armies. When Rubidus lost, he was seen sulking around the city enlisting all the unsavory knights of the streets into his army."

"Knights of the streets?" Jen asked.

"Not real knights such as yourself or those that attended your knighthood ceremony," Raguel explained. "It is a name given to the thieves, murders and dishonorable ex-soldiers who wander the streets with wickedness in their hearts."

"They sound terrible…and dangerous," Jen said.

"They are," Raguel stated. "So it did not come as a surprise, though a big disappointment, when he stole the Holy Sword from Friar Fara's death bed. Even then, Nerkon did not want to believe that his oldest friend would turn on him."

"Mysta said that the reason Nerkon and Obile took their faithful out of Stur and followed Rubidus was in hopes of leaving the Bás Plague. Was Nerkon's underlying reason because Rubidus took the Holy Sword?" Kate asked.

"Yes," Raguel shifted uneasily as he spoke. "The Holy Sword was Nerkon's to protect and to return to the Cephas Monastery. Nerkon feels his mission is to not only take back Helig, but he must also find the Holy Sword and get it back to the Monastery."

"And I will do it," Nerkon joined their walk. "But for now I must teach Kate about jousting Rubidus. He does have a couple of weaknesses that might help her defeat him."

"Look at the jousting field!" Jen exclaimed.

Kate took a deep breath. "I think I would enjoy the beauty of it a little more if I wasn't going to be part of the entertainment."

Round pavilions, made up of open sided tents with bright multicolored roofs, encircled the field. The covered shelters protected the combatants and their attendants. Beside the larger pavilions were smaller tents, just as colorful. Inside the smaller tents were the knights' favorite jousting horses, cared for by their grooms. It was up to each groom to prepare the horse for the joust by saddling it, lying on a shielding body covering cloth—a caparison—and putting an iron shield on its head. The head shield—a chanfron—would protect the horse from what could be a fatal lance hit. During the joust the groom would be close to the knight's attending squire, for his duty to take care of the horse was just as important as the squire's. If the horse faltered or fell, the knight would lose the contest.

"Raguel," Nerkon said. "Since you are acting as Kate's attending Squire, take her lances over to the judge to be measured."

Raguel gathered up Kate's three lances and walked toward the judge.

"Measured?" Kate asked.

"The judge will measure both your lances and Rubidus' lances to be sure neither of you has an advantage by having a longer lance than the other."

"Oh," Kate said. This was real and the rules were to be followed down to the lance size.

"I'm right with you," Jen said, noting the concern in Kate's eyes.

"I know you are," Kate smiled.

Jen could not shake the sick feeling building in the pit of her stomach. Rubidus had chosen to make this a real replication of battle by using sharp swords and lances. He planned on fighting this joust to the death.

> *O where does Sir Katherine lay her head?*
> *Does Sir Rubidus soon make her bed?*

Kate quickly turned to face a wandering minstrel. His look was that of a clown since he was dressed in a bright, multicolored peasant-like tunic over tight pants—one leg red the other yellow. A purple beret sat askew on his head. He strummed his lute as he sang of Kate's upcoming joust with Rubidus. His words jarred Kate. His sing-song question was of Rubidus putting her to death.

The minstrel continued to warble out his ballet of Sir Katherine and Sir Rubidus.

> *I have seen heaven, angels overflowing;*
> *Where the Eagle flies with mighty wings.*
> *I have seen caverns of darkness, Bás crawling;*
> *Where Rapio sits upon a powerful throne.*
> *Do you hear harps, stretched with strings of joy, sing from the sky?*
> *Or lyres, stretched with strings of rage, scream from beneath the ground?*
> *O where do you go Sir Katherine now?*
> *To bed by Rubidus' quick sword;*
> *Or to Helig's gate in conquering victory!*

The singing story teller bowed to Kate and continued his wandering through the camp. His tuneless song echoed eerily around him.

"Don't pay attention to him," Nerkon said. "He is here to amuse—a jester. Soon he will move on from singing non-sensible songs and amuse the crowd with his juggling and acrobatics."

"I know," Kate said. But like a ping-pong ball hit off a wall, the minstrel's chant ricocheted around in her head.

"Sir Nerkon is right," Jen stated, "You need to keep your thoughts on the match." Turning Kate's head and focus away from the minstrel, Jen stared Kate in her eyes. "You must concentrate on what Sir Nerkon has taught you for the last couple of hours."

"Okay," Kate cleared the minstrel from her head and concentrated on Jen. "Jousting takes speed, accuracy and timing." She recapped the lesson given to her by Nerkon.

"Right!" Nerkon said. "But beyond that you must remember what I taught you about his weaknesses."

"His biggest weakness is his arrogance," Kate repeated what Nerkon had told her.

"And you must use that against him," Nerkon said. "He already feels he has won the joust, so his overconfidence will be what you strike with to topple him."

"Well, he does have more experience than I do," Kate winced.

"Put that out of your head," Jen said. "You also have Sir Nerkon's other advice."

"His arrogance will make him feel invincible," Nerkon said, "so he won't be expecting you to do anything other than what a novice knight would do."

"To focus on and aim at his shield," Kate said.

"That is what he will think you will do," Nerkon reiterated his earlier line of reasoning.

"And you said to keep my lance pointed toward his shield but at the last moment, raise it and aim for his helm," Kate said.

"That is right," Nerkon said. "He will not expect you to know, or be able, to raise your lance and hit him in his head. You will take him by surprise and topple him from his horse. When that happens you have three choices—either trample him with your horse or jump off your horse and be prepared to finish the joust with your sword."

"I could not trample him," Kate stated.

"Then be prepared to fight him with your sword," Nerkon said.

"You said there were three choices," Kate observed.

"You can let him live," Nerkon frowned. "But keep in mind; he will not hesitate to trample you or run you through with his sword if the situation is reversed."

"I'll try not to let that happen," Kate said, but inside she was not sure she could kill someone in what was supposed to be a game.

"Good," Nerkon nodded in agreement. Mentally he believed Kate was ready for the joust, but she would need lots of prayers to overcome Rubidus' experience and trickery.

"Time to get you ready," Raguel said coming along side of Kate. He leaned the three wooden lances that the judge had approved against an oak tree, next to the one handed sword and a small dagger, called a rondel, that Kate would wear for the joust. A squire under Nerkon's care stood as their sentry. Raguel picked up Kate's jousting shield, a smaller version of her battle shield.

Jen followed Kate and Raguel into the pavilion that flew two banners above it—Nerkon's and the one of the Bigna Air Power. Once they stepped under the sloped top, guards quickly pulled cords holding up the rolled up sides.

Fa-thump!

Fa-thump!

Fa-thump!

Fa-thump!

Fa-thump!

Fa-thump!

The six panels fell into place enclosing the pavilion. It was time for Kate to suit up for her match with Rubidus.

"I wish I could take your place," Jen said.

"I know, cousin, but you will be close by—you will be with me in spirit," Kate said. She reached for the gambeson hanging on a makeshift mannequin. "Help me with this."

Kate obliged by holding the padded linen jacket. Kate slipped her tunic covered arms into the protective jacket that she would wear under her plate armor. Its quilted stitching held the horsehair stuffing in place.

"Itchy," Kate said squirming around.

"Be still and try not to think about it." Jen fastened the three front buttons. "It will cushion any blows to your body and will prevent the armor from chaffing you."

"Still itchy," Kate smiled, trying to deflect both of their thoughts from the upcoming joust.

"I'm sure the weight of this will make you forget the itchiness of your gambeson," Raguel said. He pointed toward a second mannequin that held a full set of jousting armor that the blacksmith had tailored just for her. Orange-red flames from six torches, tucked into top corners of the hexagon-shaped tent, reflected eerily off the spotless, shining silver metal.

Kate was gripped by the reality of the armor.

"It is your full armor against Rubidus and his vile plans," Jen said, knowing Kate's thought.

Kate nodded—her attention back at Raguel and Jen.

"Sit down and we'll start with your greaves." Raguel handed her two plate armor pieces for her legs from the knee to the ankle.

"No Velcro," Kate smiled as she snapped one of the pieces around her right leg and forced the hooks into place. "Snug." She repeated the procedure on her left leg.

"Next your sabontons," Raguel said.

"Let me," Jen said. She slipped the metal armor foot coverings on each of Kate's feet and snapped them into place. "There you go, Cinderella."

"I'll try not to lose one at the ball." Kate shook one leg. "Don't think they will come off."

"Let me help you up," Jen offered.

Taking Jen's outstretched hand, Kate pulled herself up and spread-out her arms. "Plate me," she smiled.

Raguel covered Kate's upper legs with cuisses, then grabbed her chest, back and arm armor. "Ready for the rest?" he asked.

"Go for it," Kate said.

Raguel carefully layered the metal plates onto Kate's body. He finished by sliding her gauntlets onto her hands.

Kate wiggled back and forth and then walked in a circle around Jen to gain the hang of the forty-five pounds of armor.

"You look…uh…formidable," Jen said. She stood still, holding Kate's bucket-like helmet. A sky blue plume burst forth from the top of the metal head covering.

"Thanks, but I wish some of our lighter weight modern polyethylene material was available," Kate said. "This would be the original heavy metal."

Jen laughed. "Just don't start singing."

"But surprising enough, it is very easy to move in," Kate observed. "Look!" She jogged in place and then gave a couple of 'air' punches. "A little awkward, but very manageable."

"Hello! Can I come in?"

Spinning slowly around, Kate was glad to see Petri standing in the entrance. "Come on in."

"It looks like you are ready to meet Rubidus," Petri said, but a smile did not cross his ever-serious face. He held her sword in one hand and the small rondel dagger in the other.

"As ready as I'll ever be."

Petri cocked his head to take in the over-all picture of Kate. When the vision he needed was etched in the crevasses of his mind, he slipped the sword into the sheath belted to her side and slid the dagger into the belt on the other side.

"Thank you," Kate said.

Petri put one hand on her shoulder. "May the Eagle fly overhead and bless you this day."

"Thank you," Kate whispered, acknowledging his prayer blessing.

Petri did not say another word but walked to a saddle stool in the corner of the tent and sat down. His eyes closed and he began mumbling.

"He will stay in that spot praying for you until the joust with Rubidus is over," Raguel said.

"I'm glad," Kate said. "I'll need all the prayers I can get."

"It's time to go." Nerkon stood in the doorway.

Kate took a deep breath and nodded.

"I'm with you," Jen said. She gave Kate a hug. "I'm with you." She slipped Kate's helmet over her head and pushed the hinged metal visor up so she could read Kate's eyes. Surprisingly, there was no fear radiating from Kate's deep emerald eyes, just determination.

"Let's get this done," Kate said. Her words fell out strong, her stature reflected her steadfastness. She was ready.

"Okay." Jen muscled up all the encouragement she could find inside her. She must provide Kate with a sturdy support base. She must be Kate's strength—from the sideline. "Let's go get it done." She pulled the visor down over Kate's eyes. Jen visualized herself being pulled through the visor's slits and into the armor with Kate. "I am with you all the way."

Chapter Twenty

*H*urrah! Hurrah! Hurrah!

Cheers of approval echoed though the crowd of Nerkon's Pilgers waiting for Kate when she emerged from the tent. Their knight was before them. They would support her though their enthusiastic response to each of her moves in the joust with Rubidus.

Kate, overwhelmed at their greeting, raised her right armor-plated arm in acknowledgement of their reception. At that moment the enormity of it hit her.

"Jen," Kate's voice wavered.

"You will succeed in victory for them—for Nerkon—for Bigna." Jen kept her voice and words under control to give Kate the confidence she needed right now. "You are the chosen one for this battle, but I will be close by."

Silence came from inside Kate's helmet.

"Breathe," Jen said.

"Whew!"

A heavy, sighing whistle of air slipped through the slits of Kate's metal headpiece.

Hurrah! Hurrah! Hurrah!

Hurrah! Hurrah! Hurrah!

Mobs of Pilgers pushed in closer to Kate.

Nerkon stepped between Kate and the Pilgers. Holding up both hands, he backed them away from her. "It is time for Sir Katherine to defend our honor. Show her your support with cheers, but give her room for now. There will be plenty of time after her victory for you to celebrate with her."

The Pilgers took two steps back in deference to Nerkon's words but their enthusiasm did not diminish.

Sir Katherine!

Sir Katherine!

Sir Katherine!

Taka emerged from the smaller tent where Kate's jousting horse was housed. He held tight the blue reigns of her mount.

"What..." Kate gasped.

Nerkon's powerful destrier warhorse pranced behind Taka. Its muscular, white body radiated superior strength and discipline. The strong stallion paused momentarily, its well-arched neck stiffened, its nostrils widened in anticipation of the coming battle. Even the caparison covering his body could not hide the horse's tank-like readiness. The shield protecting its head bore Kate and Jen's coat of arms—a navy blue triangle, the profile of an eagle's head inside it and a thunderbolt under it.

Kate was speechless.

"This is Des," Nerkon said. "You will ride him in your joust."

"No, no," Kate protested. "I couldn't take your best warhorse. What if something happens to him?"

"That is why I insist you use him," Nerkon said. "I want you to have every advantage possible in your joust with Rubidus. Des is the best warhorse in my stable—true and steady. But I have also trained him to respond to knee pressure rather than reins for jousting tournaments. You will need his quick reaction to beat Rubidus. He will not waver in keeping you safe in your pursuit to victory."

"But..." Kate still protested.

"Nothing will happen to him," Nerkon silenced her before she could finish. "You need him and Taka will check him after each pass."

"Thank you," Kate said. She looked into the dark brown eyes of the strong, powerful long-legged stead. Their spirits bonded immediately. "Thank you."

Taka held Des' head steady. He did not say anything, but gazed through the slits in Kate's helmet and into her almost hidden eyes. It was the same confident look he had given her the first time he let her fly her Maup solo. He gave her an affirmative nod to show her all was ready. She nodded back.

"Then saddle up, Kate," Taka said. "It's time."

"Ready?" Raguel asked. He put a one-foot high step stool on the left side of Des and held out his hand to help Kate mount her steed.

"As ready as I'll ever be," Kate answered. She took Raguel's hand, stepped onto the stool. Her gauntlet-covered left hand squeezed Raguel's before she put it on the saddle. Slipping her left foot into the stirrup, she swung her full-armored body onto the back of Des.

Kate shifted slightly atop Des until she felt she and Des were one. Having ridden horses since she was a young girl, she automatically grasped the blue reins securely in her left hand.

"Remember to sit firmly in your saddle and use your knees and thighs to grip Des," Nerkon said. "He will respond quickly to each move you make."

"I will," Kate said. "Thank you."

Nerkon put his mouth close to Des' ear and whispered, "Take care of her."

Des's head turned just enough to go eye to eye with Nerkon. Blazing determination radiated back at Nerkon. With a final stroke on Des' neck, Nerkon walked toward his box just outside the arena. From there he would have a view of his and The Mission's future. It was out of his hands.

Jen jumped onto the stool and threw her arms around Kate. Silent understanding flowed between them.

"Kate?" Jen questioned.

"I feel it too."

For a brief moment both of their lockets warmed around their necks.

"You will not be alone," Jen said. She hugged Kate again. Through the metal shell protecting Kate, Jen felt their two lockets connect. "I am as close to you as your locket."

"I know," Kate said. "Just be where I can see you."

"Of course," Jen said. She slipped the small jousting shield onto Kate's arm. "Your shield, Sir Katherine," Jen smiled, and stepped off the stool.

Des did not flinch when Kate squeezed her knees tight into his side. Kate sensed his muscular body was ready to answer her commands.

Taka gave Des' bit strap a slight tug. Des' arched head dipped briefly and leaned into Taka's hand. Taka gave him a loving stroke, let go of the bit strap and then walked toward the arena where Kate and Rubidus would meet. Des, with Kate on his back, followed Taka's lead. His four-beat ambling gait put a commanding swagger in his step. Raguel's short legs did double-time in order to walk alongside of Kate and Des. 'Ov tagged behind as the tail of the procession.

Jen watched them move away from her and started to follow.

"No, Jen." Lieg put his hand on Jen's arm and stopped her. "You cannot go into the arena with her. Only Raguel as her attending squire and Taka as Des' groom can go with her."

"And 'Ov?"

"'Ov," Lieg smiled. "'Ov will serve as Raguel's aid. He will help but you cannot go with them."

Jen watched in dismay as Kate pulled away from her. Yet, the more the distance between them became, the closer she felt. "My locket," she murmured.

"Yes," Lieg said. "Your locket will keep you and Kate connected."

Jen felt a tinge better.

"Come," Lieg said. "You will sit with Nerkon in his box. From there you will be able to see everything that happens."

Kate glanced back at Jen and realized she could not physically come with her. Her eyes did not leave Jen as she took her seat beside Nerkon. Lieg, Obile and Count Begi took seats behind them.

"She is with you," Raguel said. Instinctively, he knew Kate wished Jen was beside her. "Do you feel your locket?"

"Yes, I do," Kate said. Beneath the forty-five pounds of armor her locket radiated comfort though her body.

"Your lockets will keep Jen close to you," Raguel said. "It is time for you to focus on what is before you."

Chapter Twenty-one

*L*eading Des, Taka stopped and raised his hand. Under Taka's nonverbal command, Des did not hesitate but instantly halted his steady gait. Arching his head higher, Des stood straight, readying himself for the joust.

Kate took her attention from Raguel and glanced down the jousting court where she would do battle with Rubidus. Everything and everybody was out of the arena except for a single rope. It was stretched four feet off the ground between wooden posts and ran one-hundred feet long. The green, yellow and white striped cloth hanging from the rope created a barrier to separate Kate and Rubidus and to prevent hard-hitting collisions between them.

At the far end of the barrier Rubidus sat atop his horse—or at least Kate assumed it was Rubidus. She could not be sure as the knight who faced her was fully covered in blood red armor. A fiery red plume attached to the top of his helmet ruffled in the breeze. Only bright yellow gauntlets broke the complete darkness of the armor. His blood red shield blazed with a fiery red raven. The caparison covering his horse's body was deep red and black checkered.

"Is that Rubidus?" Kate asked Raguel

"Yes," Raguel furrowed his brow. "That is Rubidus—the Red Knight."

"Red Knight," 'Ov spit out.

"Do not let his yellow gauntlets distract you," Raguel said. "He wears them to have his foes focus on them instead of his shield or helmet. When he rides toward you he will make sure his yellow gauntlet is in the forefront in your eyesight."

Kate nodded in understanding.

"Des will ride hard and he will ride fast," Taka said. He no longer needed to stand in front of Des. Nerkon's destrier was in his starting position, waiting for the herald to give the signal. "Just tighten your knees and thighs around him, he will do the rest."

Kate nodded and tightened around Des.

"Remember," Taka said. "Like your Maup, you are one with Des and Des is one with you."

"I will remember," Kate said. She dug her knees even tighter into Des' sides. His muscles rippled beneath her.

"Here is your lance," Raguel said. He set the long pole into a half ring attached to Kate's saddle.

"Thank you," Kate said and wrapped her gauntlet covered fingers around the wooden shaft under the lance's vamplate. "This first pass will be with lances that have the steel head fitted with a coronal."

Kate looked at the crown-shaped, three-pronged cap that was placed over the sharp tip used in battle. It was put there to protect the knights.

"Blunt as those prongs are," Raguel frowned, "they can still hurt and he can still dismount you."

"I guess I'll just have to stay away from his jabs and blows," Kate smiled.

"Just be careful," Raguel repeated. "Rubidus will try to unseat you with this first run—with his first blow."

"And if he does that," Taka added, "he won't hesitate to trample you or run you through with his sword while you are on the ground."

"On this first run aim for the raven on his shield," Raguel said. "Remember. Your lance will be upright and you will lower it across your body when you are about ten feet from Rubidus."

"You don't want me to aim for his helmet?" Kate thought about what Nerkon said.

"Not this run," Raguel said. "You have never been in a match. This first run will give you practice in accuracy with your lance."

Des' front legs pranced in place, eager for the battle to begin. He had seen many battles and grew anxious to launch his body into the action.

Kate drew a long, slow breath and gathered her last minute instructions from Taka and Raguel.

"Rubidus will try to hit your weak areas," Taka said. "Keep your shield up—protect your chest and arms. He will aim for the spots where your armor connects together."

Kate knew he was talking about her underarm area where there was a gap in her armor.

"And most important, stay on Des," Taka said. "He will be in command of the ground. All you have to do is aim your lance."

Of course, Kate thought. *The most important thing—stay astride Des!*

"Careful," Raguel said, adjusting the shield in Kate's hand. "Rubidus is very devious."

"She will do fine," Taka's said. "She's been trained by the best knights in Bigna."

Raguel nodded in agreement, but concern crossed his brow. Kate was his responsibility. He looked to the sky. Wispy clouds streaked the deep blue overhead, but no living creature flew above the arena. *Where are you Eagle?*

Rubidus' mouth twitched in anger inside his blood red helmet at the other end of the run. He watched Kate interact with Taka and Raguel. Depraved thoughts of deceit burned inside him. He no longer needed the

Bás Scorpion living in the mole behind his ear to tell him what to do. He no longer needed any prompting. His own venom of hate, pulsing through his veins for years for Nerkon, consumed him.

I will put an end to this Earth World intruder and then I will kill Nerkon.

"Your lance," Abi said. Like Raguel had done for Kate, Abi set Rubidus' lance into a half-ring attached to his saddle.

Rubidus grasped the black wooden pole with his gauntlet. Overnight the five miniature pincers that were once his fingers had fused together. They were now hand size claws, growing each day toward their full, one foot long scorpion claws. Abi had modified his gauntlets to fit over them, yet still give the appearance of five fingered gloves.

Haw—haw—haw!

A callous laugh seeped from the slits in his dark helmet. This would be his last battle, but he would triumph.

"Look, Abi," Rubidus said. He held up his clawish gauntlet, spread the two claws apart and then snapped them together. "The Earth World intruder will not be able to knock my lance from my hand."

"Yes, Sir Rubidus," Abi answered. He wished he did not have to join Rubidus in Rapio's army, but he knew it was inevitable. He had made the choice to follow Rubidus—now he must pay the price.

"I will toy with her this first pass," Rubidus said looking at the coronal covering the sharp steel head of his lance. "Be ready, my old friend Abi," he snarled. "The second will be her death."

Two short snorts from Rubidus' horse's nostrils filled the air with agreement.

Chapter Twenty-two

Baraaaaaag!

The first blast from the herald's elephant trumpet echoed over the arena.

"That's the call," Raguel said.

"I will see you at the other end," Taka said. "I'll be ready to prepare Des for your second run." He struck Kate's shield with his open palm. "Keep your shield up—Godspeed."

Baraaaaaag!

"The second, and last, trumpet," Raguel said.

"Now what?" Kate asked.

"In one minute the herald will begin the three bells," Raguel answered. "When you hear the first, pull your lance from its resting place. At the second bell, set yourself mentally and physically. As soon as you hear the third bell Des will know and charge—be ready."

Raguel, like Taka, hit her shield with his open palm, but he said nothing. He picked up 'Ov so he could also hit Kate's shield.

"Godspeed, Sir Katherine," 'Ov said. His small hand smacked the crest on Kate's shield. "Godspeed."

Steam puffed from Des's nostrils. He was anxious for the fight to begin. Kate urged her stallion forward. She was ready as she would ever be.

Chink!

The chiming sound of the first bell rang over the arena. Kate pulled her resting lance from the half-ring. Gripping it tighter she made sure she had control of the long pole.

Chink!

The second call rang out.

Kate gave a quick glance toward Nerkon's box. Jen stood in anticipation of the third bell.

Beneath Kate Des was a tightly wound spring, ready to launch his body into action. Kate leaned forward to gain better vision of the playing field.

Chink!

Des did not hesitate. Kate fixed her gaze down the rope barrier and dug her heals into his side.

Charging alongside of the barrier Kate and Des barreled toward Rubidus. He held his lance out from his body and higher than she expected. Like Raguel had warned, her focus went to the yellow gauntlet holding his lance.

Focus on his shield not his gauntlet. Raguel's advice echoed in Kate's head. Immediately she shifted her line of sight to the fiery red raven on his shield.

Des did not swerve or waver.

Rubidus and his horse came toward them at freight train speed.

Judging their distance at ten feet apart, Kate lowered the tip of her lance and angled it across her body into a fighting position. Hurling toward Rubidus' at full speed and in full armor, she had difficulty keeping the tip from wavering. She stared at Rubidus shield and tried to hold her lance steady.

Whaaaam!

The shock of Rubidus' lance hitting her shield at full force crumpled her body and dislodged her from her saddle. Her left foot came out of its stirrup and flew into the air. Her body slid to the right side of Des' back.

Rubidus, sensing a sudden victory, wheeled his horse around to the side of the barrier Kate was on and waited eagerly for her to complete her fall. He was ready to come back and either trample her or run her through with his sword. A merciless euphoria pulsed though his scaled covered body. Abi ran to him, but Rubidus kicked him away. *This was his victory!*

Des sensed Kate slipping from his back. Without breaking his gait, he sidestepped into her fall. His quick action gave Kate just enough leverage to thrust down with her right foot on the ring-like stirrup. Able to gain back her balance, she pushed herself back atop Des.

Des reached the end of the barrier, braked to halt, coiled his powerful body and spun around. He was ready for the next run.

"Thank you," Kate leaned forward and whispered in Des' ear. "Thank you!"

"Very good," Taka stated.

Kate looked around Des' head. Taka was stroking the horse and checking his armor. Kate wasn't sure if he was talking to Des or her.

"Yes, very good," Raguel said. He was standing beside Des atop a small stool. "You hit his shield."

"I did?" Kate was surprised as she didn't know if her lance had touched Rubidus.

"Yes," Raguel said. "How do you feel?"

"Wasn't ready for the force of hitting a wall going forty miles an hour," Kate said, "but Des saved me." She handed Raguel the splintered lance she still held in her hand. "At least I didn't lose my lance."

"Now you know what it is like," Raguel said taking the broken lance and giving it to 'Ov.

'Ov ran the shattered pole to the side of the arena and hurled it javelin-like into a bush. Without waiting to see if he hit anything or anybody, he scampered back to Raguel.

"This time, grip firmly to Des with your legs but be prepared to give— to lean backward on the blow of Rubidus' lance. It will help keep you in your saddle."

"Should I aim for his helmet?" Kate asked, again remembering Nerkon's advice.

"Not this run," Raguel answered. "But this time Rubidus will be out to kill you so you must protect your weak areas—those places where the armor hinges." He set a new lance into the half-ring for her. "And now the lances no longer have coronals on their heads."

155

Kate looked at the pole she held in her hand. The sharp tip glistened in the bright sunlight. It was a weapon of war, not an instrument of a game. Uncomfortable at the thought of using a battle weapon to kill someone in a game, she looked toward Jen.

Jen leaned against the wooden rail that kept her from Kate. In a heartbeat she would trade places, but the rules were the rules. "Kate!" she yelled. "Feel your locket." She pointed toward her own golden heart shaped locket underneath her tunic.

Kate could not hear Jen's words over the crowd, but knew instantly what she was saying. She acknowledged Kate by pointing toward her breastplate. Her locket responded with warmth.

"At the signal Des will ride hard and fast," Taka said, coming alongside of Kate. His work with Nerkon's destrier warhorse was complete. "Keep your lance upright until you are two strides from Rubidus. Des will know when you lower it."

"I am confident he knows everything that is happening," Kate said.

Baraaaaaag!

The blast from the herald's elephant trumpet signaled the second run was beginning.

Taka did not say another word, but struck Kate's shield with his open palm.

Baraaaaaag!

"Focus on the raven on his shield," Raguel said. He hit the coat-of-arms on her shield with his hand and gave her a nod.

Des became a stone-hard statue beneath Kate.

Raguel looked toward the sky but still did not see what he was looking for. *Where are you, Eagle?*

Chink!

The first bell chimed. Kate pulled her resting lance from the half-ring.

Chink!

The second bell.

Kate leaned forward to gain better vision. Mentally she went over the next minute. Rubidus would aim for her head or underarms—those were her weak areas. She must protect them, yet at the same time hit his shield hard enough to knock him off his horse.

Chink!

Des's still body sprang forward. Kate tightened her knees against him and stared toward the blood-red suit of armor powering toward her. She held her lance upright in her right hand, waiting for the right moment to lower it.

Rubidus's yellow gauntlet did not distract her this time. She focused on the red raven on his shield.

When she felt she could wait no longer, she lowered her lance across Des' neck. Couching it in her right arm she pointed it toward his oncoming shield. She concentrated in keeping it from wavering.

Whaaaam!

Crack!

The jarring blow pushed her back in her saddle but she leaned back at the moment of impact and cushioned the blow. Her lance splintered when it hit Rubidus' shield. It moved him slightly from his firm seat in his saddle.

Clank!

Metal against metal!

Her focus was so much on the raven on his shield she forgot to bring her shield up to protect herself. Rubidus quickly saw her unskilled move and changed his lance angle at the last moment. He did not aim for her shield but instead pointed his weapon at her body. His lance slipped between her armored plates and met flesh under her unprotected arm. The steel point sliced through her heavy padded gambeson and linen under tunic, putting a two inch gash in her right bicep. Blood trickled down her arm, but she could not stop the match. If she did, Nerkon lost and Rubidus won—and what he won was the soul of the Quae of Bigna.

Kate looked over her shoulder. Rubidus had not fallen from his horse. She would have to make another run.

Des reached the end of the barrier, stopped and spun around.

Kate winced in pain and let her splintered lance fall from her hands to the ground. Her fist balled up from the pain under her arm.

"You're wounded," Raguel said. "You cannot continue." He observed the blood trickling out between the armored plates.

"Is Des okay?" Kate asked, ignoring Raguel's statement. She would not abandon the fight just because Rubidus had landed an injuring blow.

"Yes," Taka said.

"Then I must finish the fight," Kate grimaced.

"You cannot…"

"She must," Taka cut Raguel off. "The Mission is on her shoulders. Bigna is on her shoulders."

"I'll be all right." Kate looked squarely into Raguel's troubled eyes and stated, "Just tell me how to hold the lance without Rubidus knowing what is going on."

"Rubidus already knows he has wounded you so he will use this run to finish you," Taka took the lead. "This is the run you must aim for his helm—this run is when you will surprise him."

"How…" she sucked in a deep breath to overcome the shooting pain in her arm. "How can I hold my lance? I have very little strength in my right arm."

"Can you grasp it long enough to begin the run?" Taka said.

"I think so," Kate hesitantly answered.

"Can you?" Raguel questioned.

"Yes, I can," Kate exhaled out.

"Do you trust Des enough to let him carry you straight and steady without using the reigns?" Taka asked.

"Yes," Kate was definite.

"It is like flying a Maup," Taka said. "You will use your legs to stay atop him."

"And how do I hold the lance?"

"Begin by holding it up, but when it is time to lower it, let it drop into your left hand. Use your right hand only for balance. With your left hand bring the lance up and aim for Rubidus' helmet."

"No do-over," Kate said. She tried to smile under her helmet, but the pain brought a grimace into her voice instead.

"One shot!" Taka exclaimed.

"One shot," Kate concurred.

"You can do it," Raguel agreed. He knew she must carry on despite her injury.

"Sir Katherine!" 'Ov jump from behind Raguel. "Sir Katherine can do it."

Raguel picked 'Ov up.

"Godspeed, Sir Katherine!" 'Ov shouted. He struck her shield with his small hand.

"Thank you, 'Ov," Kate said.

Taka and Raguel followed 'Ov's lead and hit the crest on her shield.

Raguel searched the sky. *Are you close by Eagle?*

Chapter Twenty-three

Rubidus glared at Kate through the slits of his helmet. Beneath the heavy metal head covering, sweat dripped from his disappearing hairline over his newly formed lizard ears.

"Abi!" Rubidus shouted. His word echoed eerily around the inside of his helmet.

"I'm here, Sir Rubidus," Abi said.

"I have wounded her," Rubidus snarled. "But she did not fall. Bring me my lance with the sharpest tip."

"I have it here," Abi said and placed it in the half-ring on Rubidus' saddle.

"To her death! This time to her death!" Rubidus did not take his eyes off Kate.

Abi stood in silence.

"It is time to mortally wound the Earth World invader—time for the death blow." Heavy breathing filled the inside Rubidus's helmet.

Baraaaaaag!

Kate glanced at Jen. Jen held her forefinger and thumb an inch apart. Kate smiled. Of course! Jen wanted her to know Rubidus was small, just like an ant. Kate brought her gauntlet covered left hand to where her nose was under her helmet and wiggled her fingers to complete the routine they always did before they performed in an air show. Kate inhaled deeply. They were together in this medieval show.

Baraaaaaag!

The elephant trumpet blasted its last call to the combatants.

Kate brought her concentration back to the joust.

Chink!

The first bell chimed. Kate pulled her resting lance from the half-ring but it began to wobble. Her right arm and hand did not have the strength to hold it upright. Fighting back the pain, she let the end of the lance settle onto the saddle to give it support. Using all her mental strength she could muster, she clutched it tighter. *Lord, give me the strength to hold on just a few minutes more*, she prayed.

Des settled motionless into his coiled spring position.

Chink!

The second bell.

Kate leaned forward. A droplet of sweat trickled down her nose and splashed onto the visor. She blocked out everything except the blood red knight at the end of the barrier.

Screeeech!

Kate heard it and, without moving a muscle, took in the welcoming sound.

Raguel looked up toward the soaring bird and whispered, "I knew you would not abandon her. Thank you, Eagle."

The Eagle momentarily froze, and then swooped downward toward Kate. Three hundred feet above her he gave one flap with his giant wings and rocketed straight up toward the afternoon sun.

Chink!

Des's silent body sprang forward.

Clinching her teeth, the pain spread down her arm and through her hand. Kate balanced the lance, pushing it harder into the saddle for support. "Just a few more seconds," she whispered to herself. "Hold on."

Rubidus shortened the distance between them. His armor plating stretched to its limit over the bulging reptile body forming under it.

Kate shuffled the lance to get a better grip. *Hold on.*

Dirt kicked up from beneath Des' pounding hoofs, but his back was level and did not move.

"Now!" she yelled aloud to herself. She let go of Des' reigns and let the weight of the lance fall into her left hand. It felt awkward—much more so than it did when she had control with her right hand. She would now have to use more strategy since the weapon was guided from her weaker side and all her trust would be on Des to hold steady.

Puh-boom! Puh-boom! Puh-boom!

The sound of pounding horse hoofs was the only sound Kate heard. The crowd's noise had disappeared into silence in her head.

Her lance was directed at Rubidus' shield. Through his visor Kate saw two glowing yellow eyes stare her down.

One shot! Taka's words stuck in her head. *One shot!*

Puh-boom! Puh-boom! Puh-boom!

Rubidus charged hard. Kate felt his hatred for her propelling him toward her with his evil goal. She was Nerkon's surrogate in their fight for control of The Mission. Condescending arrogance rode with him.

Puh-boom! Puh-boom! Puh-boom!

Rubidus' blood red armor was twenty feet from her.

Instantly she changed her focus from the red raven on his shield and locked her eyes onto the bright yellow plume attached to the top of his helm. Using all the mental and physical strength she had, she pushed her lance upward with her left hand. The angle of her pole-weapon now aimed at the two glowing yellow eyes.

Surprise overtook the pompous look in Rubidus' eyes. This was a novice. She did not have the skill to aim for his helm, yet he was staring at the sharp end of her lance. He raised his lance to counter her attack, but his reaction wasn't fast enough to duck the oncoming weapon.

Whaaaam!

Clank!

Kate's lance met its mark and stuck Rubidus between his eyes.

Clang-thud!

Rubidus bounced once when he hit the ground. Stunned, he lay still.

Des raced to the end of the barrier and wheeled around. Seeing Rubidus on the ground he charged toward him. He would trample the enemy for his rider Kate. This match would be over.

Kate dropped her lance and pulled back on Des' reigns. She would not let Des kill a defenseless knight.

Rubidus watched Des run toward him and stop. He lay sill and waited for Kate to make the next move.

Kate slid from Des's back. Pain throbbed from the cut in her arm. She could no longer move her fingers. Her right arm was useless. But the joust was now hers to decide what would happen. The blow to Rubidus' head had unseated him from his horse. She was victorious. She took three steps toward Rubidus to accept his defeat. With her left hand she pulled her helm off. Rubidus, as well as everyone watching, saw Kate was declaring the match over.

"Rise, Sir Rubidus," Kate said. "The joust is over." In saying so, Kate declared his defeat, but also acknowledged that he would live. She had no desire to kill him. She looked toward Nerkon's box.

Nerkon's head bobbed slightly. Though he did not approve of Kate's decision, he accepted it. She was his surrogate—she was the one who fought the joust—she was the one who would determine the final outcome.

Jen was on her feet and making her way out of Nerkon's box. She needed to get to Kate and help her take care of the gash in her arm.

Groggy, but still aware of the situation, Rubidus stumbled to his feet. Kate had given him the moments he needed to gain his thoughts. His clawed gauntlet slowly slid down his side and gripped his sword.

This Earth World invader is foolish, Rubidus snickered to himself. *She will die today.*

Swoosh!

Rubidus drew his sword from its scabbard.

Kate realized too late what Rubidus was doing. He was not going to accept defeat. He still wanted to kill her. This was no longer about the match—no longer about Nerkon—no longer about The Mission. It was about killing her.

Swoosh!

Kate ducked just as Rubidus' sword whizzed through the air at her head. Nerkon was right; Rubidus did not hesitate to take the joust to death. Kate tried to will her right arm to move, but it was futile. The wound to her bicep was deep and the only feeling she had was the blood tricking down into her gauntlet.

Swoosh!

Clank!

Rubidus' sword met its mark on the armor covering Kate's right arm.

Kate winced with pain. She tugged at her sword with her left hand but could not get the leverage to pull it from its scabbard.

Swoosh!

Clank!

The loud ringing metallic sound of Rubidus' second blow against Kate's armor echoed around the arena.

The force behind the blow knocked Kate off balance. She staggered one step before she fell backward to the ground. In this moment Kate realized her mistake. The being inside the blood red suit of armor swinging the sword at her was not a Quae. The creature inside was no longer Sir Rubidus—a Bigna Knight, but Rubidus—a Bás scorpion.

Bweee!

Yellow glowing eyes sought out Kate. Claws gripped the sword. A bulging, green luminous body broke the metal plate armor covering it—replacing the knight's armor with the bony, scaled plates of a Bás Elite Trooper.

Bweee!

Kate stared up at the ever-growing beast. Red hair flowed over the head to its shoulders. What was once Rubidus' shield now morphed into a blood-red silhouette of a fiery raven head inside a triangle onto the scorpion-like creature's chest. The swagger of Rubidus was gone, replaced by a crusty head wagging to and fro looking for its victim—Kate.

"No!" Jen yelled. She covered the gap between her and Kate quickly, but not fast enough.

The Elite Trooper scorpion raised his sword.

Bweee!

"Die!" what was left of Rubidus the Bigna Knight yelled. "Die!"

His final feat as a Bigna Knight would be to kill Kate. He savored the thought of killing her while his nemesis Nerkon watched in horror. He would win the final battle with Nerkon. Try as he might, Nerkon could do nothing to stop him.

Bweee!

Kate raised her left arm to ward off the death blow.

Swoosh!

Sun glistened off the descending blade. It would meet Kate's head in less than a second.

Thud!

Kate did not feel the blade. The deadly blow had missed her. A shadow cast a shielding blanket over her.

Harumph!

Kate whirled her head around at the snorting sound.

"Des!" Kate whispered.

Nerkon's loyal warhorse stood over her, chest expanding from rage. Vaporous air exhaled through his flaring nose. Rubidus' sword had struck Des on his chest. The caparison covering his body softened the blow before it cut through into his flesh.

Des held his head high and steady, studying the danger before them. Blood oozing from the gash in his chest created a widening red spot on his caparison. Unfazed by the cut, he did not move away. He was Kate's protector.

Harumph!

Des' dark brown eyes locked onto the yellow eyes of Rubidus. Emitting from the eye slits of Rubidus' helmet fury burned—hatred of everything Kate stood for consumed him.

Eeeee!

Des' short, shrill, piercing cry gave the only clue to his intention. He rose to his hind feet and came down hard on Rubidus' scaled covered body.

The sword Rubidus held flew from his claws, falling loudly to the ground.

Bweee!

Rubidus stumbled slightly. His iron knight's suit fell away as his long, scaled body of a scorpion grew.

Eeeee!

Des brought his full weight down on the red-haired scorpion a second time.

Rubidus cowered away from the crushing blows. He did not want to fight Des. It was time to retreat and join Rapio. It was time for him to become one of Rapio's Elite Troopers. It was time to become part of Rapio's final war. He backed away from Des, turned and ran toward the river.

Des galloped fifty feet after him, then stopped. Rubidus was not his responsibility; Kate was entrusted into his safekeeping. He raced back to her and bent his head to nuzzle her right arm.

"Des," Kate whispered. "Thank you." She grabbed his nose strap with her left hand.

Des sensed Kate's desire and pulled her upright. She was the triumphant knight—standing tall, not lying defeated on the ground.

"Kate!" Jen ran to Kate's side. "Kate, you are hurt."

"I'm okay," Kate said, "but you must stop Rubidus. He must not get to the river."

Jen watched the disappearing back of the luminous scorpion. He was now seventy yards from them, and only fifteen feet from the edge of the Senvolte River. If he reached the river, he would disappear and become part of the expanding enemy army.

Lieg handed Jen her bow and one arrow.

"One shot," Lieg said.

"One shot," Jen repeated.

Jen held her bow over her head and remembered the commands of Mejor, the Senior Centurion from the First Cohort.

Nock! Mark! Draw!

She put the notch of the yew wood arrow onto the taut hemp string, aimed toward the fleeing Rubidus and drew it back.

Rubidus was within five feet of the river.

Loose!

The feathered arrow flew toward its target. With absolute accuracy, the arrow pierced Rubidus' scaled body just as he put one giant clawed foot into the water. Igniting into flame from the arrow strike, Rubidus spit flowing hot sparks into the air. The river water sizzled from the glowing embers hitting its surface.

Writhing from the death arrow, Rubidus' body exploded into a vivid green glaring light, blasting the area around him. Shockwaves rippled the air and kicked up dust tornadoes for one-hundred yards around the exploding scorpion. Rubidus' Elite Trooper form disintegrated into the sandy shore of the river.

Jen dropped her bow.

"One shot!" 'Ov danced around in glee. "One shot, Sir Jenifer!"

Jen smiled at 'Ov's joy, but her concern was Kate.

"Kate…" Jen began.

"Now I'm completely all right," Kate smiled. "We defeated Rubidus."

Des nudged Kate.

"Yes, Des," Kate said. "We includes you." She rubbed his head.

"I think it is time to take care of both of you," Taka said. "Both of you were injured in this battle."

"Yes, they need to be attended to," Nerkon came up on them. "But first we have to decide what to do with Abi, Rubidus' Senior Centurion. I caught him trying to slip out of the arena."

Abi, held tight in Nerkon's grip, danced on his tiptoes at the end of Nerkon's strong arm. He fell to his knees when Nerkon released his hold on his tunic.

"Sir Nerkon," Abi whimpered. "I beg your forgiveness."

"Why should I…we forgive you?" Nerkon asked.

"I did nothing wrong," Abi begged. "Rubidus forced me follow him from Stur and serve him." He hung his head low and forced his eyes to stare at the ground in mock humility.

"How could he force you?" Nerkon questioned.

"He threatened my family," Abi lied. He had no family other than Rubidus. "He said he would kill my family back home." He stole a glace up at Nerkon.

Nerkon stared Abi in his eyes. Something wasn't right, but maybe by keeping him alive he could find out more of why Rubidus turned against The Mission and what was below the river's surface.

"You shall live…for now," Nerkon said. "But Rubidus' army is to be broken up, sent on their way. They will not join any other army nor will they stay in camp. If anyone who fought under Rubidus' banner is caught in camp in one hour they will be put to death."

"Thank you, Sir Nerkon," Abi sniveled. "I will serve you well."

"You will go immediately and destroy Rubidus' red banner," Nerkon said. "Take down everything of Rubidus and destroy it. And you personally will send his army away."

"Yes, Sir Nerkon," Abi said.

"Get up!" Nerkon's voice filled with disgust. "Go…now!"

"Yes, Sir Nerkon," Abi quickly rose. He bowed and backed away from Nerkon. When he got twenty feet from Nerkon he turned and ran toward Rubidus' army. He would stay close to Nerkon and somehow report back to Rapio.

The Bás within Abi's neck burned with pleasure—a new sensation for Abi. His controlling scorpion squirmed beneath his skin. "I will do your bidding now," Abi mumbled. "Rubidus failed but I will not."

Nerkon watched Abi run. When he was out of earshot, Nerkon turned to Mejor. "Keep a close eye on him."

"Yes, Sir Nerkon," Mejor answered. "We will keep him under close watch all day and all night."

"Good," Nerkon said. Turning to Kate he said," Tonight is the time to celebrate your victory. You have won your first joust. Tonight we will have a big feast in your honor."

"Rubidus was not our objective," Kate said. She was concerned a feast would detract from their mission. "Your battles have been fought to go to Helig. Helig still needs to be taken back from the Indringers."

"Yes," Nerkon agreed. "The Mission is still our number one priority. After a good dinner we will discuss what needs to be done next."

Taka nodded. "It is good that we shall celebrate Kate's victory."

"Raguel." Nerkon waved his hand to summon the quiet guardian. "Take Kate to our physician for healing."

"Yes, Sir Nerkon," Raguel said. "Jen! Come with me to take Kate to the physician to heal her wound."

"I wouldn't be anywhere else," Jen stated.

"Taka," Nerkon added. "Take care of Des."

"Of course," Taka said. "Of course."

Chapter Twenty-four

$\mathcal{K}$ate picked up the last black and white striped one-half inch round berry from her wooden bowl with her left hand. The physician had put a healing lotion on the gash in her right bicep, but it was still sore. Her grip with her right hand was still weak.

"That was really good," she said.

"Never had a dessert so good," Jen agreed. But for Jen the fact Kate was sitting beside her, safe from Rubidus' wicked plan to kill her, was the best part of the day.

"Googy Berries are rare," Raguel said. "They only grow in the vineyards around the Cephas Monastery. Nerkon had them brought in special for this occasion."

"They are wonderful," Kate repeated herself. She was still humbled that Nerkon had declared a feast to be held in celebration of her victory over Rubidus. She looked over the knights gathered in Nerkon's tent. "As are the faithful Pilgers gathered here tonight."

Clink! Clink! Clink!

Mejor's dagger striking his goblet signaled that Nerkon would now speak to the knights.

Silence fell across the room. All attention was on Nerkon.

Nerkon rose. "Knights of Bigna! We are proud of our fellow knight, Sir Katherine. She defeated a rogue knight among us. She has rid an affliction among us. Rubidus' shield has been hung upside-down." He stopped and looked out over the knights. He need not say more about Rubidus. They knew Rubidus had dishonored the knighthood—he had become a traitor.

"But our woes are not over," Nerkon continued. "We still are on The Mission to take back Helig from the Indringers. It is our destination." He paused to let his words take hold of the knights' thoughts.

A murmur of agreement waved over of the knights.

"We can see our destination across the river," Nerkon continued, "but the river is still controlled by Elak. We must cross over the river. We must get beyond Elak's control before we can fulfill our purpose. Sir Begi has come to me with a plan. I will let him speak to you."

A roar of approval rose from the knights. Begi had proven himself in many battles. He knew how to lead a successful attack.

Begi rose and stood beside Nerkon. His scar, stretching from the top of the black leather patch covering his eye to his hairline, throbbed from the anguish of the many years in battles of war behind him and the one, what he hoped to be his last, battle ahead of him. He chose his words carefully. The knights were weary of waiting to conquer Helig, but he must inspire them to follow him across the dangerous water of the Senvolte River and storm through the gates of Helig.

"Helig is not beyond our reach," he drew in a deep breath and looked into the eyes of the knights. What he said now would either unite them in battle or discourage them into defeat. Exhaling he continued, "To cross the river my warriors have built four rafts large enough to carry a Century each. At daybreak tomorrow I will take the first raft with a Century to the other side of the river. When we are half-way across the river, Sir Fortis, my Senior Centurion, will take the second raft with a second Century on it. When they reach mid-river, the third raft will go—and then the fourth. After each raft reaches the opposite shore they will return and pick up another Century, and then another until we are all are on the other side of the river."

The knights were silent, absorbing everything Begi said.

"What about Elak?" a knight shouted. "He rules the river."

"Elak lives beneath the river!" Begi exclaimed. "We will be on the surface of the water. We will triumph over Elak! The river can be crossed."

"Helig will be ours!" Nerkon's voice reinforced Begi's claim. He wanted the knights to focus on their goal, not the river. "To Helig!"

Helig! Helig! Helig!
Helig! Helig! Helig!

The knights yelled in agreement.

The one knight who asked the question sat silent for a moment. His eyes darted around at his fellow knights. They had decided. They would not question the plan for their lives. They would follow their leaders across the river on rafts. Determined to complete their mission, they believed by tomorrow night they all would be outside the walls of Helig. Hesitant at first, the skeptic joined them in their cry. He was a Bigna Knight.

"To Helig!" he shouted.

Helig! Helig! Helig!
Helig! Helig! Helig!

There was unity amongst the knights.

Begi glanced at Nerkon.

Nerkon nodded in approval.

"When will we go over?" Kate whispered to Raguel.

Before he could answer, Jen added, "Which Century will we join on the rafts?"

"You won't take a raft," Raguel shrugged with a smile. "You will fly over with your Century—Bigna Air Power."

Jen glanced at Kate. Her lips curled at the corners in a slight grin.

Chapter Twenty-five

*D*awn seeped through the cracks of Kate and Jen's tent, giving them a hint that the new day had begun.

"Wake up, Jen!" Kate yelled, scurrying out of her bed. "The river crossing is today!"

Jen did not wait to be called twice. She jumped from under her covers, pulled on her clothes and dashed for the door. Kate followed, slowed only by her stopping at the small table to grab a piece of bread left over from the feast the night before.

"Here!" Kate broke the bread in half and gave a piece to Jen. "We don't know when we'll get to eat today."

"Thanks," Jen said. "You're always thinking."

Kate shrugged. "Only thing I'm thinking is the whole camp going across the river today and we slept in."

"I didn't hear the trumpet call," Jen said.

"Me either," Kate said. Neither excused oversleeping, but both wondered why they had not heard the call to duty.

Kate flexed her arm. No pain, no limited movement. She balled her hand into a fist. Whatever the physician had put on her had completely healed the gash from Rubidus' lance.

"Look," Kate smiled at Jen. "I'm good as new."

"Great!" Jen said. "Today Nerkon will need everyone to be their best. That includes us."

Sprinting across the camp toward the river they passed the Pilgers striking their tents, readying their gear and heading toward the river's edge. Though haste was in the Pilgers' undertaking, organization was in their every move. Each tent party, when they got to the river, found the Century banner they fought under and met up with the nine other tent parties that made their Century. Once in their Century they stood in straight lines, eight Pilgers to a line.

"Those rafts are going to be pushed to their capacity," Kate noted, looking at the size of the rafts. Big as they were, each had to hold eighty warriors, one Centurion and all the Century's gear—personal and group.

"At least we'll fly over on our Maups," Jen said.

"Too bad we don't have enough Maups to take the whole camp."

"Look!" Jen exclaimed. "Taka and Lieg have the Maups ready to go."

They rushed to where the Bigna Airpower Century gathered for the crossing. The Maups, covered in full battle gear, squatted and waited for their Mymybid riders to mount them.

"Lieg!" Jen called out.

"Ah, you decided to join us," Lieg raised one eyebrow. "We thought you might want to stay on this side of the river." He could not stop the grin that slowly crept across his face.

"We're sorry that we slept in…" Jen began and then realized Lieg was teasing them. "Well, you know us Earth World beings," she decided to join in his morning humor, "we have to have our beauty sleep."

"Of course!" Lieg no longer tried to hide the grin that now went from ear to ear.

"Not an excuse," Jen offered, "but we didn't hear the Trumpeter's call this morning."

"That is because there was no call," Lieg said.

"Why?" Jen asked.

"Sir Nerkon felt it was better to begin the crossing without taking a chance of waking Elak." Lieg answered.

"Then Nerkon does have concern about Elak in today's crossing," Kate frowned.

"Concern," Taka joined in, "but no fear."

"The river is so calm right now," Jen observed. She looked over the dawning sun sparkle off the glassy blue surface of the river. "So very peaceful."

"Peaceful right now," Lieg said. "But it probably won't stay that way, so we have a duty to do during the crossing."

"We won't be flying over the river?" Jen was confused.

"Yes," Lieg explained. "We will fly over; but, during the crossing, we will hover above the river. Our duty is to protect the rafts going across the river as best we can."

"Air support," Kate said. "I like that."

Jen nodded in agreement.

"You have just a few minutes to get into your battle gear," Raguel said, coming up beside them. "You need to put these on." He handed them their breast plates.

Quickly slipping into the light, battle weight armor, Kate noted Raguel did not appear to be ready to cross the river. "How are you going to get over the river?"

"Do not be concerned," he smiled. He handed Kate and Jen their quiver full of arrows. "I'll see you on the other side."

Kate cocked her head and wondered what he meant.

"Here," Raguel said. "You're flying outfit would not be complete without these." He handed them their 1920's flight helmets.

"Thank you," Jen said. Pulling the leather helmet onto her head and tugging the chin strap tight, she added, "Be safe, Raguel."

"Always," Raguel said. "Always."

"It is time to mount up and take to the air," Taka said. He gave Kate her sword and bow.

"And your battle weapons," Lieg said, giving Jen her sword and bow. "Hopefully, we won't need them, but Elak is very domineering and dangerous if he comes from the river's depth."

Wah—Wah!

Two, short low blasts from the First Trumpeter's long copper horn wafted over the gathering Pilgers. Needing no other signal, the First Cohort, lead by Sir Begi, marched onto the first raft. Each warrior wore a resolute face of stanch allegiance to The Mission. If there had been doubt in any of them the night before, today they would prove their right to be called The First.

"We must be over the water before the first raft casts off," Taka said. He threw his battle-ready body atop his waiting Maup, squared his shoulders over the large bird and raised his sword.

Lieg leaped on his bird and raised his sword to match Taka's. Glancing at Taka he nodded.

"For Bigna!" they shouted in unison.

On their signal, the Mymybids of the Bigna Air Power followed their lead and mounted their Maups simultaneously.

"For Bigna!" the Mymybids shouted back.

Cluck—cluck—cluck!

Cluck—cluck—cluck!

Cluck—cluck—cluck!

The Maups ran a few feet to gain speed and then became airborne. Their legs dangled several seconds and then neatly tucked into their sleek bodies. As if connected by an invisible string, each Maup lifted off in single line formation with the one ahead of it.

Cluck—cluck—cluck!

Cluck—cluck—cluck!

Cluck—cluck—cluck!

At the river's edge, Sir Begi and his First Century were pushing off from the safety of the shore. Not one Pilger looked back. All eyes faced forward toward their destination—toward Helig.

The river crossing had begun.

Chapter Twenty-six

Kate shivered at the beauty of God's creation spread out beneath her. Looking at life from the air always gave her a humbling perspective on her own existence. She pulled her left leg in tighter on her Maup to have him bank toward Jen.

"Beautiful," she yelled, leveling off beside Jen.

"Just what I was thinking," Jen yelled back.

Below them the glassy surface of the Senvolte River sparkled in the morning sun. A white tail of rippled water followed Sir Begi's raft. Standing ever alert at the front of the raft, Begi methodically scanned the still waters in all directions for any hint of trouble. He and his First Century were almost at the far shore of the river, but he did not relax his vigilance. Elak could be circling underneath him this very moment, waiting to strike.

Fortis, Begi's Senior Centurion, had pushed off from the sandy shore on the second raft and made mid-river within a few minutes. The third raft, covered with eighty Pilgers and Odo, Obile's Senior Centurion, waited for the signal to go. The crossing was going faster than anyone had contemplated.

Glancing to her right, Kate saw that Taka had the same look of preparedness that Sir Begi wore. His attention was at every undulation the rafts made in the still water. He focused on the water for any abnormality. To Jen's left, Lieg had the same intensity in his eyes.

"Keep alert!" Taka shouted at the eighty Mymybids warriors circling the river atop their Maups. "Scan the river with purpose!"

"Sir Begi has reached the other side," Jen pointed. The regimented First Century did not hesitate, but hastened their departure from the still raft.

Without waiting to be told the pilot of the vessel began his trip back across the river to ferry another Century of Pilgers to the far shore. The second raft passed him going in the opposite direction. The day would be long for the pilots of the rafts. They had many Pilgers, Centaurs and equipment to transport to safety. But at the end of the day they would be on the other side of the Senvolte River and ready to prepare for the siege of Helig. He waived to the pilot of the third boat as they passed midpoint of the river.

"It seems to be going well," Jen said to Lieg.

"Don't let your guard down," Lieg responded. "Be ready to act." His eyes never wavered from his watch on the rafts. He knew Elak's deceptiveness only too well. He had encountered the demon before.

"I'm ready." Jen tightened her legs around her Maup and squeezed the grip on her bow. And then she heard it.

Skraaa—Skraaa—Skraaa!

Skraaa—Skraaa—Skraaa!

Skraaa—Skraaa—Skraaa!

The shrill, guttural sound of the Acchim birds screamed skyward. Following their spine-chilling cry, the Acchims rose in massive form over the stone walls of Helig.

Skraaa—Skraaa—Skraaa!

Skraaa—Skraaa—Skraaa!

Skraaa—Skraaa—Skraaa!

"Kate!" Jen searched her cousin's expression.

"I hear them!" Kate responded.

Within seconds the sky darkened with the deep chestnut brown creatures. The birds, with their twelve-foot red feathered wings, red tail feathers, and bright red triangle on their chests, streaked skyward toward the Bigna Air Power.

"Hold your position!" Taka yelled.

In the front of the attacking birds was one Acchim, larger in size than the rest of the menacing flock. Its wingspan was sixteen feet of red feathered power. The deep red triangle on its chest had a raven head on it.

"An Elite Trooper?" Jen asked.

"Worse!" Taka shouted his answer."Onde!" Lieg shouted. "Onde is leading the attack."

"Onde," Jen whispered to herself. This battle was important enough for Rapio to send his high priest—the one whom he had entrusted to take the Holy Sword to Helig.

Onde, straddling the lead Acchim, was covered much like Rubidus had been in the jousting match. His armored chest plate and helmet were blood red and blazed with a fiery red raven. The darkness of his garments was broken only by the bright yellow plume attached to the top of his helmet.

"Hold your position!" Taka shouted again.

But it was too late. The Acchims, with their armored riders, were upon the Maups before their Mymybid Pilgers riders could refocus from the calmness of river to the danger in the sky.

Schhwaff!

Wap!

A Mymybid was mortally hit by an arrow and fell into the now churning river.

Schhwaff!

Schhwaff!

Schhwaff!

Kate ducked the flying arrows coming at her from the Acchim riders. Pulling an arrow from her quiver she remembered her lessons from Mejor.

Nock! Mark! Draw! Loose!

Schhwaff!

Wap!

Her arrow met its mark. An Acchim tumbled from the sky, taking its Indringer rider with him.

Just like in practice, she quickly notched one arrow after another onto the string, marked her target and drew back. But this was real battle—she did not wait for the command *loose*. She let the arrows fly toward her targets.

Schhwaff!

Wap!

Schhwaff!

Wap!

Schhwaff!

Wap!

Her hand automatically reached for another arrow after she shot the fiftieth arrow, but her quiver was empty. She tucked herself into her Maup and banked right. Jen was in her sight. She headed toward her cousin.

"Jen!" Kate shouted. "I'm out of arrows."

"Me too," Jen pointed at her quiver. "Time for hand to hand combat!" Jen drew her sword.

Kate wrapped her hand around the hilt of her sword, ready to draw it for the fight. She stopped her movement when she heard the cry from below.

Kraa—Kraa—Kraa!

With the Air Power knights distracted from their primary duty of protecting the crossing rafts, another, and much louder sound was heard.

Kraa—Kraa—Kraa!

The ravenous sound of the beast Elak broke the surface of the water a millisecond before its body slithered upward. Though smaller than Atasa, the beast was still monstrous. His fiendish dragon-like large, black eyes were set in a scaly snake-like face. A flaming three-pronged, forked lizard tongue lashed from his gaping mouth. Teeth, ready to grab and pull everything in its path to the deep chamber below the water, gleamed with acid-like saliva.

Forty foot waves rolled up and outward with his raising body. White caps splashed over the edges of the two rafts in the middle of the river.

Aaargh!

Aaargh!

Aaargh!

The crashing water upon the decks of the boats capsized the primitive rafts and washed the Pilger warriors into the swirling water. Elak's tongue whipped around the water and snatched any warrior who thrashed around trying to swim away from the chaos.

Aaargh!

Aaargh!

Aaargh!

The Pilgers struggled to fight off Elak but, heavily weighted with their battle armor, they could not retrieve their weapons nor keep their bodies afloat.

Tucking herself into the fuzzy body of her Maup, Kate turned downward toward the river in hopes of saving the flailing Pilgers. Elak's bulging soulless eyes caught sight of her streaking form and turned his attention away from the chaos in the river and on her.

"Not this time!" Kate yelled. "You don't win this time!" She aimed her Maup directly at the monster's head.

Flashes of flaming anger filled the black eyes of the beast. Elak's focus no longer was on the struggling Pilgers being sucked into the spiraling water and disappearing to their death below. Swallowing a flailing Pilger wrapped in its forked tongue, it lashed a bearlike claw at Kate.

Swish!

Its sharp talon-like nails caught Kate on her left leg.

Grimacing with the sharp pain, Kate pulled her Maup straight up, missing the second swipe from Elak's massive claws. Blood trickled down her calf into her boot. Reaching the pinnacle of their climb her hand slipped off the knob on her Maup's neck. Her hand was filled with blood but she felt no pain. She looked down at her Maup to assess the injury.

"Oh no!" Kate whispered. "Elak sliced your head!"

Blood from her Maup spilled out from a five inch slash in his neck.

"Kate!" Jen yelled, joining Kate's fight against Elak.

"I'm okay," Kate struggled out the words. "But..." She wiped the oozing blood from her Maup's neck.

"I see," Jen said. "Can you two make it back to camp?"

"We're both growing weak," Kate offered, "but we'll try."

Elak rose higher from the water toward Kate and Jen, but his eyes never took his focus from Kate. Orange-red flames belched from its gapping mouth and reflected in the black pits of his eyes.

Kraa—Kraa—Kraa!

Kate felt the heat from the flames. She twisted her body, but the gash Elak had inflected rendered her left leg numb and she grew dizzy. She could no longer give her Maup directions, and the jagged tear in his head caused him to lose his self-navigation ability.

Kraa—Kraa—Kraa!

Elak's tongue lashed out toward Kate and wrapped around her injured leg. With very little strength left, Kate could not pull away. Pulling from an inter strength her Maup extended his legs and stretched out his talons, clamping down on Elak's tongue where it left his slimy mouth.

Kraa—Kraa—Kraa!

Elak's painful cry rippled the air. His tongue momentarily went limp and loosened from Kate's leg. Her Maup did not hesitate but, from an instinctive awareness of the situation, shot straight upward—away from Elak.

Skraaa—Skraaa—Skraaa!
Skraaa—Skraaa—Skraaa!
Skraaa—Skraaa—Skraaa!

"Kate," Jen shouted. "The Acchims are retreating!" She pointed at the fleeing birds. Taka, Lieg and the Mymybids were pursuing them, but the Acchims with their larger wingspan, easily made it to safety behind the walls of Helig.

Kraa—Kraa—Kraa!

With one last blast of anger, Elak glared at Kate, and then slithered his scaly body back to the darkest depth below the surface of the water.

Waves crashed down behind Elak's vanishing body and, once again, the glassy surface of the Senvolte River sparkled in the morning sun. Two empty rafts floated silently on the still water. There were no signs of life.

"Kate," Taka said flying up beside her. "Go back to camp and take care of your wound. Turn your Maup over to the Bigna Air physician. He will tend to his wounds."

"Will he…he be…" Kate's words were muddled.

"He will be fine," Taka assured her. "Lieg and I are going to talk to Sir Begi on the far side of the river. Rapio has now managed to split our forces—Sir Begi on one side with two Centuries and Sir Nerkon on the other side with everyone else. We need to see if Sir Begi and his Pilgers are all right."

"Okay," Kate said. She didn't need to be told twice. Her leg was numb, but the rest of her body throbbed and the once trickling blood now gushed.

"I'll go with her," Jen said. "We'll see you back at camp."

"Yes, she needs you," Lieg stated. "The rest of the Bigna Air Power will fly overhead for a while to make sure the conflict is over."

"Thank you," Jen mouthed to Lieg.

Turning toward the shore where Sir Begin and his warriors were stationed, Lieg waved over his shoulder in acknowledgment of her words.

"Let's get you and your Maup taken care of," Jen said. Jen did not need to tell her Maup what to do—he knew he had to guide his fellow Maup to safety. He nudged into Kate's Maup and then took the lead back to camp.

Kate slumped into her Maup and draped her arms around his neck. "Take us home," she whispered into his ear. Her body drained, she went unconscious.

Beneath them the Senvolte River gave way to the dark force at the deepest, unending riverbed beneath its surface. Where Elak's body had slipped back into the deepest river channel, an indigo liquid oozed up and waved out in concentric circles until the whole river was opaque.

Chapter Twenty-seven

*T*he world was a hazy fuzz. Shadowy figures murmured in distant tones.

"What…where?" Kate began and tried to sit, but fell back into the soft blanket beneath her head.

"Lie back, Kate." Jen's face came within six inches of Kate's eyes. "Can you see me now? Do you know who I am?" Jen held Kate's hand tight.

"Of course. You're Jen…my cousin…my wing walker…" Kate squinted to focus. Jen was blurry, but she knew who she was.

"Well, you've been in and out of consciousness for twenty-three hours." Jen squeezed Kate's hand. "We were concerned."

"Twenty-three hours?" Kate queried.

"You are awake," Raguel's voice came from behind Jen.

"Raguel?"

"Yes, I'm here," Raguel said. "But more important Eldré is here."

"Eldré?" Kate was trying to wrap her mind around her surroundings.

"Ahhhh," Eldré exhaled, nudging Jen and Raguel to one side. "You are back with us."

"What happened?" Kate quizzed. She did not let go of Jen's hand. "The last thing I remember is…" she thought for a moment. "The last thing I remember is Elak disappearing beneath the river's surface."

"You fought Elak with much courage." Eldré took over the conversation.

"Did any of the Pilgers crossing the water survive?" Kate mentally pictured the rafts overturning under the huge swells of water caused by Elak suddenly rising from the river.

"No," Eldré answered. "They were all taken to a place deep beneath the surface."

"Then I failed." Kate's face crinkled up in distress.

"No," Eldré said. "Your battle with Elak was over before you even began. He wasn't trying to defeat you."

"Then what was he doing?"

"His battle was with Pilgers on the two rafts," Eldré said. "He was sent to the surface to send those Pilgers to a predetermined place. But more than that, he was to divide the Pilger forces. Once he accomplished that, you were only a distraction—a distraction he wanted to destroy."

"Is that why the Acchims retreated back to Helig?" Jen asked.

"Yes," Eldré said. "Though Elak would like to have continued after you, a force higher than him pulled him back."

"A force?" Kate asked.

"Perhaps Atasa or perhaps Rapio himself," Eldré shrugged.

Kate closed her eyes and thought back on the beast—black eyes staring at her from behind his scaly snake face, flaming three-pronged, forked tongue lashing out at her, and his teeth ready to devour her and her Maup. Shivering at the memory she asked, "Will he come back?"

"I don't know," Eldré answered honestly.

"When did you come...why are you here?" Kate's thoughts sped though her head. "You weren't here when we began the crossing."

"No, I wasn't," Eldré said.

"I called for her," Raguel said. "The injury Elak inflected on you was too powerful for our camp physician to heal. We needed Eldré's touch."

Kate slowly moved her leg. "It isn't numb anymore—a little sore, but not numb."

"By tonight you will be completely healed," Eldré said. "Elak inflects serious wounds, but the injury can be cured."

"Only with your healing gift," Raguel mumbled.

Eldré ignored Raguel's words. "You must drink more of this." She put a cup to Kate's mouth.

"Woo," Kate said pursing her lips. "Very sour." She wrinkled her nose and drank the rest of what was in the cup. "Jen!" Her face drained all its color and went deathly white. The room whirled around in a tornado fashion. "Jen!" she cried out.

"I'm here," Jen squeezed Kate's hand.

Eldré set the cup on the floor. "You will feel strange for a minute while the liquid does its work."

"Wow!" Kate said. As suddenly as the merry-go-round feeling began, it stopped. "Strange doesn't even begin to describe that journey."

"You okay?" Jen leaned into Kate's face.

"Yea, but don't think I want to climb on that E-ride again." Kate gave Jen a crinkled smile.

"You won't," Eldré nonchalantly said. "The potion you drank protects you from Elak's slashing claws."

"That's good," Kate blinked hard. Her eyes still felt disconnected from her head.

"Your color is coming back," Jen said. She back away from Kate's face.

"What about my Maup?" Concern filled Kate's words.

"Healed and ready to fly again," Raguel said.

"Thank you, Eldré," Kate whispered. "Thank you, Amicus."

Eldré gave Kate a crooked smile. "You're welcome, my friend."

"Eldré! Eldré!" Nerkon walked rapidly into the room. "You…all of you need to come to the river's edge."

"What is it?" Eldré asked.

"One of the warriors who was on a raft crossing the river, and pulled to its depths, has stumbled from the water. He appears to be confused and disorientated."

Eldré patted Kate's hand, "Rest and be strong for the upcoming battle." Offering Kate an ever so slight grin, she quickly followed Nerkon out of the tent.

"Help me up," Kate said to Jen.

"Eldré told you to rest," Jen said, but she knew that wasn't going to happen.

Kate put out her hand. "Help me up. I'm going."

Jen did not argue with Kate. If the situation were reversed, she would not stay down when everyone else was going toward trouble. She grabbed Kate's hand and gently pulled her up.

"At least lean on me for support," Jen said.

"Deal," Kate agreed. Her legs wobbled when she stood. "Let's go." She put her arm around Jen's shoulder.

Jen walked slowly at first but realized Kate was taking bigger steps than her. "I think your leg is healing faster than Eldré imagined."

"I'm fine," Kate said. "Let's catch up with everyone."

"Okay," Jen said. "Just hold on."

Within two minutes they joined the others dashing toward the warrior who had staggered from the depths of the river and now sat in the wet sand of the river bank. Nearing the river, they pushed through the Pilgers who formed a semicircle around the sobbing warrior.

"Ish," Jen whispered. "He looks terrible."

The baffled warrior's body was covered with green tumors. Black streaks exploded from each pus-filled, ulcerated boil, and then spider-veined across his skin.

"Tell me what happened." Eldré knelt beside the young warrior.

"Abyss…fire…trumpets," he mumbled. He looked directly at Eldré, but could not see her through his clouded pupils.

"Did you see Rapio," Eldré asked. All she saw in his eyes was a deep, hollow chasm. The clouded-cover over his pupils concealed where he had been, but did not hide the darkness, boring into the warrior's soul.

"No…no…no," the bewildered warrior stuttered out the words. "Maltzurra…Maltzurra…"

"Maltzurra!" Eldré spat out.

"Who is Maltzurra?" Jen whispered to Raguel.

"Rapio has thirteen Elite Imperial Knights. They serve as his elite guards. Maltzurra is the highest of Rapio's knights—his personal knight," Raguel answered. "He is depraved and carries out Rapio's cruel deeds."

"Abyss…fire…" the warrior repeated.

"And you chose the fire?" Eldré stated as much as asked.

"Yes…tell the Eagle…tell him I went into the fire…" His words faded.

"I will tell him," Eldré said.

The warrior's eyes rolled back into their sockets. Thick putrid smelling blood, mixed with greenish-black scum, gushed from his nose, mouth and eye sockets. Small creatures that looked like micro scorpions crawled from the scum and evaporated into the wet sand.

"He is gone," Eldré said. She put her hand over his eyes and muttered words that neither Kate nor Jen understood.

"I will take care of him," Petri said. The elf-like monk stepped from the crowd.

"Thank you," Eldré said.

The Pilgers who stood close by now slowly backed up. Whatever their fellow Pilger warrior had seen and gone though put fear into them. The same fate awaited them in the river.

"We must not wait," Eldré said to Nerkon. "We must find a way to cross the river." She stood and walked away from the river's edge.

"Agreed!" Nerkon said. He studied each of his warriors who stood around the dead Pilger. Like with the Bás Plague, if he did not do something immediately, their desire to complete The Mission would be destroyed. He followed Eldré, motioning to Kate, Jen and Raguel to come with them.

"We have no choice," Eldré told Nerkon once they were within the confines of his tent. "We must send someone into the river to find out how to stop the Bás and how we can cross the river without Elak striking us."

Filtering in from outside were the knights of highest order. Whatever was decided within this tent would affect them.

"As you saw with the warrior who escaped," Nerkon told Eldré, "there are only two choices once someone enters that domain. You either submit to Rapio's ghastly eternity or die a horrendous death from the Bás that is put into those who enter the depths."

"Yet," Eldré continued, "if someone does not go into the river and find a way…" she paused to think of the right words. "If someone does not go into the river and find a way to defeat the Bás, The Mission will be lost. If The Mission is lost, the holy city of Helig is lost."

"And Rapio…" Nerkon looked at his knights.

"And Rapio," Eldré finished his sentence, "will spread his Bás throughout Bigna."

The knights stood stiffly and silently. Each knight knew it would be one of them who would take this journey—a final journey into eternal death. They drew a community deep breath and waited for someone to step forward.

"I will go."

All eyes turned toward the voice.

"No," Jen said.

"I will go," Kate stepped away from Jen and toward Eldré. "It makes sense for me to be the one to go. First Rubidus chose me out—then Elak. I have a personal investment in this mission."

"No," Jen repeated herself.

The silence from the motionless knights was broken up only by their heavy breathing. They waited for either Nerkon or Eldré to respond.

"Kate is right," Eldré finally said. "She is the one who must go."

"Then I will go with her," Jen declared.

"You will be with her, but you will not go beneath the water with her," Eldré said.

"How…what do you mean?" Jen asked.

"You will hold her hand so when she needs to come back in a hurry you will be able to pull her back to us. Your lockets will keep you connected."

"Kate," Jen turned to her cousin. "Are you sure?"

"I guess," Kate smiled. "And Eldré gave me the potion so Elak can no longer harm me with his giant claws."

"That is true, "Eldré said. "But you must know and remember that Atasa and Rapio still can harm you. And the potion does not immune you from the Bás."

"Kate…" Jen did not have words for the uneasiness she felt.

"I will be okay," Kate assured Jen. "You will be with me."

"But how will she breathe beneath the water?" Jen asked. The realism of being underwater and not breathing hit her.

"Once you go into the Senvolte River, hold your breath for as long as you can," Eldré turned her attention directly to Kate. "You will be pulled into Rapio's domain. When you can no longer hold the air in, let it out and take a deep breath. Though the matter you fill your lungs with will be stale, you will be able to breathe."

"As long as I can breathe," Kate said, "and as long as Jen holds on to me, I'll be okay."

Jen could see in Kate's eyes that she was convincing herself as much as trying to convince others.

"Once you are Rapio's world you will see three valleys…" Eldré began.

"Three valleys?" Kate interrupted. "How will I know which way to go?"

"The three valleys," Eldré ignored Kate's question and continue, "are the three stages of the Bás. You must go through all three valleys to reach a cave—the cave of Rapio's domain. Deep inside the cave is the Beldur Chamber." She looked at Kate to be sure she wasn't going to interrupt again.

Kate stood motionless.

"The three valleys are the three stages of the Bás," Eldré repeated. "The first valley you come upon is where everyone who is lured into Rapio's world begins their dark journey. Instantly, the Bás toxic microorganisms are put into them and poison the Quae's blood system. Their skin sensations are lost because of the damage the stings of the micro Bás cause to the nerves. The weak do not resist and succumb to Rapio in just a few minutes. Often, he sends these weak back into the above-ground world with a curse hung on them—the black mole with a micro-scorpion Bás in it. With control of the Quae, the Bás scorpion manipulates the Quae into carrying out Rapio's depraved desires."

Again Eldré looked at Kate. This time she searched Kate's soul to see if she wavered in her decision to go beneath the water.

Kate wasn't moving.

"Any Quae who resists and survives the first valley is sent into the second valley," Eldré said. "There the Quae has problems breathing and have a great desire to sleep. Rapio knows once they fall asleep, the Quae is his. Stronger Quae try to keep others awake. In this stage resistance will only last, at most, one day. Irregular skin lesions begin to form and cause more nerve loss. A weakness of physical strength is common. Nasal congestion and nose bleeds begin.

"If resistance is strong, the Quae is transformed to the third and last valley—the valley of the final Bás stage. It is brought on in an insidious form to those who survive the first two onsets. It shows its signs by swelling spots on their neck. The growths begin as a red patchy rash that forms into small burgundy spots. The spots swell and knot, turning dark green. The growths are fast growing and ugly. The growths on the neck are followed by smaller ones erupting all over the body. Black veins streak from tumor to tumor, pulsating vile liquid within the Quae's body. Mental disorientation and hallucinations overtake the Quae. Resistance is usually no more than a few hours. In this stage, the Quae becomes so repulsive, others in the valley show the Quae total rejection—therefore the Quae becomes isolated, not only mentally but physically as well."

"And this was the stage the warrior was in when he came out of the river?" Jen asked.

"Yes," Eldré answered.

"You said resistance was impossible," Jen stated. "How did he..."

"I didn't say resistance was impossible," Eldré cut in. "I said resistance only lasted a few hours. But those few hours seem like days, even weeks, to the Quae who is being persecuted. In each valley if the Quae is not broken in a couple of hours, they are taken to a more macabre valley where they will suffer to the point of obedience."

"Then how did the warrior escape?" Kate's hope for finding out what she needed to do below the surface of the river and returning to the camp heightened.

"There was only one way for him to escape." Eldré explained.

"How was that?" Kate asked.

"The Wall of Fire," Eldré answered.

"The Wall of Fire?" Jen's words dripped apprehension. "That is what the warrior said."

"That was his only choice, yet he knew it would mean death," Eldré said.

"Is that how...how Kate will come back to us?" Jen's words no longer were steady.

"If it comes to that," Eldré said, "she will know what to do."

"Will Kate have to go into the Wall of Fire?" Jen repeated her question.

"You and Kate will be connected," Eldré answered. "When the time comes you will be able to pull her back to us."

"Once I go through the three valleys and find the cave, what am I looking for?" Kate asked. "How will I find the Beldur Chamber?"

"When you find the cave, you must find a way in," Eldré answered. "Once inside you will see many chambers, but you will have to go deep into the bowels of the cave to find the Beldur Chamber. Look to your locket to give you guidance."

"How will I know which chamber is the right one?" Kate repeated her question.

"The gateway to Rapio's chamber is a triangular door."

"Triangle door," Kate mulled aloud.

"Yes," Eldré responded. "You will find the answers to your questions inside the Beldur Chamber."

"What is inside the Beldur Chamber?" Jen asked.

"The Beldur Chamber is the heart of area beneath the river. In it is Rapio's throne room."

"Kate..." Jen began.

"It's okay," Kate interrupted her. "I am the one who must go...and Eldré said we will be touching all the time."

"I will be with you," Jen said, but her words were to reassure herself as much as Kate.

Chapter Twenty-eight

Raguel grabbed Jen's hand and put it on Kate's wrist. "You must not let go of Kate," he instructed. "And neither of you can let your lockets become loosened from your necks."

"I won't let go of you," Jen reassured Kate. She grasped Kate's wrist tight.

"And I won't let go of you," Kate said, reciprocating by grasping Jen's wrist so they clasped each other in a tight hand-to-wrist hold.

"Kate," Eldré said. "You will be tormented by thirst. No matter how thirsty you get, you must not drink any water once you slip beneath the water of the Senvolte River. The water will feel, smell and look cool, but it will turn to salt in your mouth. It will be just one of many allusions you will encounter once you are below."

"I will be careful," Kate assured Eldré.

"You will be tempted by many things, but remember to look to your locket."

Instinctively Kate reached for her locket. It was still around her neck, giving her comfort.

"It is time to go," Eldré said.

At the edge of the river Kate gave Jen a small smile.

Jen tried to smile back, but only one corner of her mouth rose.

"I'll be okay," Kate said. "Just don't let go of me."

"Never!" Jen tightened her grip on Kate's wrist.

The two moons of Bigna rose above the horizon, pulling a blanket of stars behind them. The Quae Knights who watched admired what Kate was going to do. One of their youngest knights was going to fight whatever evils were beneath the water of the Senvolte River. They knelt in prayer.

Kate inhaled deeply and slipped into the water. The inky, indigo blackness of the river pulled Kate into an eddy of darkness. She tumbled uncontrollably into a whirlwind of spinning, sticky, spider web substance that stuck to her skin and wrapped around her. The sound of one thousand timpani drums inside an orchestra hall reverberated through her head. Pounding on her chest made her exhale sharply.

Cough…cough…cough!

Gasping for breath, she found, as Eldré had said, the air—or whatever the matter was—was stale but she could breathe.

The deafening drums gave way to an eerie musical sound.

Waaaaa—waaaa!

"A trumpet," Kate uttered. "A trumpet crying out for me."

Waaaaa—waaaa!

"Where is it?" she spun her head around trying to locate the sound. But nothing was clear. She grabbed her locket but could not open it.

Eerie figures floated past her waving for her to follow them.

Come…come with me…come…

A new, musical tune trilled around her head.

Come…come with me…come…

Kate wanted to go toward the sing-song voice.

So enthralled with the sirens call, she didn't notice the spinning web surrounded her legs.

Come…come with me…come…

Spider threads, ever so small, enclosed the bottom half of her body. She was becoming a cocoon.

"No!" Kate screamed aloud. "No!"

You will come!

The soft singsong tone of the faceless voice turned violently dark.

"No!" Kate struggled to free herself from the shell hemming her in.

You have disobeyed the Master!

"No!" Kate thrashed about trying to disengage herself from the voice—the unseen force. The hand that connected her to Jen radiated with energy. She must hold on, but the unseen force was too powerful. Struggling drained her strength. She held tight to her locket, but could not remain conscious. Her grip loosened and her locket floated toward the surface of the water.

Kate went limp.

The power of the water and the strength of an unseen force tugged at Jen's hand. Kate was being wrenched away from her.

"I'm losing her!" Jen yelled. "She's sliding away!"

"Do not let go," Eldré responded.

"I won't!" Jen felt Kate's hand slide further from her grasp. "Something… there is a force stronger than my grip."

"Rapio's control is too strong for just one of you to fight him in his domain." Eldré knew from past experience of Rapio's power.

"I've got to do something to save her." Tears formed in Jen's eyes. She dug her heels into the slushy sand of the river bank. "What can I do?"

"Do you still have her hand?" Eldré asked.

"Yes, but barely." Jen was now pulling on Kate's slipping hand.

"You must go under with her. It is our only hope." Eldré announced.

"Anything," Jen said. She did not stop to dwell on the dangers below. "Anything to help Kate."

Raguel put his arms around Jen's waist to help anchor her. But skid marks formed in the sand where they slipped into the indigo water's edge.

"Quick!" Raguel said. "Do not let go of Kate's hand, but let me lash your other hand and wrist to mine." He grabbed a leather throng from around his boots and quickly wrapped it around Jen's wrist. Tightening it he said, "I will not let go of you."

Eldré grabbed Jen's locket tight in her small hand. "May the Eagle watch over you!" She put her other hand on the leather connecting Raguel to Jen. "And may the two of you never part!"

"I will not let go," Raguel restated. "I will bring you back to this land."

"Go!" Eldré said. "We'll be praying for you."

"Yes," Raguel agreed. "Our prayers are with you."

Taking a deep breath Jen did not let go of Kate's hand, but let herself slip into the murky water.

Chapter Twenty-nine

*P*ressure pushed into Jen's chest the deeper into the water she went. Air being sucked from her lungs, she felt they would collapse inside her burning chest. Dizziness from lack of oxygen filled her head with incoherent thoughts. She tried to pull a breath into her lungs, but the unseen force grew tighter on her chest.

From the tip of her toes the sensation of tiny insects slowly crawled up her legs until her whole body was covered with the pain of prickly pins and needles.

Jen's tongue swelled with an unquenchable thirst. Fighting the pain, she tried to make sense of the waves of different sensations flowing over her. She was rapidly losing consciousness, but she fought to hold on to Kate's hand.

Around her neck Jen's locket warmed and then glowed. From the indigo blackness of the water a pinpoint of light flashed. Her locket stretched out and locked onto the pulsating burst of light. A pencil thin beam formed between her locket and the light. Her locket towed her along the lifeline. The force tightening around her chest struggled with her locket for Jen's life, but the locket did not waver from its path toward the shinny object it sought.

The force surrounding Jen's body gave one last crushing squeeze on her chest. She watched bubbles rise from her nose and mouth. Unnerved by seeing the last amount of her oxygen slowly rise to the surface, she gave into the pressure and gasped to suck in air. To her surprise, a life-giving substance filled her lungs. Tingling and numbness crept over her body, replacing the pain of stinging insects.

The inky blackness of the murky water gave up the fight with Jen and pushed her out onto a small space. Unhindered by the struggle with the unseen force, she found herself wedged between a bolder and Kate. She still clung to Kate's wrist, but Kate's hand was limp and unconscious.

"Kate?" Jen shook Kate's shoulder. "Kate?"

"Ugghhhhhh…" Kate groaned.

"Kate," Jen sighed. "Thank God, you're alive."

"Jen? What are you doing here?" The familiar sound of Jen's voice stirred Kate to a blurry consciousness. "What happened?" She raised her head but fell back. "My mouth…filled with cotton…thirsty…I'm so thirsty…"

"Don't move," Jen commanded.

"Where…" but words didn't come to Kate.

"Lie still," Jen repeated her command. She looked around. A bubbling brook flowed next to them. It was crystal-clear blue and its coolness blew over their bodies. "Stay still."

Jen cupped her hands and scooped up the thirst quenching sparking liquid.

"No!" Kate hoarsely whispered, knocking the water from Jen's hands. Her memory slowly crept back into her mind. "Remember what Eldré said; *don't drink any water once you slip beneath the water of the Senvolte River.*"

"I momentarily forgot," Jen said. She looked at the ground where the water splashed from her hands. Crusty salt crystals grew into small stalagmites. The stream evaporated, leaving a pencil thin drizzle of water seeping into the ground. "My mind became confused and I wasn't thinking straight." She quickly wiped her hands on her pants. "Eldré was right about the strange things and allusions."

"We'll have to watch each other closely," Kate said. "We are in Rapio's domain. Temptation will abound and we must overcome whatever is thrown at us. We have to look to our lockets to give us guidance and strength."

"It's gone!" Jen's voice was filled with alarm when she looked at her wrist.

"Your locket is gone?" The alarm in Kate's voice matched Jen's.

"No…no…not my locket." Jen put her hand on her neck to feel the assurance her locket was still there.

"Then what's gone?" Kate asked.

"The leather throng connecting me to Raguel."

"Leather throng?" Kate questioned. "Raguel? And what are you doing here?"

Jen realized Kate did not understand. "As soon as you went into the water, your hand began slipping from my grip. I was losing you…"

"Oh, that is what I felt," Kate said. "When I went under a force hit me and I became disorientated and started hallucinating. The force began communicating with me…it was…it was a soothing…singing voice. I didn't want to resist the call to follow…to follow the voice. I felt myself drifting…drifting into a beautiful, angel-hair like web. I was spinning and spinning—being wrapped inside the spun glass cloud. Suddenly the voice turned dark…evil, telling me I had not been obedient. I couldn't hold on to a logical thought, and unconsciousness started to overtake me. As I struggled with the force I felt a strong pull on the hand that you held. It was as if the force and you were fighting for me."

"That must have been when I felt your hand slipping from mine," Jen shivered. "I was afraid I was losing you…" She put her hand on Kate's hand. "I was terrified you would be lost to…to whatever is below the Senvolte River."

Kate semi-smiled. "But you didn't give up. You didn't let go. You came after me."

Jen squeezed Kate's hand. "We're a team, cousin."

"Yes, we are," Kate smiled. "After I felt the struggle for my hand, I went unconscious."

"I found you unconscious," Jen said.

"Oh," Kate said. "I remember something else. Just before I went unconscious my locket pulled tight against its chain and floated toward the surface of the river—like it was searching for something. I felt an energy coming from it—connecting it to something."

"That must have been when Eldré prayed over my locket and the leather thong connecting me to Raguel."

"My locket was searching for yours," Kate stated.

"After I slipped into the water I saw a small light flash," Jen said. "That must have been your locket because mine stretched out and locked onto the pulsating light. Our lockets linked together and guided me to you." Jen looked at her wrist again. "But the leather thong was our connection to the world above the river. How will we get back?"

Kate examined Jen's wrist. A slight glow shimmered from where Raguel had lashed them together.

"Maybe it's still here." Kate touched Jen's wrist. Glitter-like flakes floated upward. "I think we'll just have to have faith you and Raguel are still connected."

Jen touched her wrist. Tightness tugged at her hand and more sparkling flakes rose. "Faith we'll have."

"I wonder where we go from here," Kate pondered. She sat upright and leaned back against the boulder, but quickly moved away. "What is that?"

"Nothing good," Jen answered. She leaned closer to the boulder, and then examined the rock walls around them. They dripped with slime, the same putrid-smelling, greenish-black scum that gushed from the warrior's nose and mouth who stumbled out of the river. Micro-scorpions moved inside the slime.

"Don't touch the walls!" Kate exclaimed.

"Not to worry," Jen replied. "Yuck." She stood and took a step backwards. The rock she stepped on moved beneath her foot.

"Don't..." Kate yelled and pulled Jen toward her.

"What?" Jen asked.

"The stone you stepped on isn't a stone at all," Kate said. "Look!"

Jen glared at the rock that Kate had pulled her off. It looked like the rest of the orange brown incrusted rocks on the path where she stood, but it suddenly wriggled sideways and jetted off into the distance.

"What was that?" Jen asked

"Some sort of a Stonefish I would imagine," Kate answered.

"Stonefish?"

"If you disturbed it, it would have put up its spines and stung you. If it is like an Earth World Stonefish, its venom is deadly. At best it would have temporarily paralyzed you."

"At best?" Jen raised one eyebrow.

"It didn't happen," Kate gave a halfway grin. "But we will have to be extra careful while we are down here."

Jen continued to look in the direction where the Stonefish had disappeared.

"I think we need to look to our lockets," Kate said. "We seem to be at a loss as to directions and a plan."

"Agreed." Jen opened her locket to get a bearing. Before her was the place where she stood. A path led away from the boulder they hid behind. "I guess it's onward." She stretched her neck and offered Kate her hand.

"Thanks," Kate pulled herself up. Standing she got a better view of the dark chasms of Rapio's realm. They stood on the edge of a cliff that overlooked a series of three small valleys below. Smoke rose from fires in various campsites. The activity of creatures moving about was abundant, but in slow motion. At the far end of the strange scene was a ghostly mountain with one huge entrance.

High above them the Indigo blue of the river met a cobalt substance in a whirlpool of a violent storm. Flashes of red lightning collided with bolts of white lighting in a battle for the area. "Are we in the Obex?" Jen asked. "I don't know," Kate answered. She surveyed the celestial-type sphere they were under. The dark gray sky was streaked with the green-blue of the Obex instead of sparking stars. The combating red and white lighting rumbled in the distance. "It has the look of the Obex, but we are not being wildly tossed about."

"Perhaps it is a different part of the Obex." Jen frowned.

"Perhaps we have been pulled to the underside of the Obex—into a worse place than the Obex itself."

"No doubt this is a worse place," Kate agreed. "Not as physically violent, but much more spine-chilling. We were sent here to find out how the Bás can be defeated and how the Pilgers can cross the Senvolte River so they can conquer Helig. I suppose we need head forward."

"Does your locket show anything more than mine?" Jen asked.

"The same path," Kate said. "It seems to be leading us through the valleys toward that mountain with the entrance."

"Do you think that is the cave entrance that will lead us to Rapio's Beldur Chamber?" Jen asked.

"We'll find out," Kate answered. "I suppose it is one foot in front of the other, trusting we will be told what to do."

"Then let's do it," Jen took a deep breath. "Ready?" She exhaled.

"Ready," Kate nodded. "At least as ready as I'll ever be."

Jen touched her wrist again. The slight tug and small shimmering glow assured her Raguel was still with them.

Chapter Thirty

*T*he air hung with the smell of decaying creatures—a stench that stuck in Kate's and Jen's nostrils as they made their way into the first valley. The color of the valley was dirt brown—creating the vision of a grim and neglected place. Lean-to tents gave the Quae, who were scattered randomly in the valley, a small amount of shelter from the cold, drafty refuge for the short time they would be in this purgatory. The air hung chilly and uncomfortable, yet a desert hot wind whistled through the camp.

Huddles of Quae squatted next to multitudes of campfires. They clustered together in hopes of understanding their fate.

"Look over there," Kate said, nodding in the direction of one of the campfires. "That group looks like three of Sir Begi's warriors who were on the third raft."

"Let's see if they know what is going on," Jen said.

Kate and Jen walked fifty yards and stopped short of the campfire. The three Quae stared into the flames that licked around the sides of the ever-burning logs. Two of the warriors looked up occasionally at any movement around them but did not speak. Fear and desolation covered their faces.

"What is this camp?" Jen asked one of the Quae warriors.

"Go away," the Quae warrior responded.

"We're here to help," Jen offered.

"You cannot help us," the warrior moaned. "There is no help for us."

"We are traveling toward death," the second warrior said. His eyes reflected his words.

"They have accepted their fate," the third warrior said. He did not look up from staring at the firefly embers crackling from the burning logs.

"You will too, Odo," the first warrior sobbed. "You will too."

"Odo?" Kate turned to the one they called by name. "Aren't you a First Centurion in Sir Obile's army?"

"Yes," Odo answered. "Or at least I was before I was sucked beneath the water."

"What does he mean…that you will accept your fate too?" Jen asked.

"See." Odo pulled at his sleeve to show them an ulcerated red rash. "We all have this and yet we cannot physically feel anything anymore. But inside us the pain is unbearable."

"What happened?" Kate asked.

"When we were pulled beneath the water, we were tossed to and fro and then spit out onto this desert sand," Odo began his answer. "As far as I can understand, it is a place between life and death. Within seconds we were covered with small scorpion-like creatures. They quickly buried their scaly bodies under our skin. I was at Stur when the Bás infected the city. These bugs looked and affected us the same, only ten times as bad. We became weak and hallucinatory."

"We believe the bugs are Bás scorpions," Kate said. "Only these Bás scorpions have much stronger venom to infect you than the ones at Stur."

"I know," Odo agreed. "Most of the warriors on the raft with us went crazy and did not resist the scorpions. The hot wind that continually blows through the camp is the dark voice that lures the weak to succumb to the Bás. Once you surrender, the skin lesions disappear and the many scorpions are replaced by a black mole with one micro-scorpion in it."

Kate looked around for someone who had been healed, but everyone in her eyesight was weak and covered in the same ulcerated rash as Odo and his two companions.

"How do you know this?" Kate asked.

"We have watched it happen to all those who surrender," Odo answered. "The hot wind whispers constantly in our ears about our destiny."

"What does it say?" Jen asked.

203

"To surrender and we can join our family above the river," Odo answered.

"To surrender?" Kate's eyebrow went up. "To what? To who?"

"Rapio!" Odo spit out his one word, simple answer.

Aaargh…

Aaargh…

The two warriors who warmed themselves by the fire fell to their knees. Odo stepped away from them. He motioned for Kate and Jen to step back.

"There is nothing you can do for them," Odo declared.

Aaargh…

Aaargh…

The two warriors grabbed their necks and wreathed around on the ground. They collapsed face first into the sand. Raising their heads they uttered in unison, *Rapio.* Instantly their bodies cleared of the rash and a black mole appeared on their neck. Even from the twelve feet separating them, Jen could see the baby Bás squirming inside the warriors' moles.

And then the two Quae warriors evaporated.

"What…?" Kate blinked in disbelief.

"They are now in Rapio's service," Odo said. "This," he waved his hand around to indicate the desolate land where they stood, "is a place where we are brought to exist between life and death. Rapio keeps us alive, but we are forced to choose between life as his follower or an unpleasant death. Once we were pulled beneath the water and entered his domain our fate has been to bow before him or die. If you bow down, you may be sent back above the river to spread the Bás."

"Like Rubidus," Kate stated.

"Yes, Rubidus was controlled by a Bás," Odo stated. "Once controlled, Rapio gives each Quae a limited power to show miraculous-looking signs to get others to follow. I watched it in Rubidus, but I finally figured out that his signs were false, a magician's trickery. Rapio controls the individual through controlling the micro-scorpion because he communicates with the scorpion."

"You said that once a Quae bows down he may be sent back above the river," Kate said. "What happens to those who submit and are not sent above the river?"

"I don't know for sure," Odo said, "but it is whispered that Rapio keeps others in slavery down here to someday become part of the final war —Război."

"But you have not succumbed to the Bás," Jen stated.

"No," Odo said, "but I do not live under any allusion that I have escaped. My fate has yet to be decided."

Shreeeeeeeeeeeeee!

The hot wind that wafted through the camp shrieked a wicked cry and kicked up the sand into a small tornado. Bodiless and eyeless it focused its attention on Kate, Jen and Odo. Working itself into a fury, it picked up speed and, like a skilled surgeon, cut between Kate and Jen and took Odo off in its whirling path. As quick as it had whipped into a raging tornado, it quieted back into a whistling hot wind.

"Where did Odo go?" Jen asked.

"According to what Eldré said, if a Quae fights and survives this valley, he will be sent to a second valley," Kate answered.

"We need to hurry on though the next valleys," Jen said. She fingered her locket. "Our object is not the valleys but the Beldur Chamber inside the cave at the far side of the three valleys."

Kate stayed close to Jen as they climbed the hillside until they reach the peak of the hill overlooking the second valley. Unlike the dirt brown first valley, the second valley was green and lush.

"Didn't expect this," Jen said. "It's almost beautiful."

"It is…" Kate began, "but let's be cautious as we cross it."

Halfway down the hill Kate slipped but caught herself before she stumbled down the rest of the way.

Kneeling on one knee, she smiled up at Jen. "This velvety moss' silky texture is just as slippery and hard to walk on as the moss we first saw in Gudsrika."

"Moss?" Jen's left eyebrow rose. "Gudsrika?"

"Yes, isn't it beautiful?" Kate fingered the fuzzy-soft, damp green carpet her knee sank into. "I can almost see Raguel showing us stepping stones." She laughed at the memory of Gudsrika.

"Kate?" Jen's words were measured. "I don't see moss."

"You don't?" Kate asked. "But you said it was beautiful."

"All around me are the blue flowers with yellow centers that we first saw on Gudsrika," Jen said. "They are beautiful; in fact I can smell their clove-like scent." She inhaled deeply. Her head filled with the delightful smell and made her eyes close. "I could easily curl up in this blanket of flowers and take a nap."

"Jen!" Kate jumped up. "We are seeing what we want to see. We are hallucinating."

"Hallucinating?"

"Remember Eldré said we would encounter many allusions and tempted by many things," Kate said.

"Yes, I remember," Jen nodded. "And she said to turn to our lockets." She put her open hand on her locket.

"Didn't she say when someone enters the second valley they have problems breathing and have a desire to sleep?"

"Yes, but what does that have to do with us seeing moss and blue flowers?"

"You just said you would like to curl up and take a nap." Kate's shook her head to clear her thoughts. "I believe there is something in this valley to cause hypnogogic hallucinations…"

"Hypno…what?" Jen queried.

"Hypnogogic hallucinations," Kate explained, "are hallucinations that occur just before someone goes to sleep. You can see, hear, feel and even smell the hallucination. They cause confusion and may even cause sleep paralysis, where you become physically unable to move. That would go along with what Eldré said—a weakness of the Quae's physical strength is common in this valley. If that is what this valley is all about then, unlike the first valley where extreme pain is caused, in this valley everyone is lulled into a false sense of joy—of serenity. With that peace they have a great desire to sleep. Eldré said that Rapio knows once they fall asleep the Quae is his."

"Then none of this is real," Jen stated. She stooped, picked a blue flower and held it to her nose. "I can smell the strong scent of cloves."

"And yet to me, you are holding nothing and are sniffing at your fingers," Kate said.

Jen snapped her hand open and let the cool breeze she felt blow the imaginary flower from her fingers. Though she could see and smell the flower, Kate was right, she held nothing.

"Take my hand," Kate said. "And hold on to your locket with your other hand. Hopefully, our lockets can break the hallucinatory power."

Jen did as Kate told her. The earth beneath their feet shook violently for a moment, knocking them to the ground. The hallucinations of blue flowers and velvety green moss whirled around them in a blur of brilliant colors. They held tightly onto each other and their lockets. A flash of colored sheet-lightening lit the air around them and then dissipated.

Stillness created a vacuum around them.

"Jen," Kate whispered. "Open your eyes."

"There is no beauty…no velvety moss…no scented flowers," Jen said.

Their hallucinations stripped away, the second valley had the hint of the look of the first—the color of dirt brown and ash gray. But this valley was even more grim and neglected as the first one. The same chilly air hung on them and the same hot wind whistled through the valley, yet this one looked as if a raging fire had scorched the ground. A hostile, colorless mountain, with spiky peaks, circled around them, threatening their very existence.

"Kate, are you okay?" Jen asked

"I think so," Kate answered. "I'm a little woozy, but I think I'm okay."

Jen stared at Kate. "You look a little pale." She touched Kate's face. "And you feel clammy."

"Maybe a little residue from the hallucination," Kate smiled, but her insides were racing with anxiety. "I'm okay." Her statement was for her as much as for Jen.

Jen read Kate's face and knew she wasn't being forthright, but also knew they had to push on. "Promise you'll tell me if you feel worse."

"I promise," Kate held up her right hand to gesture a solemn assurance.

"Look!" Jen exclaimed. "There's Odo." She pointed toward a rock outcropping with Odo leaning up against it. "Let's see what he has found out about this valley."

"If he has found out anything," Kate uttered her questionable validation of seeing Odo.

"Odo," Jen yelled out to the Pilger warrior. "Odo."

Kate and Jen jogged toward Odo.

"Kate! Jen!" Odo called to them. "You have found this paradise."

"Odo you must fight this," Kate said to him. "This is not a paradise, it is a hallucination."

"No," Odo smiled. "See the beautiful oak tree I lean against." He stroked the gray rock. "And look at the clear, blue lake before us—listen to the soft sound of the lyres playing music."

"No, Odo," Kate said. "It is not real."

"But it is," Odo grinned. "It is just as I remember the country of my youth."

"Odo," Jen joined in. "You must fight what you see—what you smell— what you hear. It is not real."

"Come," Odo ignored their words. "Come sit with me on the grassy shore." He lay down and closed his eyes. "I'm so tired." His body shuddered involuntarily as he relaxed.

"Jen," Kate yelled. "We've got to get him on his feet and keep him awake. His muscles have begun twitching which means he is beginning to fall asleep. If he does, he will belong to Rapio."

Together they pulled Odo to his feet and walked him for a few minutes.

"Odo!" Jen yelled in hopes of reaching his subconscious. "Odo!"

He responded by physically jerking himself awake.

"What?" Odo stared at Kate and Jen. "Where are we?" He slumped down to the ground. "It was beautiful, but now it is ugly."

"He is no longer hallucinating," Kate said. "We have awakened him back to reality."

"What is happening to me?" Odo asked.

"You have fought the power of Rapio in his second valley and you have won," Jen said.

"Won?" Odo questioned. "What have I won? And at what price?"

"You have beaten Rapio," Jen said. She did not want to think about the price Odo might pay.

"I have never heard of a Pilger beating Rapio," Odo's face saddened. "Maybe it would have been better to give in to him while I was in this valley." He looked at the skin lesions forming on his body. Red patchy spots on his neck began swelling into tumorous lumps. "I do not know what awaits me, but I do not think Rapio will let me win again."

"You have beaten him twice, Odo," Kate encouraged him. "Whatever happens, you have won."

Shreeeeeeeeeeeeee!

The hot wind that wafted through the desert valley shrieked its wicked cry again.

Shreeeeeeeeeeeeee!

"Thank you," Odo said to Kate and Jen. "Remember me as you see me here—a victor." His breathing was irregular.

"We will," Jen said.

Shreeeeeeeeeeeeee!

"My fate is coming for me," Odo cried. "I will fight a good fight to the end." He sucked in deeply to get air into his congested nose and lungs.

Shreeeeeeeeeeeeee!

The bodiless spiteful wind did not kick up the sand into a small tornado as it had before, but snatched Odo's body off his feet and whipped him around like a ragdoll hanging from a speeding car's open window. Before Kate and Jen could grab him, he was gone.

Silence fell on the valley.

"Do you think he is strong enough to hold out in the third valley?" Jen asked.

"I don't know," Kate answered, "but I do know we also have to move on." She looked at the other Quae wandering in the valley. Most had smiles on their faces and were laying down in their allusions to sleep. Rapio had their souls for eternity.

Sssblam!

The explosiveness of a series of rockets shooting toward the gray sky filled the air.

Sssblam!

Sssblam!

Kaboom!

The dome that covered this domain streaked with orange red sheet lighting as the missiles exploded against the floor of the Obex.

Brrum—Brrum—Brrrum—

The soil rumbled beneath their feet. Surface ground waves rolled toward them at jet speed.

Brrum—Brrum—Brrrum—

"Earthquake!" Kate yelled.

"Hold on to me," Jen yelled back. She grabbed Kate and pulled her close.

The power from the moving terrain knocked them to the ground.

"Hold on," Jen repeated.

Brrum—Brrum—Brrrum—

Fissures split open the ground around them. With each ripple of the ground, Kate and Jen slipped downward. The ominous mountains that surrounded the valley crumbled. They quickly collapsed and sank into the desert surface. Something beneath the surface swallowed the mountains, creating an endless black-hole.

Sssblam!

Sssblam!

Kaboom!

Brrum—Brrum—Brrrum—

One last massive ear-shattering explosive and tsunami wave of the ground kept Kate and Jen in their prone position.

Silence!

Kate and Jen found themselves a few feet from the rim of a mammoth chasm. They inched their way to the edge of the darkness, making sure they did not get swallowed up with the debris tumbling into the sink-hole. Below them lay a steep-sided ravine, carved deep by the hot wind that was omnipresent in the other two valleys. Dark shadows from formless creatures crept eerily around the canyon walls. Low, remote wailing echoed through-out the abyss. Like the ghostly figures in the Obex, these beings echoed tormenting sounds.

"It looks like a brown and gray Grand Canyon," Jen said.

"Only the Grand Canyon is beautiful," Kate responded. "This canyon oozes of a hideous wickedness."

"Agreed," Jen said. She rolled onto her back to scan her surroundings. Everything had disappeared and they were enclosed in a vacuum of browns and grays. The land around them was flat and went on forever. Far above them was the Obex—a dark indigo blue swirling mass that formed the barrier between them and Bigna.

Without turning over she opened her locket. Before her was a non-path leading down the sides of the canyon that lead to a cave entrance at the far end of the hostile chasm. It was clear they were to go to the bottom and then on to the Beldur Chamber.

"It looks like we have to go into the abyss to find what we are looking for," Jen said.

"I'm seeing the same thing in my locket," Kate said. "And I think our destination is that glowing cavern over there."

Jen turned over to gaze into the desolate gorge below them. She saw the opening in the wall that Kate pointed to. "How could I have missed that flaming cave?"

"I think the gates are not open all the time," Kate answered. "When I first looked I did not see it, and then it suddenly appeared and those eight green luminous scorpions came out and stood guard."

Jen looked at her open locket again. A small, distant flame glowed in the vision. It had not been there when she looked before. "I think you are right. We will have to time our entrance into the cave carefully."

"Those scorpions belong to Rapio's Elite Troopers," Kate said. "See the red triangle on their chests with the raven head inside it?"

"And they are wearing blood-red helmets with the red plume on the top and carry blood-red shields blazed with the raven head on them," Jen noted.

"Except for the red plume on their helmet, they look just like Rubidus did in his jostling match with me." Kate shuttered at the memory.

While they studied the Elite Troopers, a thousand smaller green luminous scorpions spilled out of the opening of the cave. They wore black helmets with no plume flowing from the top. Their shields were black, but still were emblazed with the fiery red raven on them.

"Rapio's regular warriors?" Jen asked.

"That would be my guess," Kate answered.

"I wonder why the warriors came out of the chamber," Jen pondered aloud.

"We won't know until we get closer," Kate frowned. "Ready?"

"As ready as I'll ever be," Jen shrugged.

Chapter Thirty-one

*K*ate dug her heels deep into the dirt to keep her footing on the steep incline. Loose rocks did not make the descent into the valley any easier. Adding to her distraction was that the shadowy figures they had seen on the canyon's walls were now whirling around them in an eerie dance.

Jen's every movement down the side of the cavern was that of the surefooted athlete that she was, but she knew Kate was a little less agile. She looked back at Kate and slowed down. Jen saw in Kate's face her thoughts of the formless creatures. "Try to ignore them. I don't believe they are here to hurt us."

"I think you are right," Kate said. She momentarily stopped. A clammy breeze wrapped around her but did not tighten. "In fact, I think they want us to help them."

"We can't," Jen frowned.

"I know," Kate continued down the incline. "I know. We are here for something else."

At the floor of the canyon, Jen picked her way along the edge so they would not be discovered by Rapio's army that now formed a semicircle around what looked like an altar. Beside the altar was a blood-red shield blazed with a raven head on it. A black sword leaned against the shield.

The Elite Troopers marched quickly to line a pathway between the gate of the cavern and the altar. The gate again shut and faded into the side of the canyon. What once had been and opening to the inside of the mountain, now only the rockiness of the side of the canyon showed.

Jen picked a spot behind a saw-toothed bolder and squatted down. She motioned for Kate to do the same. Rapio's regular scorpion warriors stood silent and waited for the Elite Troopers to give them a signal. The eight Elite Troopers' crusty heads wagged to and fro, looking for disorder in the regular warriors.

BWEEE—BWEEE!

The signal from the Commander of the Elite Troopers was spoken.

Bweee—Bweee—Bweee!

Bweee—Bweee—Bweee!

Bweee—Bweee—Bweee!

The thousand warriors began their chant.

Bweee—Bweee—Bweee!

Bweee—Bweee—Bweee!

Bweee—Bweee—Bweee!

Kate and Jen put their hands over their ears to soften the nails-across-a-blackboard squeaky sound pulsating off the canyon walls in a rhythmic high pitch.

Bweee—Bweee—Bweee!

Bweee—Bweee—Bweee!

Bweee—Bweee—Bweee!

The cadenced became louder. The thousand green luminous scorpions stomped their heavy, clawed feet in the tempo of their chant. Dirt puffed up from the heavy pounding of their in-place march.

Baraaaaaag!

The blast from an elephant trumpet echoed over Rapio's scorpion army.

Instant silence.

Instant stillness.

The gate to Rapio's domain once again appeared in the walls of the canyon.

Kate shifted her position. "What's happening?"

"Don't know," Jen said, "but all eyes are on that gate."

Baraaaaaag!

A second bass-sounding blast from the trumpet rang out.

Creeeak!

A harsh sound of rusty hinges on the huge gate resounded its opening.

Creeeak!

For a moment the open gate indicated only a black void inside the cave.

Sssblam!

Sssblam!

Kaboom!

The same explosiveness of the sheet-lighting Kate and Jen heard and saw when the second valley gobbled itself up and fell into the black hole, spilled out from the cavern. Kate and Jen scrunched lower behind the rock and grabbed each other's hand. The energy waves from the explosion whipped around their protective boulder, kicking up small rocks and the ash-like dirt near them.

Sssblam!

Sssblam!

Kaboom!

Kate and Jen peeked around the boulder. From the mist of the orange-red fiery substance lighting up the opening of the chamber, a figure emerged.

"Oh!" Kate gasped.

Daunting, the figure wore a black ankle length robe with an over tunic of blood red. Black onyx stones formed the profile of the head of a raven on the glowing gold breastplate that hung from his neck. The raven's eye, a single ruby, reflected a connection to a sinister lord. A black turban, with a gold headband, sat on his head. In his right hand he held a scepter with a golden raven at the end. His left hand was covered with a golden gauntlet, which he formed into a fist.

But more disturbing to Kate and Jen was the figure had the head of a raven, yet the bare feet protruding at the bottom of the robe was that of a Quae. This figure was part raven and part Quae.

"Onde," Jen whispered. "Rapio's high priest."

Onde thrust both arms into the air and marched toward the altar.

The Elite Troopers bowed as he passed them. The warriors in the regular army followed suit. Upon reaching the raised altar, he pointed his scepter toward the chamber opening and then to the canyon wall behind the regular army.

"Rapio is the one!" Onde shouted out. "Rapio!"

Sssblam!

Sssblam!

The orange-red fiery substance lighting up the opening of the chamber streaked over the bowing army and hit the wall behind them. The wall exploded into a fiery furnace. Flares of hot gases sizzled white from the intense heat. Scales on the bodies of the scorpion warriors closest to the wall crackled and smoldered, but the warriors knew not to move. To do so would bring instant death from the Elite Troopers.

Onde once again pointed his scepter toward the opening leading to the Beldur Chamber and raised his golden gauntlet-covered hand. Again he closed his gold-covered fist.

"Bring out the slave!" Onde yelled. "He will be an example to all!"

Maltzurra, Rapio's personal knight, stepped from the opening. A head taller than the Elite Troopers, his scorpion scales were deep red, giving him the look of wearing armor. A bright yellow plume was attached to the top of his red helmet. His blood red shield blazed with a fiery red raven. He raised his black steel sword over his head.

"Rapio!" Maltzurra shouted. He then tugged on a chain that held the slave.

A weak form stumbled from the darkness into the blazing light from the fire wall. He covered his eyes to protect them from the heat. Looking around he showed signs of mental disorientation. His body was covered in dark green tumors. Black veins streaked from one tumor to another one, pulsating Bás scorpions through the liquid of his body.

"Oh no," Kate muffled her cry. "Odo."

Jen stared in disbelief. They had freed him from his pleasant hallucinations of the second valley to suffer this fate. She felt Kate move.

"No," Jen said. "We cannot help him."

Kate crouched down again. "I know." She lowered her head into her hands to gather her thoughts.

Jen reached over and wiped a tear from Kate's eyes. "I understand, but we have to be strong."

Bweee—Bweee—Bweee!

Bweee—Bweee—Bweee!

Bweee—Bweee—Bweee!

The sounds from the warriors grew louder as Maltzurra led Odo toward the altar.

Bweee—Bweee—Bweee!

Bweee—Bweee—Bweee!

Bweee—Bweee—Bweee!

Maltzurra bowed to Onde when he reached the altar. Onde stood tall—his eyes never strayed from Odo.

"Kneel, slave Odo," Onde ordered. "Kneel to your lord, Rapio!"

Odo did not move.

"Kneel!" Onde ordered again.

Odo straightened his back as much as he could. The black-green tumors swelled up and throbbed beyond his pain threshold, but he did not yield to Onde's command.

Aaargh!

The anguished cries of the Quae who hunkered down in fear in the third valley could be heard echoing off the steep walls of the last valley of hope for them. They felt Odo's pain every time he refused to surrender. They knew their fate would be the same as his.

Ker-thump!

The blunt side of Maltzurra's black sword hit the back of Odo's knees.

"Kneel!" Maltzurra shouted.

Odo stumbled into a kneeling position before Priest Onde. He tried to rise up, but Onde held him down with his golden gauntlet covered hand.

Maltzurra picked up the blood-red shield that leaned against the altar and laid it on the top of the raised rock structure. Grabbing the black sword, he pointed its tip toward the open, darkened cave and then handed it to the high priest Onde. The high priest waved the menacing steel sword above Odo's head. Each wave of the sword agitated the pulsating Bás scorpions within Odo.

Aaargh!

Odo could not control the anguish cry of the pain he felt, but he still controlled his thoughts.

"Yield your eternity to Rapio," Onde said.

"No...no," Odo whispered.

Onde pointed his scepter toward the fiery wall. The swirling reddish-orange, sun-hot heat flamed outward toward Odo. As if guided by tunnel vision eyes, sparks flew from the flames and stuck Odo's bare back.

Aaargh!

Odo's shriek was heard by the throngs of Quae waiting their fate.

"We can eliminate the pain—your suffering," Onde sneered.

"No..." Odo maintained, but his resolute was getting weaker.

Onde swung the steel sword from side to side of Odo's head—each swing barely missing his neck.

Aaargh!

Mercilessness, the high priest and Maltzurra watched Odo scream out as the Bás moved in rhythm of the swinging sword.

The Elite Troopers and regular army stood at attention, not daring to move, not daring to even blink. Their doom would be that of Odo's if they showed any empathetic emotion.

Aaargh!

"You have a choice," Onde soothed. "Say yes. Give your eternity to Rapio."

Aaargh!

"Say yes or you will live for eternity with the agony of the tumors—you will live for eternity with the Bás crawling inside you—forever in pain, never to be relived.

Aaargh!

Onde pointed his scepter at the flaming wall again. The hot, swirling wall exploded, spurting out fire balls flaring up to a thousand degrees. A blazing sphere rolled beside the kneeling Odo.

"Or you can always throw yourself into the unknown," Onde pointed toward the blast furnace wall.

Aaargh!

Odo's pain overtook his reasoning ability.

"Say it!" Onde ordered.

"Yes...yes," Odo whimpered. "Yes...Rapio..."

"Well done," the priest smirked. He laid the flat of the black sword blade on Odo's head. "I call you into Rapio's knighthood. I call you for Rapio's own." He waved the sword above Odo's head. "Pledge your allegiance to Rapio," he demanded.

"I pledge...I...I..." Odo still fought the battle within him.

"Louder!" Onde shouted. "Loud enough for the heavens to hear!"

"I pledge...I pledge my eternity to Rapio." Odo wept.

The deed was done.

Onde tapped Odo on his head with the black sword.

"Rise, Sir Odo," Onde ordered. "Rise to serve your lord, Rapio."

Odo rose and instantly the growths on his neck and the black veins streaking from tumor to tumor disappeared. His mental state returned. His appearance was restored to the same figure as before he was snatched beneath the Senvolte River—snatched into Rapio's hellish domain.

Onde lifted the sword from Odo's head and took the shield from beside the altar. He presented them to Odo.

Odo reluctantly put the shield on his arm and sheathed the sword. Tears streamed down his cheeks.

The High Priest Onde put his hand on Odo's neck under his left ear.

Aaargh!

The overbearing pain stunned Odo's body. He wobbled under the stabbing throbbing in his neck.

"One last thing," the high priest said. "Your shield will display the division of the Quae army you go back to. But you will carry a messenger of Rapio with you." He lifted his hand and a small black tumor remained. Inside an iridescent green dot could be seen. "Your overseer will be with you to guide you in your ways. Do not try to fight it or you will die a slow, horrified death."

Vreeeeeeeeeeeeeeeew!

With the high-pitched squeal from Onde's raven mouth, Odo disappeared.

Onde pointed his scepter toward the fiery wall and then to the opening to the chamber.

"Rapio is the one!" Onde shouted. "Rapio!"

Sssblam!

Sssblam!

The orange-red fiery substance reversed its previous act and streaked toward the dark opening of the cave. The menacing void exploded into sheet lighting and spilled onto the valley's floor, forming a flowing, hot, five-foot wide carpet between the opening and the altar. Onde stepped upon the smoldering flames and was instantly pulled into the fiery opening.

Sssblam!

Sssblam!

With one last explosion the lighting disappeared, taking Onde with it. Maltzurra quickly followed Onde.

Rapio's Elite Troopers and regular scorpion warriors marched after Maltzurra.

"What just happened?" Jen whispered.

"I don't know," Kate whispered back, "but we need to hurry and get behind the regular army so we can get through that opening before it closes again."

Chapter Thirty-two

*K*ate and Jen dashed from their hiding place and managed to merge with the tail end of the regular army scorpions. Crouching down, they scurried though the dark opening. Once inside they broke ranks and tucked themselves into a narrow crevice in the side of the cave.

Huddling together, Kate and Jen hunkered down and listened to the orderly noise of the army marching. An icy wind blew around them.

Creeeak!

The harsh sound of rusty hinges on the huge gate closing signaled the last scorpions were inside.

BAAAM!

Inky darkness engulfed Kate and Jen. They were locked inside the rocks—inside Rapio's macabre domain.

Boosh!

Boosh!

Boosh!

Flaming torches on the walls flared up, giving their surroundings an eerie light.

Kate reached for Jen and found her hand. Neither uttered a word in fear their presence would be discovered. Slowly their eyes adjusted to the flickering light. They were in a large cave chamber, the size of a domed football field. Six passageways branched off the huge room. Tapered stalactites hung from the ceiling high above them and dripped the same putrid smelling greenish black slime Kate and Jen first saw on the walls of their hiding place overlooking the three valleys.

The floor of the cavern was a gooey, muddy substance that slowly flowed at molasses speed from an unseen underground source. The shadowy figures they could make out did not sink into the goo, but seem to slide along the top of it.

Kate pointed to their feet. The gooey substance sluggishly moved beneath them. Like the other creatures they did not sink into it.

Jen shrugged in the same disbelief as Kate.

Surveying the room they discovered, the shadowy figures were of two kinds—Rapio's army of scorpions and Quae. The soldiers of Rapio's army carried four-foot whip batons and marched around giving orders to the Quae.

"Those Quae don't seem to be infected with the tumors of Bás," Kate observed.

"No, they don't," Jen said.

Bweee—Bweee—Bweee!

A scorpion raised his baton and flogged a Quae until he fell to the ground. The moving floor oozed around the Quae. For a moment the Quae struggled, and then was sucked into the floor and disappeared.

"Quicksand!" Kate gasped. "The floor is alive."

Bweee—Bweee—Bweee!

Bweee—Bweee—Bweee!

The other Quae working in the cavern shrank away from the scorpion.

Bweee—Bweee—Bweee!

Bweee—Bweee—Bweee!

"These Quae are slaves," Jen whispered. "The choices given to Odo—these Quae must have given their eternity to Rapio."

"It must be true what Odo said, that not all who give their eternity to Rapio are sent back above the river," Kate observed. "It looks like most who make that decision are kept here as slaves."

Bweee—Bweee—Bweee!

Bweee—Bweee—Bweee!

Bweee—Bweee—Bweee!

The army scorpions shouted out to the Quae slaves, giving them orders to get back to work. Though they spoke different languages, the Quae understood the dominance the scorpions had over them. They were the oppressed with no escape.

"Which way do we go?" Kate whispered.

"Remember what Eldré said—look to our lockets," Jen answered. She snapped open the clasp of her locket. The swirling cloud gave way to a moving picture of the same domed room they were in. At the far end, in one of the dark passageways, a small light flashed. "I think we're to follow the third passageway. The small light flashed a burst of light twice.

"Our ever faithful GPS lockets," Kate smiled. She stared into her locket. It showed the same passageway. "That must be the corridor to the Beldur Chamber."

"And Eldré said the Beldur Chamber is where we will find the answers to our questions."

Kate and Jen waited a moment until the creatures roaming about the large cavern room seemed more occupied with their duties than any intruder they might find. They eased from their hiding place and edged their way to the third passageway. Once inside they slowed down and looked at their lockets. The movie picture swirling inside their golden cases mapped out a path that would take them into the heart of the cavern—into Rapio's throne room—into the Beldur Chamber.

"I'll lead," Jen offered.

"Right," Kate agreed.

They both knew Jen's athletic skills would sense where to step and how to miss any hazardous footing. She would find the safest path to the Chamber.

The rocky, narrow passageway was difficult to navigate by the irregular light of the flickering flames of the torches placed on the walls. Jen trusted her locket to take them where they were to go. Down—down—down, they followed the path deeper into Rapio's domain. Slime on the wall moved with baby Bás ready to be chosen to be put into a Quae as an overseer.

"Oh," Kate gasped, slipping on a moving rock.

"Careful," Jen said. "There are a lot of Stonefish along our path."

"So I just discovered." Kate stood still and looked at the wiggly stones beneath the muddy floor. "But the floor is also becoming more solid, and not made up of that gooey quicksand we saw in the big room."

"That's true," Kate said, "but still just as dangerous." Another stonefish squirmed under Kate's foot. This time she was ready and lifted her foot when it first moved.

Down—down—down, deeper they descended. The putrid stench emitting from the slimy walls stuck in their nostrils. Hot, humid air pushed against their bodies. The torches that once lit their path were no longer stuck into the walls of the cave. Step by step they journeyed deeper into murky shadows, lit only by the iridescent glow from the green luminous baby scorpions wiggling beneath the slime of the walls.

"Look," Jen said, pointing at a gaping hole in the wall. "Do you think that's the Beldur Chamber?"

Kate eased around Jen. She quietly crept to the opening and looked in.

"Oh no," Kate stifled her words.

Jen leaned over Kate's shoulder and looked into the shadowy cavern. She quickly drew back from the horror chamber she saw. Three Quae, covered with greenish tumors, huddled together while four army scorpions towered above them. Hundreds of other Quae were held back against the slimy cavern walls by other army scorpions.

Bweee—Bweee—Bweee!

The eerie sounds of the scorpions filled the room.

Bweee—Bweee—Bweee!

One scorpion cracked his whip baton in the air over the Quae heads. The second crack of his whip hit the head of one of the Quae.

Aaargh!

Bweee—Bweee—Bweee!

"No...." the huddling Quae whimpered.

Bweee—Bweee—Bweee!

The scorpion's whip hit the huddled group two...three...four times—flogging the whimpering group into submission.

Kate couldn't watch any longer. She turned away from the chamber opening. This must have been where Odo spent time before Maltzurra drug him out to kneel before High Priest Onde. A tear trickled down her cheek.

Knowing they could do nothing right now for this group, Jen wiped Kate's tear away and motioned for them to move on down the corridor. Sticking close together they followed the twisting trail Jen's locket put before them. They scurried past four more horror chambers like the first one, not stopping to watch the terror in the faces of the Quae, but still hearing the cries of agony.

Down—down—down they went. Finally they heard muffled sounds unlike the cries coming from the horror chambers. The droning noise was voice-like, but with undistinguishable words. The sounds came from ink blackness before them. Jen stopped abruptly and put her finger to her lips. Edging their way quickly and quietly toward the sounds, they found an outcropping of rocks to hide behind. Jen motioned to Kate to crouch down. From this place they would be able to see what was ahead of them.

Easing up, they peeked around the bolder into the crevice below them.

"Oh!" Flabbergasted, Kate dropped to her knees.

"It's huge," Jen whispered.

"And endless," Kate added.

A massive, dark endless void of space, with a spiraling circle of galactic rocks forming a ring leading to another cavernous abyss, was in front of them. Massive meteors and small meteorites sped through the dark space, smashing into each other in volatile explosions, but missing the triangular door that floated freely inside the ring of chaos.

"Whew!" Jen exhaled.

"Agreed," Kate said.

"Do you think that triangular door leads to the Beldur Chamber?" Jen asked.

"Eldré said the entrance to Rapio's throne room would be a triangular door," Kate answered. "That must be it."

"But how do we get to it?"

Jen opened her locket. From the spiraling galactic rock ring rocks began breaking off from their orbital course.

"Look!" Jen held her open locket to where Kate could see the picture inside.

"Those rocks are forming a bridge, or at least giving us stepping stones to cross over," Kate stated.

"It's pretty clear we're to follow the *grey rock road*," Jen joked.

"I'd feel better if it was yellow brick, a solid road, not meteorite-stones floating in space," Kate smiled. "Those rocks don't look too steady. And we'll have to jump from one to the next."

"A challenge," Jen said, "but we can do it." She looked at the spinning rocks.

"Just like wing-walking in a breeze," Kate offered. She had wing-walked, but she much preferred to pilot the airplane while Jen did her acrobatics on the wings.

"Yes," Jen agreed. "Just like wing-walking." She knew Kate's preference of piloting, not acrobatics.

Kate nodded.

"No one seems to be on guard. Let's go," Jen said, ignoring the obvious hazardous path.

Kate stifled an inside chuckled. Why would Rapio need a guard for this fortress? It was a spinning galaxy, deep inside a dark, unknown world. No, not many an intruder would dare try to infiltrate this fortress.

Just as Jen suspected, the rocks whirling around made an unsteady path. She took the lead and, after looking again for guards, jumped quickly from one spinning rock to another. Kate followed closely until they reached the glowing triangular door. Rocking back and forth on the last whirling stepping stone, she surveyed the area to fine the best place to jump that would give them cover to plan their next move. Making a decision, she leapt behind the corner of the triangle door and signaled Kate to follow.

Jen looked into her locket. Before them was the Beldur Chamber—an endless world of its own. She pointed at the picture in her locket and then the edge of the door where they stood. A path through the open door, but nothing else was given to them. Beyond the door was the emptiness of space.

"Faith," Kate said.

"I suppose so," Jen agreed. "Ready?"

Kate nodded.

"Three—two—one—"

Together, they stepped over the triangular door's threshold.

Chapter Thirty-three

*O*nce they stepped over the triangular door's threshold, they stood in a dimly lit void—no walls, no floor—no other life form existed outside of them. Kate spun around to survey the area.

"Where is the door?" she asked.

Jen turned around to find the gateway they just stepped through, but it was not there. Gone—everything gone. The slimy walls—the damp corridor—the chambers of horror—were all gone. They floated freely in space.

"Where..." Before Kate could get the words out, her locket warmed and glowed brilliant blue. "Jen?"

"Mine too," Jen said.

From the blackness where they stood, their lockets pulsed with bursts of vivid cobalt blue light beams—with each burst their lockets searched for a path.

"It's like when we were in the Diamond Passage," Kate said. "Remember Raguel said that our lockets are sensitive as to the direction we need to take and the journey we are on while we are in Bigna. Our lockets are finding us a way."

"Somehow I don't think we will see snowflakes and beautiful colors in this passageway," Jen frowned.

Kate and Jen stood silent while their lockets blinked. The blue pulsating beams from their lockets crossed each other a dozen times before they found their common target —a single small, reddish light. Melting together into one steady cobalt blue beam, they formed a narrow, glassy surfaced footpath, leading Kate and Jen toward their next destination.

"I think we've found out the where," Kate said.

"Faith and trust in our lockets," Jen responded.

"Let's go," Kate said. She did not want to linger in the nothingness any longer. She did not know where the deep blue path would take them, but she knew they were exposed to the unknown where they stood.

Blackness surrounding them, the shaft of light they dashed over was all they could see. The small, red glowing light their lockets drew them toward blazed brighter with each step they took.

Boosh!

A burning ball of fire went over their heads.

Boosh!

Another ball of fire went over their heads, this time a little closer.

Boosh—viiiip!

A third ball of fire came at Kate and Jen, but when it reached them it encircled their bodies. Spinning around them at a high speed, the fireball captured them inside and pulled them toward the blazing light at the end of the blue glassy path they were on. They stopped running, but the spinning flames tightened around them and continued their forward movement.

Boosh!

Boosh!

Boosh!

More burning fireballs from the reddish light sped at and around them.

"Grab my hand," Kate yelled.

"Got you," Jen said, clasping tight to Kate.

Boosh!

Boosh!

Boosh!

Unlike the Diamond Passageway of sparkling diamonds, the kaleidoscopic effects of the flaming spheres pulsated strobe-like flashes. The silence from the void they were in was broken only by the vibration of the blazing balls swirling past them. Even the ring of fire spinning around them made no noise.

Within seconds, the small, reddish light at the end of their path became a giant gateway to another chamber—another world. The force that held them tight pulled them ever closer to the fiery door.

"Fight it," Kate yelled.

"I am," Jen responded.

It did no good. The force that held them was stronger than all the fight they put up. They couldn't break away. In less than a second they would be thrown through that door.

Klunk!

Viiiip!

The blue light from their lockets broke off the path they were on and threw up a barrier between them and the blazing light.

Wham!

Fa-thud!

The impact of hitting the blue barrier with full force knocked Kate and Jen to their knees. Their lockets had broken the spinning fireball force that held them and drew them into the blazing hole. They no longer were captive to the unseen force.

Sploosh!

The blue barrier melted and before them was a fiery porthole to a chamber, but the force that held them was gone. The glassy path they were on was gone. Black void was behind them—a fiery ringed door in front of them. And though the gateway was a glowing ring of reddish flames they felt no heat. They could see inside without fear of being burned.

Easing closer to the opening to get a better look, Kate and Jen drew back at what they saw.

"I think we've reached the heart of the Beldur Chamber," Kate whispered.

"Rapio's throne room," Jen whispered back.

Unlike the void they had just passed through, they now looked at a well-defined chamber. The size of two domed football fields side by side, it was smaller than Kate and Jen had anticipated. Splotches of green patina formed on the stone walls, floor and ceiling. The patina gave the hint that underneath the rock laid layers of copper, aged and tarnished by thick acidic rain-like moisture that dripped from the top of the chamber and oozed down the stone. Carved in various large outcroppings of patina were profiles of ravens.

Parent Bás scorpion spun threads of muddy goop that hung from the four hundred fifty foot ceiling, creating nests for their young. As each egg was laid, the semi-liquid, sticky substance formed into a long stalactite that glowed with the luminous green of baby Bás. Tiki torches, on long wood poles, wedged in crevices in the walls, bounced their flickering light off the patina glazed walls and added to the ghostly green glow from the cocooned baby Bás.

A fire-fall, slightly smaller than the size of Niagara Falls, thundered down one side of the cavern and disappeared into a fissure at its bottom. Flares from the fire-fall, like water on a hot skittle, sizzled and exploded around the fracture.

The patina rock floor was split into two halves by a glassy, black, obsidian, rock path that led to a Fire Opal throne at the end. The throne, each facet of the large opal chiseled to reflect every ray of light in the room, was translucent in appearance. The chair glowed orange-red from the eerie light of the chamber. Ten yards in front of the throne was an altar made from the same Fire Opal, almost impossible to see in its transparent state.

"That must be Rapio's throne and altar," Kate whispered.

Jen nodded. "But where is Rapio?"

One hundred of Rapio's Elite Trooper scorpions stood at attention fifty yards in front of the raging wall of fire. Another one hundred stood at attention on the other side of the chamber. Their chests blazed with blood-red silhouettes of the raven they served. Their crusty heads did not move but waited for an order from their leader.

"We'll have to have a really good plan before we step though this porthole," Jen pointed at the Elite Troopers.

"Our lockets," Kate opened her golden necklace.

Jen did the same.

"It's showing us stepping through this gateway," Kate said.

"And the path takes us behind that statue of a raven." Jen pointed to one of two orange-red opal sculptures of thirty-foot ravens, their wings stretched high above their heads, their raven pebbly claws clamped to the floor. The two stood, one on each side of the gateway, guarding the entrance to Rapio's throne room.

"Are you sure?" Jen squinted to get a better look.

"I'm sure," Kate said.

"Then let's go." Jen looked at the fiery ring that was the entrance to the throne room. Shrugging, she stepped through the ring to the other side. Kate was at her heels. Quietly, they scurried behind one of the statues.

Baraaaaaag!

The blare from the elephant trumpet was the signal for all Elite Troopers to stand a little straighter. In unison their scaly heads turned toward a black, obsidian-framed entryway to the left side of the throne and altar. The tunnel behind the opening was as dark as the glassy rocks and gave no clue as to what was inside.

Kate and Jen joined the Troopers in looking toward the blackness.

Baraaaaaag!

The trumpet resounded again through the chamber.

Emerging from the darkness of the tunnel, twelve Elite Imperial Knights marched in unison to the beat of an unheard drum in their heads. With their scorpion scales a blood red, they looked much like Maltzurra, but instead of the bright yellow plume attached to the top of their helmets, a deep red plume was affixed. Their blood red shields blazed with a fiery red raven. Strapped to their sides were red swords. They took up an attention stance, six on each side of the Fire Opel throne.

"Rapio's knights," Kate whispered.

Jen nodded in agreement.

Baraaaaaag!

Maltzurra, his yellow plume rippling in the still air, stepped from the tunnel. Onde stood beside him, his arms outstretched. He carried a sword with a golden filigreed handle. On each side of the handle was a silver triangle, inlaid with hundreds of small diamonds. Inside the center of each triangle was a two inch ruby, in the shape of an eagle profile. The blade, pure silver that had been honed to razor sharpness, glistened in the flickering light of the chamber.

"He has the Holy Sword," Kate said in a soft voice.

"Perhaps we can steal it back before we go back to camp," Jen reasoned. They watched Maltzurra and Onde stride out of the tunnel's darkness.

"Oh…" Kate gasped.

Jen just stared.

Trailing behind Maltzurra and Onde was Rocas, Raguel's twin brother who had turned his back on the Eagle and pledged his loyalty to Rapio. His elf-like body scrunched down, ready to shape-shift into a rat if necessary. His round black eyes shifted from side to side, suspicious of everything around him.

Maltzurra and Rocas made their way quickly, yet in a royal way, to the foot of the opal throne. They did not speak but waited for their master. Onde laid the Holy Sword on the altar in front of Rapio's throne and stood stiff backed, waiting for his master.

Baraaaaaag!

Baraaaaaag!

Baraaaaaag!

Three blasts of the horn. All eyes were on the darkened tunnel. The silence of the chamber was broken only by dripping of the acid-rain substance running down the walls.

Sssblam!

Sssblam!

Kaboom!

Fireballs exploded from the darkness. Flames roared around the obsidian doorway. An orange-red fiery quicksilver liquid lit up the tunnel and quickly flowed out and formed a hot, heavy silvery metallic carpet between the opening and the throne.

Out of the chaos materialize a being—the body of a human, the head of a raven.

"Rapio!" Kate said.

"Rapio," Jen agreed.

Chapter Thirty-four

Rapio stood silent for a moment. His raven head did not move. Ink black feathers flowed back from his glossy black beak and down his back. He wore a tar black monk's robe, tied with a blood red double-cord around his waist and fitted to allow his two ink-black feathered wings to extend out the back. Kate was surprised at the simplicity of his robe. Not the clothing she expected of the ruler of the dark domain.

Two human-like arms, covered with pebbly-raven skin, projected from the sleeves. Hands, with spindly fingers and claws instead of fingernails, gripped a scepter in one and leather-bound book in the other.

Kate squinted, but could not tell what the book was. She gestured to Jen with her hands the question, *what's the book?*

"His holy book?" Jen offered as a question.

Kate studied Rapio's face—anger, deceit, malice oozed through the pores of his feathered skin. Eyes, blacker than she had ever encountered—soulless, ruthless, depraved —two bottomless pits, scanned the room, scrutinizing every servant of his kingdom.

Badaboom!

Rapio's eyes turned from black to lavender glass. Exploding purple fire spit from them and encircled his body.

Badaboom!

The electrifying ring of purple fire still whirling around him, Rapio spread his wings to their full fifteen feet.

Everyone in the chamber went to their knees to kneel before him.

"Rapio, our lord!" Onde shouted out. "Rapio! Rapio! Rapio!"

Rapio! Rapio! Rapio!

Rapio! Rapio! Rapio!

Everyone in the chamber took up Onde's chant.

Rapio! Rapio! Rapio!

Rapio! Rapio! Rapio!

Satisfied his servants were under his power, Rapio drew down his wings, melted his eyes from lavender glass back to black pits and swaggered over to the altar. He handed Onde his scepter, laid the book upon the altar and picked up the Holy Sword.

His clawed right hand wrapped around the handle of the sword that contained miraculous power. Brandishing the Holy Sword over his raven head, he pointed the silver blade toward each of the four cardinal directions of the compass.

"From the north—the south—the east—and the west, I am the mighty force that will fall over the Quae of Bigna. I will weaken their bodies—weaken their minds—destroy their mission—destroy their faith. I will crush the enemy into defeat."

"Rapio, our lord!" Onde shouted. "Rapio! Rapio! Rapio!"

Rapio! Rapio! Rapio!

Rapio! Rapio! Rapio!

"He has twisted Friar Fara's speech to the Pilgers before the Battle of Stur," Kate whispered.

"The great liar and deceiver," Jen responded.

Smugness sweep over Rapio's face. His hardened beak twisted into an arrogant sneer. He nodded to Onde and strutted to take his place on his throne. Overlooking his kneeling servants, he decided he would have them stay in that position. He liked them worshiping to him.

Rapio played with the bejeweled hilt of the Holy Sword for a few minutes before he spoke.

"Onde," Rapio finally said. "Take your place beside me. My knights, rise for council."

"What is on your mind today?" Rapio asked Onde.

"My lord," Onde began. "We have been very successful in releasing the Bás scorpions into the Quae Pilgers. We have them stopped on the far side of the Senvolte River. They cannot cross over. Elak has complete control of their path to Helig. If they do not make it to Helig and take it back, history of the Earth World will forever be changed."

"True," Rapio sneered. He liked what he heard.

"Maltzurra and I have held council with your knights," Onde pointed to the twelve knights standing guard around Rapio. "We think it is time to attack the Earth World direct. We think it is time to release the Bás into the Earth World."

Rapio's raven-skinned hands dug his claws into the hilt of the Holy Sword. He searched each knight for a weakness.

"No," Rapio scoffed. "When I conquer the Quae, there will be no Earth World."

"True, my lord," Rocus nodded in agreement with Rapio's words. He had not been brought directly into the discussion, yet decided to interject his opinion. He flashed a sneer of authority at Onde. Only he, Rocus, rode with and on Rapio—only he was Rapio's constant attendant—only he truly had Rapio's ear.

"But we could conquer both at the same time," Onde tried once again. "We can send the Bás through the Obex into the Earth Word."

Rapio dug his claws deeper into the Holy Sword. He searched the knights again for flaws in their loyalty to him. Why did he put up with such incompetence? He would make the decision of when and where to destroy the Earth World.

"The Bás do not affect Earth people in the same way as they do Bigna Quae," Rapio sneered.

"How so, Lord Rapio?" Rocus asked. He would appease Rapio in every way he could.

"Earth people can be saved…even cured with a blast of two trumpets of hammered silver, blown by the holy woman. The holy woman must blow only one, but both silver trumpets must be made at the same time. The Bás bugs can kill their bodies but not their souls. No, not the Bás Plague, but I will send to the Earth World another plague for their souls."

"You are so cunning," Rocus purred.

"But of course I am," Rapio mocked Rocus' statement.

"And the silver trumpets will not save the Quae from the Bás?" Rocus asked.

Rapio started at his little creature. "It could," he laughed. "But the Pilgers believe trumpets are made to lead them to their battles above ground. They do not know the two silver trumpets will also battle the Bás from my domain. When both trumpets are sounded together, one by the holy woman and one by the holy man, the blasts from the trumpet would stop the Bás from spreading among the Quae."

"Then those we…you have sent above with the Bás could be rid of their Bás with just a blow of the silver trumpets?" Rocus was concerned.

Rapio's sarcastic laugh chilled the chamber. "Not the Quae with my Bás already in them. For the Bás to leave them Mysta, the Holy Man, must wave the Holy Sword above them while the holy woman blows a silver horn. And I have the Holy Sword." He stroked the silver sword he gripped with his clawed hand and smirked. "Yes, I have their magical sword."

"My lord," Rocus bowed. "You will reign forever."

"Of course I will," Rapio sneered. "But for now I have a plan for Bigna—one that could also destroy the Earth World."

"And what is that?" Rocus bowed.

"Not now," Rapio said. "Bigna World is the big plan, but for now we will send even more Bás into Domare by infecting even more Quae. They will give it to other Quae and the Bás will spread across Bigna—just like at Stur." Indifferently, Rapio waved his hand. "Simple, so simple."

"So simple," Rocus agreed.

"What you see here is just a start, Rocus," Rapio laughed. "It is time to conquer Domare and then on to victory over Bigna."

Onde was quiet. He feared he had angered Rapio. He shuffled his Quae feet. Rapio could destroy him—send him into servitude as a Quae—with a snap of his clawed fingers.

Rapio stood. With his curved nailed fingers he grabbed the collar of feathers around his neck and pulled them into a hood over his head. His face disappeared into the blackness. Now all that looked into the chamber full of his followers was a black hole —malicious and ominous in its emptiness.

The Holy Sword was weighty, even for Rapio. He walked to the altar and laid it upon the book. Inside the darkened hood, his beak turned up at the corners. With the Holy Sword he would conquer Bigna. For now, he would sit upon his throne and rule his kingdom.

Rocus trailed behind his master, waiting to serve.

"We have to get back to Eldré and tell her about the two silver trumpets," Jen whispered.

Kate nodded. "What about the Holy Sword?"

Jen looked at the distance between them and the Holy Sword. Even with their athletic abilities, they would not be able to grab the sword and find an escape route pass all of Rapio's followers. "We'll have to leave it for now. We need to get back to save the Quae who are not infected with the Bás."

Kate exhaled in frustration. She knew Jen was right. "Perhaps Eldré can help us find a way to recover it once we get back."

Jen motioned toward the gateway they had come through. It was ten yards behind them, but they would have to dash out in the open to get through it. She hoped once they jumped through the opening their lockets would provide a path for them.

"Ready?" Jen whispered. She put her hand on the foot of the raven statue.

Kate leaned back against the statue to protect their hiding a little longer. She felt the statue move slightly. She looked at Jen.

"I felt it too…" Jen began but it was too late.

The raven statues they hid beneath turned their heads and stared at Kate and Jen. Their beaks opened and they belted out harsh, croaky calls.

Caaawwwww!

Caaawwwww!

The statues were alive.

Caaawwwww!

Caaawwwww!

The harsh call sounded the alarm that intruders had breached Rapio's throne room.

Chapter Thirty-five

Caaawwwww!
    Caaawwwww!
Rapio swung his head in the direction of his Fire Opal Raven guards.
Caaawwwww!
Caaawwwww!
The Fire Opal Ravens spread their wings and blocked Kate and Jen's exit from the throne room.

Instantly, twenty-five Elite Troopers broke ranks and swarmed Kate and Jen.

"Run!" Jen yelled, but she knew there was nowhere to run or to hide.

Instantly, the crusty bodies of the Elite Troopers were upon them.

"Well, well, well," Rapio smirked. "Who do we have here?"

Kate and Jen fought to free themselves from their captors, but the pincher-claws of the four Elite Troopers holding them tightened around their flailing arms.

"Bring them to me!" Rapio ordered.

Kate and Jen struggled to no avail, as they were dragged down the black, glassy, obsidian path that led to Rapio. Rapio took his position beside the altar and picked up the Holy Sword.

"Kneel before your master!" From within the dark feathered hood, Rapio's merciless words fell. Kate and Jen saw nothing but the black, ominous void.

"Let go of us," Jen yelled at the troopers. But the crusty claws of the troopers pushed down on their shoulders and forced them to kneel before Rapio.

"Well, well, well," Rapio repeated. He lifted the Holy Sword and fingered the blade. The pure silver glistened. For a millisecond one sparkle from the blade flashed toward Kate and Jen. In that instant their lockets pressed into their chests.

Kate looked at Jen.

Jen's eyes blinked twice. She understood.

The Holy Sword and their lockets were communicating.

"Katherine Morgan Phillips and Jennifer Morgan Fillmore from the Earth World," Rapio sneered. He stroked the leather bound book on the altar. "Ah, your names are written, but in my book? This is a surprise. I have only hoped—and surely did not expect to gather you so soon—if at all." He opened the book to a blank page. "No, not even a hint I would be the one to write your name." With one hand he pushed the hood of feathers from around his face. His black, soulless eyes focused on them. "But I accept the gift."

Kate and Jen's lockets continued to press hot into their skin. They would have to read their lockets without opening them. They would have to read each other without speaking.

Kate glanced at Jen. Jen's eyes were directed at the sword.

Of course! Kate thought. We have been sent to take back one of Cephas Monastery's ancient holy relics.

Jen broke her stare at the sword and looked over at Kate. They were thinking the same thing—The Holy Sword. They must rescue the Holy Sword. To thoroughly rid the Quae of the Bás they must take back the sword.

"Your struggle against me is fruitless," Rapio snarled. "You are in my domain and I have already conquered you."

"Never!" Kate and Jen yelled in unison.

"Today—I command you to cross over into my eternity!" Rapio waved the sword above the altar. "Today—your mouth will open up and say my name. Today—your heart will melt before me. Today—your life will become obedient to worship me."

"Never!"

With both hands gripping the golden filigreed handle of the Holy Sword, Rapio raised it high above his head. The sword blazed in majestic glory—Rapio's clawed-hand frozen to the hilt. The pebbly raven skin on his arm glowed until his whole body radiated a ghoulish purple. Lavender lightning radiated from the tip of the sword. Rapio smirked and let the tip fall upon one of his Elite Troopers holding Kate and Jen.

The trooper's eyes glowed green for a moment before his whole body ignited into flame. He spit glowing hot sparks from his mouth, exploded into a vivid green glaring light and then disintegrated into the ground.

Kate and Jen squinted from the brightness of the exploding green inferno.

The three remaining Elite Troopers flinched slightly, loosening their vise grip on Kate and Jen.

Rapio sadistically kicked the smoldering ashes of the trooper toward Kate and Jen.

"You see," he glared into their eyes, "with this magical sword all I have to do is touch you and you are gone." He waved the sword above their heads and then laid it upon the altar.

Kate and Jen knew they needed a plan—fast. They folded their hands in front of them. They would communicate with hand signals, much like they did when they preformed their wing-walking, high in the air.

"You will come to me now," Rapio held out his hands.

"Never!"

"Then you will beg me to release you from your pain—the pain in which I will always control you."

Anger breached his tightened beak.

Rapio's ink black wings spread out. A gust of icy wind blew through the chamber.

"Onde!" Rapio shouted.

Onde dashed to Rapio's side.

"Onde," Rapio smirked. "Go find the best two of my baby Bás."

Onde scurried off to a one foot square notch in the wall. The inside glowed incandescent green from Bás. He carefully put his hand in and lifted out two squirming, luminous green scorpions, one-half inch long, and dropped them into a small jar.

"My lord," Rocus said. "Bás? I thought Earth World beings would not be affected by the Bás?"

"Not if I allowed these two Earth World beings out of my domain," Rapio said. "But I have no intention of sending them back above. They will be mine—they will serve me in this world, in my world."

Onde set the jar with the baby Bás on the altar.

Kate and Jen looked at the infectious insects. Their time was running out.

Jen put her two index fingers together to indicate she would snatch the sword.

Kate twiddled one thumb upward to say she understood.

"Soon these two babies will be part of you." Rapio held up one of the green bugs. "And then you will not fight me."

Jen glanced back at the entrance. The two Fire Opal statues still guarded the way out. She looked left and right. Nothing to the left—the wall of fire on the right.

"Katherine," Rapio said. "You will be the first to come to me."

Jen watched Rapio's insidious actions and made a quick decision. She pointed in the direction of the wall of fire.

Kate twiddled a thumb and put out three fingers—they would go on the count of three.

Rapio stepped in front of Kate. The Elite Troopers holding Kate and Jen took three steps backward and bowed down to Rapio.

Rapio let the baby Bás crawl around on his outstretched cupped, hand. The small green scorpion skirted around the claws at the end of Rapio's fingers.

"Yes, my little one," Rapio said to the baby scorpion, "I have chosen you for a special task—your host is from the Earth World."

Rapio put his hand next to Kate's face. Icy cold radiated from the claws at the tips of his fingers. He let the scorpion crawl from his hand onto her cheek. Kate involuntarily shuttered under the insect's legs scratching at her tender skin.

"Ouch!" Kate flinched when the scorpion sunk his pincher tail into her cheek.

Rapio scooped the baby bug off her face.

"Not just yet," he said to the scorpion. "Soon she will be yours—soon she will be mine." He delighted in toying with Kate.

Jen watched the horror show taking place next to her in disbelief. She could not wait any longer. She began her countdown. Clasping her hands together where Kate could see them, she pressed her index, middle and ring fingers together—then she closed them in a timed beat—ring fingers closed—middle fingers closed—index fingers...

Both Kate and Jen bolted forward at the same time. Kate collided with Rapio, knocking him down to his knees. Jen dashed up the one step of the altar and grabbed the Holy Sword.

Surprised by the sudden movement of Kate and Jen, the Elite Troopers were temporarily stunned. Without the capability to think for themselves, they looked to Rapio. Rapio held up his hand to stop them. He turned to his twelve Elite Imperial Knights.

"Go after them!" Rapio yelled. There was no place for Kate and Jen to run. Why not let his Imperial Knights have the pleasure of the pursuit and capture?

Jen reached the wall of fire just behind Kate. Flares from the fire-fall exploded at their feet.

Sssblam!

Sssblam!

Kaboom!

The fire-fall stopped them from going any further. The Imperial Knights caught up with them, but hesitated at completely closing the gap for fear of getting too close to the fire. Their blood red scorpion scales glistened from the blaze of the fire. Each had his shield raised to protect his body from the searing heat.

Sssblam!

Sssblam!

Kaboom!

Fireballs sped over Kate and Jen's heads.

"Do not let them escape!" The roar of Rapio echoed off the chamber's walls.

Kate and Jen edged closer to the blazing furnace. Jen felt the hairs on the back of her neck sizzling from the heat.

"We cannot stay in Rapio's domain," Kate stated. "But maybe…" her words dwindled off.

"We cannot stay, no maybe," Jen looked back at Rapio. He spread his wings out in rage, creating an icy wind that whipped though the cave.

The Imperial Knights, also aware of Rapio's wrath, began edging closer to Kate and Jen.

"Kate!" Jen exclaimed. "You have a red rash forming on your cheek." She grabbed Kate and looked closer at her face.

"Are you saying…what… I'm infected?" Kate's words were incoherent.

"We have to get you out of here—back to Bigna—back to Eldré. She must be the holy woman Rapio said could save Earth people."

"How…how can we get back?" Kate asked. Her thoughts were becoming confused.

Jen looked up at the blazing wall of fire before them. An image formed out of the flames. Calling to them was a Quae Pilger knight—his silver armor glistened with the flames licking up his sides. He stood with a drawn sword in one hand and a pure white shield with an Eagle on it in the other.

"Jen," Kate struggled for words. "Remember what Eldré said about going into the Wall of Fire to get back to them—*If it comes to that, she will know what to do*. I think she was talking about this moment …but I can't think…I can't decide…"

From Jen's wrist a slight glow shimmered from where Raguel had lashed them together. Glitter-like flakes floated upward. What had Raguel said, *I will not let go. I will bring you back to this land.*" Could it be that she was still connected to Raguel? She prayed it was so.

"Our lockets!" Jen quickly opened her locket. Inside was a wall of fire.

"My locket…is…is hot," Kate whispered. Words were failing her.

"I don't think we have a choice," Jen quickly grabbed Kate's hand. It was hot to the touch—almost as hot as the blazing fire in front of them. "I think the only way back is to go into the wall of fire."

"My mind…my thoughts are fading fast," Kate forced out in a raspy voice. The rash spots on her face were quickly turning into dark green tumors. "It's up to you…"

"Ready?" Jen exhaled.

Kate's dry mouth opened in agreement, but words would not come from her lips. Her mind swirled with irrational thoughts. She leaned dizzily into Jen. Jen tucked the Holy Sword between them and put her arms around Kate.

"Three—two—one—"

Jen tightened her hug around Kate. Without any more hesitation she jumped into the reddish-orange flames that lashed out at them from the searing wall of fire.

Chapter Thirty-six

Sun-hot fire flares blasted Kate and Jen when they jumped into the fire wall. Hot, exploding spheres of fire and gale-force wind whipped them around in a fiery tornado, but the heat did not singe their skin. The torrent waves of the deadly Senvolte River, filled with the destructive Bás Plague firestorm, swirled around them. Expecting the searing heat would burn them, they were surprised when an icy air stripped their body of the blaze around them.

But the relief from the heat being stripped away was replaced by the suddenness of ice cube cold. Freezing rain pelted their bodies. The supercooled, large liquid drops froze into tiny ice puddles when they impacted with their skin. A thin glaze spread out from the ice spots and built up on their bodies. Jen saw this once before when she and Kate were caught in a storm and their de-icing equipment failed. Their airplane's wings covered with a glaze of ice—pretty to look at but deadly for flying. They had quickly descended into warmer air to safety.

This time she did not have an option of going to a warmer altitude. They were tumbling out of control. There was no altitude—no up, no down—no higher, no lower.

"Kate!" Jen yelled over the howling wind. "Kate!"

No response. Kate was limp, her arms and legs were like those of a rag doll being blown lifelessly in the wind.

Jen hugged Kate tighter. She could not let Kate be torn from her grip or she would be lost for eternity in the icy furnace. The bitter cold glaze spun around them as a moth spins a cocoon. Soon it would not be the heat that Jen had feared would kill them—they would freeze to death.

Scorching gusts, mixed with the biting cold wind, was quickly turning their cocoon into a dry, burning ice prison. Tumbling at jet speed, Jen could not focus on anything in her surroundings, but it would do her no good anyway as she had no control of their direction—their destination— or their destiny. Struggling hard she could not break the ice shell forming around them.

From inside Jen's tunic her locket moved—slightly at first—but enough to give Jen hope. Wiggling from her neckline, her locket magnetically connected to Kate's locket. Firmly connected, the two lockets pulsated a ray of blue light—then a second ray of light—a third.

Jen began to lose consciousness under the pressure of the cocoon around them.

The pulsating cobalt blue light from Kate's and Jen's lockets locked on a small, diamond light. Jen felt a tug on her wrist. Their tumbling stopped.

Like a string on a yo-yo, the bright blue ray of light pulled Kate and Jen toward the ever-increasing brightness of the diamond light. From the darkness, kaleidoscopic effects of a noon sun dancing off millions of Marquise cut diamonds, strobe lights radiated around them.

"The...the Diamond Passageway," Jen coughed out to Kate. "Our lockets... have found the...have found the Diamond Passageway."

Kate did not respond.

Rocketing over their lockets' blue path at the speed of light, the icy cocoon melted away. The blasting spheres of fire, gale-force wind and freezing rain that pelted their bodies exploded in one abrupt, violent tornado and then dissipated into the darkness behind them.

Spring fresh, cool air brushed over their faces. Jen, though weak herself, clung tight to the unconscious Kate.

Boosh!

The lockets' force that pulled them toward the diamond light, gently nudged them out onto the bank of the Senvolte River. Hitting the solid ground, they rolled apart, the Holy Sword slid from between them.

"Jen! Kate!"

Jen opened her eyes. The two moons of Bigna shone above her. The knights of Quae still knelt in prayer.

"Jen! Jen!" Raguel said.

Jen smiled and lifted her arm. She was still lashed to Raguel.

"Thank you," Jen mouthed.

"You are okay," Raguel said. "That is all I need…" but he cut off his words when he saw the unconscious Kate. The tumors blistering her body sent out black veins toward her heart.

"Eldré!" Raguel yelled.

"I'm right here," Eldré put her hand on Raguel's back. "I see."

"What can you do?" Raguel asked.

Jen quickly untied the leather strap connecting her and Raguel and put her face close to Kate's. "Kate! Kate, can you hear me?"

Kate's eyelids did not move. Her chest rose and fell in labored breathing.

Eldré tugged gently on Jen. "Let me look at her."

Reluctantly Jen moved back, but not far.

Still studying Kate, Eldré asked, "Jen, tell me exactly what happened once you went beneath the water."

Jen's mind whirled trying to remember it all. Quickly, but acutely, she spun the tale of what happened to Kate and her. Eldré's eyes never left Kate.

"…and then we threw ourselves…well, really I pull us into the wall of fire," Jen summed up.

"Mmmm," Eldré said.

"When we went into the Wall of Fire," Jen asked, "did we go into the Obex? It didn't feel like the Obex."

"No," a voice behind Jen answered.

"Mysta? When did you come to the camp?" Jen asked, very happy to see the High Priest of the Cephas Monastery.

"Eldré sent word that you and Kate were beneath the Senvolte River," Mysta said. The Holy Sword Kate and Jen had rescued from Rapio was securely in Mysta's hand. "It was time for me to come to the battlefield."

"I am so glad you are here," Jen jumped up and hugged the monk. "So much has happened."

"So I heard," Mysta said. "And no, you were not in the Obex. The Obex is the barrier between the Earth World and Bigna. When you went into the Wall of Fire you were still in Rapio's domain. You were still very close to him."

"What was the coldness that we felt in the firewall?" Jen asked.

"Rapio's domain is burning with sulfuric heat," Raguel said. "But Rapio himself lives in cold darkness. What you felt was Rapio reaching out for you."

Jen shuttered at the thought that Rapio came close to enclosing them in the ice cocoon.

"You are safe now," Mysta offered. "Your lockets found the portal back to us."

"The Diamond Passageway?" Jen asked.

"Yes," Mysta answered.

"He has a book on his altar," Jen said. She broke her hug with Mysta to get close to Kate again.

"His Eternal Book contains the names of the souls Rapio has gathered for eternity," Eldré said.

"Eternal Book?" Jen asked.

"Eternal books have no past, present or future," Eldré frowned. "All souls Rapio gathers before the end of time, before Război, are in his book."

"He said our names were written, but he did not expect them to be in his book," Jen said. "What did he mean?"

Kate groaned.

"You said Rapio told his council that Earth World beings could be cured with a blast of two trumpets of hammered silver, blown by the holy woman," Eldré said. She did not answer Jen's question.

"Yes," Jen answered. "Kate and I thought that might be you."

"We must hurry to make the trumpets to cure Kate," Eldré frowned, but still did not answer Jen's question.

Nerkon stepped up. "I will have my silversmiths make two trumpets."

"Make them of your purest silver, straight, two feet long," Eldré instructed, "with the bells decorated with a chiseled figure of the Eagle flying toward the sun. The mouthpiece will be cut to fit perfectly to create flawless notes."

"As you wish," Nerkon concurred.

"And I will go to assist your silversmiths," Mysta offered. To finish the silver trumpets in time for Kate to be cured Mysta would have to conjure up magical power that only he possessed. He carefully placed the Holy Sword across Kate's chest.

"Hurry," Jen urged. She could see the Bás spreading beneath Kate's skin. "Why did Kate become infected yet I did not?"

"When Rapio placed the baby Bás on her cheek, the Bás must have stung her with a portion of its venom," Eldré said. "Also, it could be when she bumped into Rapio when you escaped he transferred the Bás that was in his hand onto her."

"I should have bumped him," Jen said.

"No," Eldré said. "Your plan was a good one. You run faster than Kate. She could not have grabbed the Holy Sword and made it to the Wall of Fire before Rapio's guards caught her."

The fire keeping Kate and Jen warm flickered. Raguel quickly threw logs onto the dying coals. Firefly embers danced skyward as the brushwood lit into flames.

"Hang on," Jen said to Kate. "Hang on." In the distance she heard the hammering of the silversmith. She held Kate's hand tightly.

Eldré stroked Kate's face and mumbled in a language Jen did not understand. With each passing minute Kate breathed a little shallower.

Kate looked toward the noise from the silversmith's anvil. *Hurry*, she silently prayed. *Hurry.*

"They are finished!" Mysta ran to where Kate laid. In each hand he carried a trumpet of hammered silver. Handing one to Eldré he said, "It is up to you, Holy Woman."

Eldré's magnificent ground length red silk robe swished when she stood and took the trumpet from his hand. Stretching to bring herself to her full four feet, she stood dignified before them. The silver mouthpiece glistened, reflecting her lips as she placed them on the miraculous musical instrument.

Huuuuum!

The sound from the bell of the trumpet was soft, buzzing like that of a humming bird flitting from flower to flower. Lulling and peaceful.

Huuuuum!

The Holy Sword on Kate's chest radiated brilliance with each note.

Huuuuum—Claaaaang!

The peaceful buzz changed. Eldré added a note that raised the tune up an octave, to a loud, harsh metallic sound.

Huuuuum—Claaaaang!

Each time she blew the notes, the noise around Kate reverberated unforgiving echoes.

Huuuuum—Claaaaang!

The trumpet sound was so loud Jen wanted to put her hands over her ears, but she did not let go of Kate's hand.

Huuuuum—Claaaaang!

Kate's face glowed an iridescent green from the baby Bás beneath her skin.

Huuuuum—Claaaaang!

The luminous tumor on Kate's cheek grew to the size of a lime, brightened and exploded.

Huuuuum!

The music of the trumpet was again soft and peaceful.

Kate bolted upright.

Eldré placed her tiny hand on Kate's cheek and mumbled her mysterious language. The tumors, the black veins and the Bás all disappeared. Only a small red spot showed where, moments before, the Bás was blasted from Kate's body by the music of the silver trumpet.

"Kate!" Jen said. "You're back."

Kate smiled. The last thing she remembered was Jen saying *Three—two—one*—and then falling into the Wall of Fire. "How long was I out?"

Jen's face scrunched up. Days? Weeks? She didn't know.

Mysta saw Jen's dilemma. "For you the time you spent beneath the river is immeasurable. That is the way it is in Rapio's domain. For us, it was but a few minutes."

Kate put her hand on her the fading red spot on her cheek. It itched like a mosquito bite.

"That is where the Bás was," Mysta said.

"The Bás?" Kate was confused. "I remember Rapio let a Bás crawl around on my cheek but I thought he took it back."

"Long story," Jen squeezed Kate's hand. "I'll tell you the details later."

Kate shuttered at the thought she had carried a Bás within her. "Is it gone? Will I have any after effects?"

"We do not think so," Mysta said. He glanced at Eldré. Their eyes met in the knowledge that the question Kate asked was unknown. No one from the Earth World had ever been host to a Bás. They did not know if Kate would have problems later on.

"Mysta, Rapio said when both silver trumpets sounded together by the holy woman and holy man, the blasts from the trumpet would stop the Bás from spreading among the Quae," Jen said.

"We believe you have found the cure," Mysta said.

"Then we need to begin," Kate said. She was relieved that her contracting a Bás served a purpose.

"Not tonight," Eldré stated. "The trumpets must be blown at dawn. It is when the battle for the souls of the Quae begins."

"Sleep tonight," Mysta said. "Tomorrow we conquer the Bás—tomorrow we conquer the city of Helig."

"A good night's sleep will be welcome," Jen said.

Kate nodded in agreement. Her eyes were already closing.

Chapter Thirty-seven

*T*he smell of coffee wafted though the opening of the tent. Jen rolled over in peaceful drowsiness.

"Jen," Kate whispered.

"Mmmmm," was Jen's response.

"Jen!" Kate shook Jen. "Time to rise and shine."

Jen bolted up. "What time is it?" Sleep still clung to her mind.

"I saw Mysta leave his tent," Kate responded. "I think he and Eldré are preparing to blow the silver trumpets."

Jen did not wait for another word. Slipping her boots on, she pulled herself to a standing position. "I'm ready." She looked at Kate. "And you are already dressed."

"Couldn't sleep," Kate smiled. "I'm too excited that we might really be able to rid the Quae of the Bás today."

"Sounds good," Jen said.

They rushed out the tent door and dashed to the river's edge.

"Glad you are here," Mysta said. He stood among the leaders of the Quae Pilgers. "Eldré and I have readied the trumpets." He handed Kate and Jen wooden mugs filled with coffee-like liquid.

Kate and Jen accepted the cups. They enjoyed the warmth of the drink every morning. It had the biting taste and strong aroma of coffee, but it was made from a local plant.

"Thanks to you, we know now what Rapio's plan is for the Quae," Mysta said. "His plan to send Bás into Domare and then spread his control from the Quae in Domare to the Quae in all of Bigna has slowed down. He wants to get the Bás out at a more rapid pace. For him, he is not gathering souls for his eternity and the end times, final war of Război fast enough. He is getting ready to release an epidemic on the Quae population. Stur was his test city for his malady. And it worked—to a degree."

"More so than we would like," Nerkon said.

"Unfortunately, that is true," Mysta agreed. "Rapio has infected multitudes of the Quae and sent them back into Bigna to pass the Bás on to the healthy Quae. By doing this, he has interconnected the Quae to himself. He plans on these Quae to do his bidding in the wars to come."

"Then there are Quae who carry the Bás who live among the Quae of Bigna?" Kate asked.

"Yes," Mysta said. "Hopefully, today we will rid all of the Bás from the Quae of Bigna."

"Sir Nerkon! Sir Nerkon!" Mejor, Nerkon's Senior Centurion, ran up to the group. "Something has happened at the tent of Abi."

"Abi?" Nerkon asked, not expecting an answer. "It seems my distrust for him since the day Rubidus was exterminated was for a reason." He followed close behind Mejor.

Kate and Jen looked at Mysta.

"Go," Mysta said. "We still have time before the morning sun rises. Eldré and I will guard the silver trumpets."

Scurrying after Nerkon, it did not take Kate and Jen long to catch him outside Abi's tent. But instead of finding Abi in rebellion as they suspected, he laid dead, an arrow through his heart. The arrow was accurately shot through a small, vulnerable spot in his body armor.

"Who did this?" Nerkon asked. He stared at the onlookers. No one stepped forward.

Kate and Jen moved closer to Abi's body. A black mole behind his left ear still wiggled.

"He has a Bás scorpion controlling him," Kate said, stepping back.

"I couldn't let him do it…I couldn't…" a knight stumbled from beside Abi's tent.

"Sir Odo?" Jen questioned.

The knight, who had traveled through Rapio's three valleys and finally submitted to the torturous pain of the Bás throbbing through his body, fell to his knees.

"I couldn't...." Odo crawled toward Kate and Jen.

"Couldn't let him do what?" Kate knelt down to listen to Odo.

"Spread...spread Rapio's...the Bás..." Tears trickled down Odo's cheek. "Forgive me..."

"Odo," Kate whispered to the fallen knight. "You won. You beat the Bás scorpion Rapio put in you."

Odo smiled slightly. "Remember me to the Eagle," he whispered. His body went limp. The Bás had taken his body, but not his soul.

Kate brushed Odo's hair back. The Bás scorpion was still alive. "Quick!" she yelled to Raguel. "Bring me the Holy Sword."

Bwee—Bwee—Bwee!

The Bás scorpions from Odo and Abi were being called back by their master, Rapio.

Bwee—Bwee—Bwee!

Bwee—Bwee—Bwee!

The micro-scorpions' tails slashed through the translucent skin of their hosts.

Bwee—Bwee—Bwee!

Bwee—Bwee—Bwee!

Once outside the Quae bodies, the small bugs grew until they became luminous-green five foot tall scorpions.

Raguel ran with the Holy Sword to Kate. "Here. It's up to you."

Kate took the Holy Sword from Raguel's hands.

"Not this time," Kate yelled. She slashed the head from one of the green bodies. The headless scorpion ran directionless a few steps and exploded into a fiery ball.

Bwee—Bwee—Bwee!

Angered, the other five foot scorpion came at Kate. She plunged forward and thrust the tip of the Holy Sword into the thick scales of the body the Bás.

Bwee—Bwee—Bwee!

Wounded, but not dead, the giant bug continued his quest for Kate.

Bwee—Bwee—Bwee!

Raising the sword high, she plunged forward again, this time landing the tip of the sword between the thin, tapered eyes of the monster.

Bwee—Bwee—Bwee!

The Bás staggered backward and collapsed. His body squirmed in agony before bursting into flame; hurling embers at the Quae Pilgers watching.

Kate felt an arm slide around her shoulders. "Good job, cousin."

Kate gave Jen a half-hearted grin. "Odo was faithful to the end."

"Yes," he was."

"And he will be rewarded for it," Mysta said coming along side of them. "But the battle is not finished and the sun is just over the horizon." He took the Holy Sword from Kate's hand. "We must get back to the silver trumpets."

On the crude wooden table in front of Nerkon's meeting tent, the two trumpets of hammered silver glittered in the dawning of a new day. Mysta laid the Holy Sword between them. He and Eldré bowed to each other.

"First they are going to place a protection on the Quae of Bigna who have not been infected with Rapio's Bás," Raguel whispered to Kate and Jen.

"It is time," Mysta said. He picked up one silver trumpet and handed it to Eldré. Wrapping his hand around the other trumpet he nodded to Eldré. Turning slightly, they both faced north.

"Those from the North," Mysta said.

Huuuuum!

Eldré blew the sweet note of the peaceful humming bird.

Claaaaang!

Mysta's harsh metallic sound overpowered Eldré note.

Huuuuuuuuuuuuum!

Eldré blew the sweet note higher and longer, until the music from her trumpet blocked the harsh metallic sound of Mysta's trumpet.

Eldré and Mysta turned ninety degrees.

"Those from the East," Mysta said.

Huuuuum!

Eldré's note wafted eastward.

Claaaaang!

Mysta's harsh metallic sound overlaid Eldré's note.

Huuuuuuuuuuuuum!

Eldré's melodic note again blocked Mysta's harsh tone.

Eldré and Mysta turned ninety degrees.

"Those from the South," Mysta said.

Huuuuum!

Claaaaang!

Huuuuuuuuuuuuum!

Eldré and Mysta turned ninety degrees.

"Those from the West," Mysta said.

Huuuuum!

Claaaaang!

Huuuuuuuuuuuuum!

Eldré and Mysta turned to each other and bowed. Returning his trumpet to the wooden table, Mysta picked up the Holy Sword.

"Now they will banish the Bás from the Quae who have been infected," Raguel told Kate and Jen. "Because you rescued the Holy Sword, many will be saved."

Mysta took his position beside Eldré. With two hands he pointed the shining blade of the sword toward the sky. His hands glowed golden.

"It is just like when Fria Fara sent the Pilgers into the Battle of Stur," Kate whispered.

Huuuuuuuuuuuum!

Eldré sounded one long note while Mysta pointed the Holy Sword to all four cardinal directions of the compass and stated, "From the north—the east—the south—the west, the mighty force will come within you and rid you of the controller in you. The mighty force will rid you of your Bás."

Again Eldré and Mysta turned to each other and bowed. Eldré placed her silver trumpet on the wooden table and Mysta put the Holy Sword between the two musical redeemers.

Eldré put out her hands toward Kate and Jen. She wanted them to join her and Mysta. Grasping each by a hand, she held their arms up for the gathered Quae Pilgers to see.

"Sir Katherine! Sir Jennifer!" Eldré announced to the crowd.

Hurrah!

Hurrah!

Hurrah!

Mysta held up his right hand. The Pilgers quieted.

"Today we stopped the Bás sent by Rapio to destroy us," Mysta said.

Hurrah!

Hurrah!

Hurrah!

"Today we were able to do this because Sir Katherine and Sir Jennifer risked their lives—risked their souls and went into the depths of Rapio's domain to rescue the Holy Sword and find the cure from the Bás."

Hurrah! Sir Katherine—Sir Jennifer!

Hurrah! Sir Katherine—Sir Jennifer!

Mysta held up his hand again. Silence from the Pilgers.

"In two hours you will cross the Senvolte River and take back the city of Helig," Mysta said. "Some of you were at the Battle of Stur." He stopped speaking and picked up the Holy Sword. Raising the sword skyward he continued, "You remember the Holy Sword and Friar Fara. Today I give you his words.

"From the north—the south—the east—and the west, a mighty force will fall upon you," Mysta repeated Friar Fara's words. "The force will fall upon you to strengthen your body—strengthen your mind—strengthen your mission—strengthen your faith. The enemy will not defeat you, but you will crush them. Today you go onward to Helig to defeat the Indringers."

Helig!

Helig!

Helig!

The crowded cheered in agreement.

"Rest for two hours," Mysta said. "Prepare for the battle ahead."

Hurrah!

Hurrah!

Hurrah!

Hurrah!

Hurrah!

The cheering of the Pilgers faded away as they walked away from Mysta's words to gather under the banners of their divisions. They would prepare for the upcoming battle. They would be ready for the afternoon's charge on Helig.

"Take the Holy Sword," Mysta said to Nerkon. "Draw from its power."

"Thank you," Nerkon said, accepting the sword. He walked to his tent and disappeared.

Eldré continued to hold on to Kate and Jen. "You stopped Rapio from gathering more Quae for his eternity. You have stopped his plan—this time."

"This time?" Jen asked.

"Rapio lost another battle, not the war," Eldré said.

"Come with us." Taka said. He and Lieg did not leave with the rest of the Quae. "There is still much to be done before the Quae cross the river."

"Go," Eldré said. "Perhaps even fly your Maups." She smiled from the secret she held inside. "Yes, go fly your Maups."

Chapter Thirty-eight

Eldré released her hold on Kate and Jen and walked over to Mysta. In a language only the two of them understood, they carried on a conversation.

"I think Eldré has a good idea," Lieg said. "We can do a little reconnaissance before the battle. Let's go fly."

"Sounds good to me," Jen said. It would be good to get into the air again.

"Me too," Kate agreed.

Their Maups were ready for them when they approached the stables.

"You knew that Eldré would tell us to come with you to fly," Kate grinned.

"Yes," Taka smiled. "And what pilot wouldn't jump at the chance to fly?"

Kate boosted herself onto the waiting back of her Maup. She snuggled her face into his neck and stroked the hard knots under his ears. "Once again you and I," she whispered into his ear. Her Maup leaned his neck into her. He unfolded his long legs and rose off the ground, readying himself for flight.

Jen threw herself onto her Maup and openly said, "Okay, big boy, today you and I will conquer the skies." Her Maup lifted his head higher in understanding. He unfolded his legs and stood.

Taka and Lieg were already on their Maups. Taka winked at Lieg. With Taka's signal they both kicked the sides of their Maups. Today they would do reconnaissance, but also have some fun with Kate and Jen. Both knew time was short.

Kate caught their playful gesture and kicked her Maup to urge him to follow Taka and Lieg. With her command her Maup took to the air.

Cluk—cluk—cluk!

Kate's Maup sounded his tongue-clicking cry as he took flight.

"Licet volare si in tergo aquilae volat," Kate yelled as she turned to see the shocked expression on Jen's face.

"Oh no you don't," Jen laughed. Her competitive spirit aroused, she kicked the sides of her Maup to nudge him into the air. He ran a few steps to gain speed and then became airborne. His legs dangled for a moment and then he folded his legs and tucked them into his body.

Cluk—cluk—cluk!

Jen's Maup's tongue-clicking cry echoed over the campsite as he caught up with Kate. Jen gave Kate a thumbs-up. They were flying again.

Taka and Lieg lead Kate and Jen in a three-sixty turn around the cheering Quae Pilgers readying themselves for battle. The Pilgers gave Kate and Jen one more loud, vocal recognition before they made the march to Helig. Leveling their Maups off, Taka and Lieg set out toward the Holy City.

Glancing at the white caps whipping up on the dark blue Senvolte River, Kate involuntarily shuttered. She took a deep breath and grasped the knobs of her Maup tighter.

"Look past the river," Jen yelled. But, she too felt a pit in her stomach.

Kate exhaled, dug her legs tighter into her Maup and looked at the city walls of Helig ahead of her. Above the city walls the flag of the Indringer army flew—a black flag with a luminous green scorpion on it.

Massive stone towers, evenly placed along the outside city walls, cast ominous shadows on the scorched plain surrounding Helig. A few Yew trees still stood, but when the Indringers conquered Helig Onde ordered everything that belonged to the Quae to be burned.

Reaching the outside of the city walls, Taka held up his hand for the four of them to go into a holding pattern until they knew what the situation within the city was. They did not have to wait long.

Schhwaff!

Schhwaff!
Schhwaff!
Schhwaff!

From the top of the walls Indringer warriors shot arrows at them.

"It looks like Rapio has sent Onde back to Helig to protect the city," Lieg yelled. "Sir Nerkon and the Pilgers won't be able to create a surprise attack."

Taka pointed upward, indicating they should go up—they needed to get out of the range of the archers.

Banking to the left, the four flew in formation in an upward spiral until they could see the arrows falling short of their target. Lieg pointed toward the city. Flying high they were able to see behind the walls and what kind of fortification Onde had prepared.

"Wow!" was all Kate could say as they crested the towers and looked down on Onde's defense.

Machines capable of lofting missiles made of rocks, steel and burning torches were placed on the ramparts, waiting for the Pilgers. Thousands of Indringers, dressed in intimidating black armor, stalked the walkway at the top of the wall. They yelled orders at Quae who had been captured at Helig's fall and forced into slavery. Buckets of pitch, ready to be boiled and poured on the any Pilger who dared to scale the wall, were being placed beneath well placed gaps in the wall.

In the courtyard, twenty-thousand regular army Indringers stood at attention. Their battle gear on, they did not dare move a muscle less Onde would order their death.

Bwee—Bwee—Bwee!

All movement inside the city wall stopped. All eyes turned toward a building at the far end of the courtyard, a building that was heavily guarded.

"A king's keep?" Kate asked.

"Yes," Lieg answered.

Bwee—Bwee—Bwee!

From the entrance of the king's keep, twenty Elite Troopers marched out and made a corridor, ten on each side. They looked around the courtyard. Nothing dared move. This signaled the Senior Elite Trooper, who waited at the entrance of the keep, to stride through the doorway.

Taking one step out, the Senior Trooper stopped; his blood red scales glistened in the sun. Cranking his crusty head from side to side he surveyed the area. With radar precision in his dark eyes, he searched for any hidden danger.

No danger on the ground.

No danger inside the buildings.

No danger on the walls.

Far above him his senses picked up the danger—Quae.

The Senior Trooper took three more steps outside the king's keep and pointed upward. Drawing an arrow from his quiver he set the notches in the string of his bow. Carefully aiming he shot the arrow skyward.

Schhwaff!

His arrow barely missed Kate.

Schhwaff!

The Senior Trooper's second arrow nicked Kate's Maup in his wing. Instinctively she pulled her Maup into a climb.

Schhwaff!

The third arrow fell short and low of Kate.

Jen, Taka and Lieg joined Kate at the higher altitude.

"How…" Kate looked at Lieg.

"That is Onde's number one Elite Trooper," Lieg cut in with an answer. "He is like Nerkon's Senior Centurion, Mejor. As such, Onde has given his Senior Elite Trooper a limited amount of magical power."

"Obviously," Taka added, "some of the magic is in his arrows."

Baraaaaaag!

The blare from the elephant trumpet drew the foursomes' eyes back to the courtyard below.

Baraaaaaag!

All heads within the Helig's city walls turned toward the entrance to the king's keep.

Baraaaaaag!

One more blast of the trumpet announced the arrival of the king of Helig.

"Onde," Kate shuttered.

The Senior Elite Trooper's attention was no longer on the four Maups and their riders. He bowed when Onde stepped through the entrance. Everyone and everything on and within the city walls followed the Senior Elite Trooper's act.

Onde's black ankle-length robe with an over tunic of blood-red flowed around him with each step he took. His right hand held the scepter with a golden raven and his left hand was covered with the golden gauntlet. But he had traded the black turban with the gold headband of the High Priest for a king's crown of black gold and bejeweled with rubies.

Onde surveyed his subjects bowing to him and then immediately turned his attention to the air. He pointed his scepter toward Kate, Jen, Taka and Lieg.

"Rapio!" Onde shouted out, calling on his master. "Rapio!"

Sssblam!

Sssblam!

Orange-red lightning bolts streaked upward, but missed their marks.

"Time to go," Taka yelled.

Kate, Jen and Lieg did not wait for another order. All four kicked their Maups, ducked their heads into the peach fuzzed necks of the Maups and flew redline speed to leave Helig.

Sssblam!

Sssblam!

Onde's fiery electrical discharges exploded behind them, causing shock waves to rock the air around them.

Chapter Thirty-nine

*K*ate, Jen and Lieg stood beside Taka. Landing their Maups from their reconnaissance mission, they immediately went to Nerkon. What they had learned could decide the outcome of the Battle of Helig. Nerkon called on Obile and Begi to gather their knights for a council with the four scouts.

"Yes," Taka said. "Onde is back in Helig." He addressed Nerkon, but all of the Quae Pilger knights gathered at the council meeting to hear his words.

"Onde is back from Rapio's domain and stands as the Indringers' king," Taka continued.

"We can defeat Onde," Nerkon said. He fingered the hilt of the Holy Sword. "Onde is mortal—once a Quae like us. We can take back Helig."

Helig!

Victory!

The knights' voices rose with enthusiasm.

"Onde is mortal, but he carries magical power," Taka said. "And he has prepared the Indringers for battle. They are waiting for your attack, but you can overcome their defense."

"Is there a weakness in their defense?" a skeptical knight asked.

Nerkon shot the knight a sideward glance, but the question was on his mind also.

"You will have to take them head-on," Lieg answered. "Your faith will prevail for your victory."

Kate looked at Jen. Jen's eyes said it all. They both knew the first wave trying to climb the wall would be met with burning pitch, Greek fire and arrows from a thousand archers.

"Prepare yourself and your warriors—it is time to cross the river," Nerkon told his knights. "We will be at the city walls in two hours and ready ourselves for the attack." He did not want his warriors to have time to think and run. He must take advantage of the reconnaissance mission.

Helig!

Victory!

"But how will we cross the river?" the same skeptical knight asked.

"I will take care of the river." Mysta stepped forward. "The Senvolte River will be sealed up to never flow again."

"But how…" the knight began but Mysta held up his hand to stop the doubting knight.

"It will be done," Mysta said.

Eldré stepped forward and handed Mysta one of the hammered silver trumpets. She held the other one close to her side, tucked into the folds of her red silk robe. Together they walked to the edge of the river. In concert, they turned to face the boiling, dark indigo blue water. Somewhere deep below the surface an angry Elak awaited for the first Quae who dared to step into his territory.

The Quae Pilgers who waited for their orders no longer milled around the camp, but gathered on the shores of the river to see what their fate would be. All of their eyes now darted between the two trumpeters and the raging river.

Huuuuuuuuuum!

Huuuuuuuuuum!

Eldré and Mysta held the musical notes blasting from the bells of their silver trumpets for one minute and then they were silent for a minute.

Huuuuuuuuuum!

Huuuuuuuuuum!

Eldré and Mysta repeated their one minute notes, followed by a one minute of silence, seven times. Upon completing their cycle, they once again blew their silver trumpets.

Huuuuuuuuuuuuuuuuuuuum!

Huuuuuuuuuuuuuuuuum!

This time they did not stop at one minute, or at two or three, but continued the harmonic sound for seven minutes. At the end of seven minutes Eldré and Mysta stepped back from the edge of the river and held their hammered silver trumpets high into the air.

Kate looked up to where the trumpets pointed. She nudged Jen.

Squinting, Jen looked up. High above them the Eagle made lazy eight circles.

Swooooosh!!!

The sound of water rushing though the air brought Kate and Jen's attention back to the river.

Swooooosh!!!

The water of the Senvolte rose into a fifty-foot tidal wave, and then surged over the large gray, stone tower that rose midstream. Unable to withstand the force of the increasing power of the rolling water, the tower crumbled and dissolved, as sugar cubes in hot coffee.

Kraa—Kraa—Kraa!

Elak's guttural roar bubbled up above the sound of the surging waves. From the angry water where the tower disappeared, the angered Elak rose. His monstrous two large black eyes, set in his scaly snake-like face, moved upward until his full dragon body was exposed to the above world of Bigna.

Kraa—Kraa—Kraa!

Elak's focus was on Eldré and Mysta. His forked lizard tongue lashed out from his mouth toward them, but an invisible shield around them did not let it hit its target. The acid-like saliva that dripped from his teeth sizzled when it hit the water of the Senvolte River.

Kraa—Kraa—Kraa!

Elak's rage grew—but the raging water surrounding him began swirling into a whirlpool.

Kraa—Kraa—Kraa!

Eldré's and Mysta's strength was being drained from the battle between them and Elak, but they did not let their two trumpets of hammered silver drop.

Crash!

With one last dying echo, the river bellowed a rock-pounding crash against the shoreline and then sucked its liquid power into an ever enlarging whirlpool.

Kraa—Kraa—Kraa!

Elak bellowed one last time. He could no longer fight the power coming from Eldré and Mysta. His bulging eyes switched focus from Eldré and Mysta to Kate and Jen. Soullessness behind them, he did not take them from Kate and Jen until his scaly snake-like face was sucked into the violent indigo whirlpool.

Imploding into itself, the river followed Elak into the dark chasms of the darkness below. What was once a mighty waterway, the Senvolte River was now a stream two feet wide.

Silent awe was all the Quae Pilgers could muster up.

Eldré and Mysta let the hammered silver trumpets drop to their sides.

"The Senvolte River will never flow again," Mysta broke the silence. "And the Volgo will flow into the Zout Lake."

"And from this day," Eldré continued Mysta's thought, "the Zout Lake will be dead to all living things. It will be made so salty it cannot sustain life."

"Have your Senior Trumpeter blow his trumpet to call everyone to gather to march on to Helig," Mysta told Nerkon. "Blast your trumpet as the signal to set out for battle."

Chapter Forty

Nerkon, Obile and Begi stood before their Pilger warriors. The Bigna Air Power circled above them. The Holy City of Helig seemed so much closer. The Senvolte River and Elak were no longer a threat—no longer an obstacle. The Quae Pilgers would continue The Mission. They would march on Helig this day. They would take down the black flag of the Indringers that flew above the Holy City walls.

"You are ready," Mysta told Nerkon. "Today is your day to take back Helig for the Quae."

"Thank you," Nerkon said. "It is time to talk to everyone committed to The Mission. Thank you again." He handed Mysta the Holy Sword. "It has served us well."

Mysta smiled and stepped back next to Eldré to listen to Nerkon address his warriors.

Nerkon turned to Kate and Jen. "Thank you for all you have done. We would not be here today if you had not joined us."

"And we will be with you until you no longer need us," Jen stated. Kate and Jen stood next to Taka and Lieg. They would join the Bigna Air Power after Nerkon gave the order to begin the march to Helig.

Nerkon gave a nod to Jen and Kate as a soldier going to war and leaving his daughters at the airport terminal. They would find out soon enough what he knew. He mounted his horse, stood tall in the stirrups and turned to face the Pilgers.

"The Indringers want death for you," Nerkon shouted, so as to be heard by the thousands of Quae Pilgers waiting to take back Helig. "But today you are to set your mind on the spirit of life and of victory. Today we will fight side by side for the honor and glory of Bigna. I pledge my honor to guard your honor and life. We will fight until the holy city of Helig is ours again. Today we will go forward! We will never fear or turn from our enemy."

Nerkon!

Nerkon!

Nerkon!

The cry of support rippled across the warriors.

A Pilger in the far back of the warriors jumped onto a tree stump and shouted, "We will follow you to the walls of Helig."

"Not to the walls," Nerkon's voice rose. "Not to the walls of Helig," he repeated, "but over the walls of Helig—over the walls to defeat our enemy and gain victory."

Helig!

Helig!

Victory!

Victory!

"Keep your faith!" Nerkon drew his sword from its sheath. Pointing it toward the sky he shouted, "Hoist your swords! Raise your shields! Victory!"

Obile and Begi followed Nerkon's lead and thrust their swords into the air.

"Victory!" Obile and Begi shouted as one. "Onward to Helig! Victory!"

Helig!

Helig!

Onward to Helig!

Victory!

Victory!

The Pilgers picked up on Obile and Begi's battle cry.

Baraag!

Nerkon's First Trumpeter sounded one short blast on his trumpet. The signal was clear—their destiny was understood—Nerkon called the Quae Pilgers to set out toward Helig.

Nerkon was the first to ride his horse across the small stream that once was the Senvolte River. Obile and Begi followed him. They sat tall in their saddles to show their strength and how they would lead their warriors to the completion of The Mission. The Quae Pilger's faith fully restored, they did not hesitate to follow their leaders. Their chant confirmed their unwavering belief in their destiny.

Helig!

Helig!

Helig!

Victory!

Victory!

Victory!

Mysta leaned over and whispered something to Eldré. She nodded and Mysta stepped away from her. With both hands he held the Holy Sword and pointed it toward the sky. It was back in the hands of the Cephas Monastery monks. Far above Mysta the Eagle dipped one wing and then continued to circle.

"Until we meet again," Taka said to Kate. He jumped onto his Maup and nudged it into flight.

Cluk-cluk-cluk

Lieg hugged Jen. "Fly like an eagle my friend." Like Taka he mounted his Maup, kicked its sides and took off. He disappeared into the bright sun.

Cluk-cluk-cluk

Taka turned back and swooped up Mysta and the Holy Sword. The two flew in the direction of the Cephas Monastery.

"Taka and Lieg are not going to fight the Battle of Helig?" Kate was confused.

"No," Eldré answered. "They, like Mysta, belong to Cephas. The Holy Sword is back where it belongs. Their duty to the Quae Pilgers, to The Mission, is complete."

Jen's Maup nuzzled her hand. She looked into his eyes. He was leaving her.

"Kate?" Jen questioned. "Kate, what is happening?"

Kate was hugging her Maup's neck. She did not know why, but she knew he was also going to fly away without her.

Without waiting for Kate and Jen to give them orders, their Maup ran a few feet, picked up their legs and folded them under their sleek bodies.

Cluk-cluk-cluk

Cluk-cluk-cluk

Kate and Jen watched the white peach fuzzed bird-like creatures spread their beautiful eight foot orange feathered wings and take flight after Taka and Mysta. Both felt a pit in their stomach as they watched their friends fly away.

"We are not going on to Helig either, are we?" Kate asked.

"No," Eldré answered. "You have also completed your work in Bigna."

Kate watched Nerkon, Obile and Begi lead their warriors toward the city walls of Helig. Dust billowed up from thousands of Pilgers feet marching to battle.

"We need to tell them to go home as soon as they take back Helig," Kate said to Eldré. "How can we explain that if they don't go home they will fight for another two-hundred years? In the end it will become a no win for anyone."

"You cannot," Eldré answered. "Quae, like men in your Earth World, must live their own history. The Mission will go on until both sides are victims and neither side is victorious. You cannot change it. Your journey here is finished. You stopped Rapio's Bás Plague against the Quae and put the Holy Sword back in the hands of the monks at Cephas Monastery."

"Will we return to Bigna?" Jen asked.

Eldré gave an ever-so-slight smile. "Only the Eagle knows where your journey will take you."

"But we didn't get to say good-by to Mysta—to Taka or Lieg," Jen said.

"Or how much they mean to us," Kate added.

"They know," Eldré half-smiled. "They know."

Badaroom!

Badaroom!

The rumbling bass-drum sound of the Obex was low and distant at first, but abruptly gave way to vibrating the air around Kate and Jen.

Badaroom!

Badaroom!

"Eldré?" Kate questioned.

"Raguel and the Eagle will take care of you now, Amicis—my friends."
Eldré stretched her four-foot body out and reached toward the sky.

From the center of the sun, Lieg dove from his unseen place, gathered
up Eldré and soared toward the Cephas Monastery.

Badaroom!

Badaroom!

The ground shook and heaved under Kate and Jen's feet.

Kate opened her locket. "Jen, our grandparents' picture is coming
back. We are going back to our Earth World."

Badaroom!

Badaroom!

The sound of the Obex grew louder.

"We have to leave," Raguel yelled.

Kate looked to where she last saw Nerkon. The dust from marching
feet had enveloped every Quae. She could no longer see the Pilgers—or
the Holy City.

"We have to leave…now," Raguel repeated.

Badaroom!

Badaroom!

Chapter Forty-one

*D*ust, rocks and what little water was left from the Senvolte River swirled around Kate, Jen and Raguel in a multicolor whirlwind, turning the ground they stood on into a patchy green and brown carpet of moss and clay. Roots, from the massive oak tree they found when they first popped through the Obex into Bigna, protruded through the ground. Growing hundreds of years in seconds, the tree rose to its full height, filling its branches with fist-sized acorns.

Badaroom!

Badaroom!

The Obex covered one-half of their view.

Like a plane rotating on its axis, the soil beneath Kate, Jen and Raguel's feet rolled left. Bigna was disappearing and they were being spilled into the Obex.

Badaroom!

Badaroom!

The Obex's power pulled at them.

"Grab the tree!" Kate yelled.

Kate and Jen reached out and managed to grasp a hold of a low hanging branch of the mighty oak.

"Hold on!" Kate yelled, but she was sliding off her firm foundation and one hand slipped from the branch she held to. Only two fingers and thumb of her other hand kept her from falling into the Obex.

"Grab my hand," Jen yelled. She reached out and grasped Kate's free hand. "I won't let go."

"Let go of the tree," Raguel yelled.

"We'll fall off the edge of the...of Bigna...off into the Obex," Kate yelled back. Her feet slipped and lifted off the ground.

"Trust me," Raguel yelled. "Have faith." He let his body drift from the solid soil he stood on. His silky, copper red hair glowed as he tumbled away from them.

Kate looked at Jen and gritted her teeth. "Faith, he says."

"Faith," Jen repeated. She tightened her grip on Kate's hand and took a deep breath. "On the count..."

"Ready," Kate exhaled.

"Three...two...one..."

They let their hands slip the security of the branch, and plummeted into space after Raguel.

Badaroom!

Badaroom!

Immediately they were engulfed in a shockwave of blue gel. Flashes of orange-red flame lit their surroundings long enough for them to know they were tumbling out of control in the Obex.

Kraa! Kraa! Kraa!

An icy cold breeze touched Kate's cheek.

Rapio was near.

Kraa! Kraa! Kraa!

The dry ice air sucked the oxygen from Kate and Jen. Pressure on their chests tightened.

Kraa! Kraa! Kraa!

"Kate," Jen yelled. "Hold on to your locket with your free hand." She did not let go of the tight grip she had on Kate's other hand.

Both grasped their lockets and squeezed tight.

Screeeech!

The Eagle's protective cry enveloped them.

Poof!

Their tumbling abruptly stopped. They were surrounded by soft feathers.

Screeeech!

"Hang on," Raguel said. "Hang on."

"Raguel?" Jen questioned.

"Hang on," Raguel repeated.

"Eagle?" Kate whispered.

Before any answers could be given, they were spinning and tumbling from the violence of the Obex into a murky blue, white-streaked tunnel, much like the tunnel the Eagle had created for them in Gudsrika. The ear-shattering howl of wind of the Obex, with all its horror, was all around them, but they safely sat on the back of the Eagle.

"Oh!" Kate looked back. She stared into the black, soulless eyes of Rapio—his form was that of the giant ink-black raven. On his back Rocus clutched onto his master. However Rocus' focus was not on Kate and Jen but on Raguel.

Rocus raised one hand into a fist. His mouth snarled at the edges.

"Not today, my brother," Raguel yelled. "Not today."

Rapio's fifteen foot, ink black wings spread out. A gust of icy wind blew through the tunnel.

Kraa! Kraa! Kraa!

The low guttural cry of Rapio mixed with the eerie rumbling of the Obex as he and Rocus disappeared into the churning blue gel.

Screeeech!

Kaboom—Prbttt!

The Eagle, with Kate, Jen and Raguel on his back, squirted from the icy tunnel and for a moment flew in the tranquility of a fluffy cloud.

Screeeech!

"Until we meet again," Raguel said. "Licet volare si in tergo aquilae volat."

A gentle breeze brushed Kate and Jen's cheeks. *On the back of an Eagle* it whispered. The wind tenderly lifted them from their secure position atop the Eagle and free-floated them slowly until their feet touched the solid ground of the airport's black asphalt tarmac. They wore their leather flight jackets and sported their silk scarves around their necks.

Kate put her hand into her jacket pocket. "FOD," Kate said. She pulled out the aluminum washer and screw she had put into her jacket pocket before the dust tornado took them away from the air show.

Throngs of people were still posing for pictures beside the static displays to get their best pose with the pilots and airplanes. Other air show spectators were still staking out their places along the side of the runway to watch the air demonstrations.

Kate and Jen shaded their eyes and looked into the cloudless blue canopy above them.

Screeeech!

The Eagle, his powerful brown and white wings fully spread, caught a rising thermal and soared heavenward. A small copper red field mouse hunkered down on his back.

"Until we meet again," Kate said.

"Fly high, my friend," Jen said. "Fly high and free."

He brought me up out of the pit
of destruction, out of the miry clay,

And He set my feet upon a rock,
making my footsteps firm.

Psalm 40:2

*C*arole Bailey is a lifelong reader of fantasy, mystery and humor. As a child she developed a vivid imagination and a love of flying. Uniting the two, she began writing. After years as a college faculty member in California, she now resides among the Saguaro cacti of Arizona.

*P*hotography by Caleb Hale.